THOUGH grimy, the yellow sign fixed to the elevated highway's support post stated clearly: PARK AT YOUR OWN RISK. Norah wasn't the only one who ignored it. So when she heard the footsteps behind her she assumed it was another driver.

Subconsciously, she continued to listen to that other set of footsteps that were like an echo of her own. They remained behind her, deliberately maintaining distance. To test, she stopped. He stopped. She started, so did he.

Quickly Norah slipped behind one of the support posts and drew her gun. "Police officer," she called out. "Stop where you are." She waited a bit, but by now there was nothing to see. Whoever had been following her was gone.

Relieved, Norah put the gun back into her handbag and came out from behind the pillar. She took out her keys but before reaching the door, she stopped and spun around just in time to see a hulking figure silhouetted against the luminosity of the water. Raising his weapon, the big man moved in and lunged. . . .

Fawcett Crest Books
by Lillian O'Donnell:

☐ AFTERSHOCK   24479 $2.50

☐ THE CHILDREN'S ZOO   24498 $2.50

THE CHILDREN'S ZOO

Lillian O'Donnell

FAWCETT CREST • NEW YORK

THE CHILDREN'S ZOO

THIS BOOK CONTAINS THE COMPLETE TEXT OF THE
ORIGINAL HARDCOVER EDITION.

Published by Fawcett Crest Books, CBS Educational and
Professional Publishing, a division of CBS Inc., by arrange-
ment with G.P. Putnam's Sons.

Copyright © 1981 by Lillian O'Donnell

ALL RIGHTS RESERVED

ISBN: 0-449-24498-9

The author gratefully acknowledges permission from The
Associated Press to reprint the article on violent teens.

Printed in the United States of America

First Fawcett Crest Printing: April 1982

10 9 8 7 6 5 4 3 2 1

Chapter I

"Trick or treat!"

The call startled Bill March. He hadn't expected to hear it in this staid neighborhood, certainly not at this hour. It was close to midnight, and he would have expected that all little ghosties and ghoulies would be safely tucked into their beds and dreaming the dreams brought on by overstuffed tummies. His arm, resting lightly around his young wife's waist, tightened protectively. They had been married four months and Ruth was pregnant. It was a warm night with a full moon so they had decided to cross from their new co-op on Montague Street over to the Brooklyn Heights promenade for a short stroll before turning in. They had been standing at the railing and looking out across the silver-plated waters toward the dark silhouette of lower Manhattan when they heard the jeering call.

Sensing her husband's unease, Ruth March raised her head from his shoulder and looked up into his face inquiringly.

"Kids," he said.

"Trick or treat!"

The shouts rang out again and the menace was palpable. It quickly disabused Bill March of any notion that these were

5

harmless neighborhood youngsters and that he might be able to ignore them. He wasn't afraid. At twenty-nine, though slight in build, March was strong and fit, more so than he appeared. He'd been a finalist in the Golden Gloves, lightweight division, and he still went a few rounds a week at the New York A.C. on Fifty-ninth. He could take care of himself against a bunch of rowdy teenagers, but he didn't want Ruth frightened. He was thinking fast. Money would placate them, of course. Unfortunately, all he had on him was some loose change. He looked back over his shoulder to gauge what he'd have to deal with.

He barely had time to note that there were four of them—white, thirteen or fourteen years old, neither costumed nor masked but wearing ordinary pants and windbreakers—before the first volley hit him full in the face. He flinched at the impact, felt whatever they'd thrown break and release a gelatinous goo, sticky and foul-smelling, drip down into his neck. Eggs! He nearly laughed aloud. They were throwing rotten eggs. They were just children after all, children out for some mischief.

"Knock it off!" he yelled. "It's not funny. Knock it off."

The next barrage got him in the eyes. Instinctively, he closed them, put an arm up to shield himself. Too late. The impact forced bits of shell into the eyeball, lacerating it and causing fluid material necessary to the eye's function to seep out from beneath the lids. All March knew was that his eyes smarted. He blinked rapidly to clear them and to ease the burning. That only released more of the valuable fluid. He bent over in his pain, and seeing him hunched and helpless, they pelted him anew.

"Stop it! Stop it!" Ruth March screamed. Trembling, she got in front of her husband and in trying to protect him was splattered herself. The slimy mess was in her hair; it made a disgusting splotch on the shoulder of her suede jacket. "Oh, please, stop . . ." She was crying. "Please, please . . ."

The boys laughed uproariously. They slapped and pounded each other. The more the frightened woman wept, the more they howled. It was the distant bleep of a police siren that finally dispersed them.

"Are you all right, darling?" Ruth asked anxiously; it wasn't like Bill not to fight back.

"Kids, just kids," he muttered, but he didn't straighten up.

6

The burning in his eyes was worse. He kept them closed and reached out a probing hand. "Honey? I think I'd better get to a hospital. Will you help me?"

He let her lead him. He stumbled, but he would not open his eyes. He was afraid to. If he did, he might not be able to see.

Karl Wespo walked down Tenth Street to where he'd left his car. He'd had a few too many, but he was okay to drive. Sure he was. A while back—he couldn't say exactly when, whenever the party broke up, whoever or whatever the party had been for—anyhow, several drinks ago, Sam Cirillo had offered to drive him home. He'd refused. Sam was a good buddy, and Karl Wespo would give the shirt off his back to a buddy, but not the keys to his car. Never. He would not ever admit that he wasn't fit to drive. At thirty-six, Karl still lived at home. The car, his beautiful red Ferrari, was his badge of independence, his statement of who and what he was. Besides, if he turned up without it, Mama would know for sure that he'd been drinking. That last consideration wiped out the fleeting notion of taking a cab. He'd be okay! Once behind the wheel, he'd be okay. Wasn't he always? First, though, he had to find the car. Where in hell had he parked?

He didn't notice the group of young blacks who had been loitering at the corner of Sixth Avenue near the all-night hamburger joint, and who now detached themselves from the building against which they'd been leaning to fall in step behind him. If he had, it wouldn't have mattered. Karl Wespo was six foot three, two hundred and twenty-seven pounds. He worked in the family business at the Fulton Fish Market and was accustomed to dealing with men who reasoned with their fists. He knew all the tricks of the street fighter. Any punk would take one look at Karl Wespo and steer clear—when he was sober. It was all too evident that on this occasion Wespo was drunk, so the five youngsters followed gleefully and, for the time, silently.

"Where the shit did I put it?" Wespo muttered to himself and shuffled to a stop in the middle of the sidewalk. He hadn't come this far in the car; he was sure of it because he would have noticed and remembered the boarded-up porno theater. He turned around and found himself staring straight at the boys. He felt a moment's panic, but it was over what

7

had happened to his car, not the boys; to him they were objects, street impedimenta like trash cans and fire plugs. He turned and started to retrace his steps.

Stifling their mirth, they reversed too and closed in a circle around him.

"Trick or treat," they chanted. "Trick or treat." Sing-song style. "How about it, mister? What's it going to be?"

Wespo flicked them aside like flies. "Get lost." He'd spotted his car, its red-and-silver perfection gleaming in the moonlight. It was directly across the street where he'd known it would be. With a smug grin, he lurched out into the middle of the road.

The gang lined up along the edge of the sidewalk.

"Trick or treat, mister. Last chance."

Wespo didn't even bother to look around. "I told you, fuck off." He found his keys and bent to open the car door.

Rocks came out of pockets. One grazed Karl Wespo's temple. Another hit the Ferrari's windshield, shattering the glass into a sunburst. More rocks scratched and dented the perfect finish, put dents in fenders and doors. When the rocks were used up, they rushed the vehicle. They swarmed over the hood, hacking at it, bouncing up and down on it. A rasping rush of air indicated a tire had been slashed. Blood trickled down the side of Karl Wespo's face, but he didn't notice, didn't run for cover. He stood in a daze and watched the violation of the only thing he truly cared about. But not for long. With a tremor that shook his whole massive frame, that cleared the alcohol from his brain, he came out of it.

"Get away from that car! Get away!" he roared.

The shrieks of glee died. Next, the three boys on the hood stopped jumping. What they saw in the big man's red face made them slide off and start running.

Moving deliberately, Wespo grabbed two who hadn't got away by their jacket collars. "I'm going to give you the beating of your lives," he told them.

But they wrenched themselves free to run after their buddies and left him standing in the empty street to stare at what they'd done. The tears came to his eyes. *God damned little bastards!* He'd get them for this, he told himself.

They'd disappeared. Where? Around a corner, of course. Which corner? He didn't know, but he'd find them. He started walking down the middle of the road. When he got to the intersection he looked right. Nobody. Then left. There they were, lying in wait—not with rocks but with guns. They got him in both knees. He tried to keep moving, but the pain was excruciating. It brought him down. It wasn't enough for the pack. They continued to pour bullets into him until their guns were empty.

Shortly after midnight, after the park had officially closed, three figures dressed all in black except for soiled white jogging shoes scaled the wall of the Sixty-fifth Street transverse at Fifth Avenue. Traffic was sparse at that hour. It came through the transverse from the West Side in clusters regulated by the lights. It was a matter of letting one cluster go by and making the move before the next arrived. The move consisted of breaching the low parapet, jumping across to the inner wall, a matter of a couple of feet, throwing the rope ladder over the spiked railing and climbing down into the zoo. Piece of cake.

The animals stirred uneasily in their sleep. The modest dun wood ducks raised their heads. The splendid white geese with their dramatic orange bills and orange webbed feet ruffled their feathers, got up, and waddled to the railing squawking as always for a handout. The two elegant black swans from Denmark arched their long, aristocratic necks inquisitively—they were mute by nature and would be the only ones to make no sound when the terror struck. The fowl were housed in the open at the center of the menagerie, in the contact pit, so that the children could see them and pet them. Being most exposed, they were most sensitive to the intrusion. The pigs, sheep, donkeys, the raccoons being more sheltered in the stalls and huts along the perimeter, slept on—for a while longer.

The last of the three black-clad figures jumped from the bottom rung of the rope ladder and landed silently on rubber soles. By prearrangement, the three picked their way to an open area in the middle of the compound. At a nod from the leader, they spread out. One wielded a baseball bat, one a knife, the last had only his bare hands.

The howls and screams of the wounded and dying animals were piteous. The rabbits, guinea pigs, the lone raven, protected because they were in cages, nevertheless panicked. They thrashed and clawed at the very bars that saved their

9

lives. The cacophony of terror was transmitted to the wild beasts in the main menagerie where the lions responded with low rumbles and the panthers paced restlessly.

Raul Pelletier had clocked in from his first round and was settling down to a coffee break. He had just opened the big thermos his wife filled for him and poured a steaming cup when he heard the sounds of agony. Pelletier was a short, thick-set man in his fifties, a man of both spiritual and physical courage who had already been tested. He didn't hesitate. He put his cup down and ran.

A low iron fence separated the two sections of the zoo. Pelletier didn't bother to unlock the gate, he simply vaulted over. The second fence was too high; he had to stop and use his keys to get beyond the walls which had been erected to protect the creatures whose dying cries colored the black night red.

"Who's there?" the night watchman yelled as he pushed the heavy plate-glass door open. "What's going on?" he demanded as though the animals could tell him.

He didn't need to flash his light. Enough illumination spilled down from the transverse and the moon was bright enough for him to see the horror all too plainly. He started to shout a warning. Instead of words blood poured out of his mouth.

Ha. Halloween.

The sun shone bright on All Saints' Day.

Norah and Joe came out of St. Vincent Ferrer's after the six-thirty A.M. mass and stopped for a moment at the top of the steps to adjust their vision after the mellow darkness inside.

"Have you made up your mind?" Joe asked somewhat diffidently because Norah had been oddly touchy on the subject.

Sergeant Norah Mulcahaney was nearly as tall as her husband, now a detective captain. She held herself very straight and looked directly into his dark eyes, then quickly away. "Not yet," she answered and started down the steps to the street.

The sun brought out the auburn glints in her dark brown hair that she was wearing long again and that today she had tied back with a green silk scarf. She was fit and trim now as

10

when he'd married her, Joe Capretto thought, watching her; she hadn't changed. No, he corrected himself, she had changed, subtly and gradually, and, he realized with a sudden jolt, quite markedly. Norah stood five nine in her stocking feet. At that height and with her elongated bone structure she couldn't look dumpy, but when he'd first met her she'd been close. Capretto smiled, remembering his Norah as a rookie—naive, eager, and dedicated to becoming a good police officer. And she had succeeded, he thought. She'd also slimmed down and learned how to dress. The fact was that a certain inner radiance hidden before and which Joe himself had had to learn to see and appreciate was now quite evident to all. There was now about Sergeant Norah Mulcahaney an aura of assurance, both personal and professional, which she'd earned over the years and to which Joe knew he had contributed . . . in both departments.

One thing hadn't changed—he smiled ruefully to himself as he ran down the church steps after her—the thrust of her jaw when she was upset. Norah's eyes were a deep blue and framed by well-defined eyebrows and naturally thick lashes; her skin was clear and finely textured; her lips, soft and full—all in good balance but for that square, blunt jaw. Well as he knew his Norah, her reaction in this particular matter confounded Joe. He read her signal clearly, but he was also losing patience. He caught up to her.

"I think you owe Jim Felix some kind of answer and soon, by the end of the week anyway," he said, matching his stride to hers. "You can't expect him to hold the job for you forever."

"I don't."

"So?"

She shrugged. "I'm still thinking."

"What's to think about, for God's sake?"

There was an edge to his voice which Norah recognized in the same way that he recognized the jut of her jaw. Though he was a Latin, Joseph Antony Capretto had his temper under good control. He was understanding of her moods, but not indulgent. After a reasonable period he would demand that she snap out of it. She was aware that she was now approaching the end of that reasonable period.

"I told you; I'm not sure I want to make a change. I like it where I am."

Joe took a deep breath, held it, then blew it out with a short

11

explosion. That, as Norah had also learned, was a safety valve for his temper. "I thought you'd be enthusiastic," he continued mildly enough. "I thought you'd grab at the chance to be on the Homicide Task Force. It's a lot like Homicide North used to be. It's the most prestigious detective assignment in the city. What's more, the work is right up your alley. It's what you like and what you're good at." They turned the corner at Sixty-eighth where Joe parked his car. "What's the problem, *cara*?"

While Norah, becoming more poised and sophisticated, had slimmed down, Joe, settling into the complacency of a happy married life, had put on weight. Ten years older than Norah, he was still a good-looking man. His face was dark and bold, dominated by a high brow and the classically straight Roman nose. His jet black hair was showing some gray, but the gray was coming in most obligingly right at the temples. Before marrying, Capretto had been the squad swinger in a style that by today's standard would be accorded an indulgent smile. A sergeant on the elite and now defunct Homicide North, Joe had been efficient, a good detective, but no workaholic. When he married he accepted the responsibility of building security for his family and he set himself to studying. From sergeant he made lieutenant, then captain. Gradually and without regret, he shifted to administration. He was now working out of the One-three for his old boss, Deputy Inspector James Felix. Except for a short interval during which he had been assigned to Narcotics, Joe and Norah had always worked, if not together, at least out of the same command. But now Norah remained at the old stand, Fourth Homicide Division across the park on Eighty-second Street.

Joe's dark eyes were somber; his heavy eyebrows almost crossed into a frown. "What's the matter, darling? Is it that you don't want to come downtown? Is it that you'd rather not be working with me?"

She stopped dead in the middle of the sidewalk. "Whatever gave you that idea? I love working with you or near you. You've taught me everything I know."

"You didn't need me to teach you." Nevertheless, he was pleased that she had said it and he leaned forward to plant a quick, light kiss on her lips. "So? What's up? What's bugging you? If you think I rigged the offer, forget it. Felix was the

12

one who put your name on the list along with about a dozen others. Deland picked you."

"The Chief did? Himself?"

"That's right."

She brightened, then shook her head and started walking again. "I wouldn't fit in."

"What?" Joe hurried after her, grabbed her hand, and pulled her around. "I can't believe you said that."

They stood just outside the entrance of the remodeled brownstone in which they had an apartment and faced each other. Joe challenged: Norah glared back. Out of the corner of her eye, Norah glimpsed a woman hugging a bag of groceries in both arms stop a short distance off and watch them, open-mouthed.

"I guess I'm smartening up," Norah replied.

"I don't believe that."

"Well, thank you. Thank you very much."

"You know what I mean."

"Sure." She smiled and the tightness around her jaw eased. Linking her arm through his, Norah steered Joe toward the entrance. Catching the bystander's eyes, she waved over her shoulder.

Disappointed, but not embarrassed, the woman took a fresh grip on her groceries and moved on.

"I just want to look in on Toni; make sure she's up and gets breakfast," Norah explained to her husband.

He frowned. They'd planned to grab a bite together at a fast-food place, then pick up his car. He would then drive Norah to work and continue on to his office downtown. Norah kept her car in the precinct lot for use during the shift. "Toni's okay," Joe said. "She can feed herself and get herself to school. You fuss over the child too much!"

Norah shrugged. "I like to fuss. She's a sweet girl. It gives me pleasure."

They had no child of their own. They'd tried to adopt and it hadn't worked. It was a disappointment they no longer talked about. The family, on both sides, had stopped asking when they intended to have children. Even Joe's mother, the redoubtable Signora Emilia, no longer cast sly and hopeful glances at her daughter-in-law's belly.

Toni, Antonia DeVecchi, was Joe's sister's girl. She was staying with them for a couple of weeks while Lena and her

13

husband, Jake, were in Puerto Rico celebrating their fifteenth wedding anniversary. The four DeVecchi children had been farmed out among the family—Joe had seven sisters in all. He and Norah got Toni because Toni was the oldest, twelve, and able to look after herself while they were working. And because Norah had asked to have her. It was working out fine. Joe was glad to see the joy Norah derived from the child and the way the child responded to Norah, but he was also worried about what would happen when Toni went home again. The happier Norah was now, the more engrossed and involved she became with the girl, the harder it would be for her to adjust when she was gone.

"You're spoiling Toni," he warned.

"Oh, I don't think so. She's pretty level-headed. You don't have to come up if you don't want to."

"Well . . ." Joe studied his wife. Her color was high: her dark blue eyes alight with anticipation; she couldn't wait to get upstairs to the child. "I really don't have that much time."

"I'll take a taxi," she said and with a quick, perfunctory kiss dismissed him and went quickly, almost on the run, inside. The door swung shut in Joe's face.

That Norah's maternal feelings were being regenerated by the visit, Joe understood, but there was more to it. She seemed lately to be avoiding him, to be using the child as an excuse to keep him at arm's length. What was bugging her? What in hell could it be that she wouldn't tell him about it?

14

Chapter II

"Homicide, Sergeant Mulcahaney."

The call came in to Fourth Division at precisely 8:02 A.M. With one hand Norah picked up the receiver and with the other reached for her pad and pencil. She made notes out of habit, but no notes were necessary. She listened without comment, then hung up. Collecting her jacket and her shoulder-strap purse, both hanging from the back of her chair, she got into the jacket on her way out of the squad room. Before she was out of the station house, she had in her hand the keys to the gray Honda Civic, a replacement for the Pinto which had been fire-bombed three months before.

Once inside the park she cut on to the pedestrian paths as being the most direct route. She drove slowly. There weren't many pedestrians in the park at that hour—most of the joggers had already done their daily stint and so had the dog walkers; only a handful of business people were using the path as a shortcut to offices on the East Side—nevertheless, Norah wasn't anxious to run anybody down. At fifteen miles an hour, she had plenty of time to observe and absorb the early serenity of the park. The leaves were turning and were predominantly yellow. By contrast the green of the grass was so sharp it seemed almost artificial. A smoky lushness scented the air: autumn flaunting her opulence before withering into winter.

Norah picked up speed across the empty mall, down through a dark underpass, then turned right and entered a high iron gate. Aside from the blue-and-white park-precinct patrol car at the official entrance to the zoo, she was the first on the scene. The others, specialists and technicians, had farther to come of course; nevertheless she'd hurried because she'd found that once they arrived a certain atmosphere and individuality of the crime was lost in their turmoil.

Getting out of the Honda, she walked to the filigreed arch and read the legend cut into the marble slab just below:

THE CHILDREN'S ZOO
A Gift to the Children of the City of New York
by
Governor and Mrs. Herbert H. Lehman
1960

Norah took a deep breath, straightened her shoulders, and walked up the three steps into the arcade-style building, passing through the single corridor and emerging on the other side into the zoo proper.

Her first impression was of time stopped, of utter stillness and complete absence of sound or motion. To her right, the patrolman, notebook in hand, stood over the body of the victim, partially shielding it from her view. To her left, two men and a gray-haired, hunchbacked woman, all three dressed in dark green Parks Department fatigues, seemed to be in a state of suspended animation. What Norah saw between the groups made her gasp and like them also freeze. She had been told that some animals had been killed, but she had not been prepared for the carnage. Nothing, no matter how detailed, could have prepared her.

A soft breeze wafted into the enclosure which was below street level and with it a soft flurry of leaves sifted down. It broke the spell. Norah stirred and slowly, reluctantly, moved toward the contact pit dominated by the giant wooden Jonah's whale around which the dead bodies of ducks, geese, swans lay in untidy heaps, their long slender necks obscenely twisted. From there she turned right and began the sad tour.

16

The first structure she approached bore a sign: The Three Little Pigs. There were only two inside, butchered, lying on blood-soaked straw. The Cow Barn was next. The cows cringed at her approach, but they were okay; their size apparently had saved them. Inside MacDonald's Farm the sheep had had their throats cut. As Norah crossed over a small bridge to the Rabbit Hutch, the rabbits, well protected behind mesh screening, scurried frantically to the farthest corner away from her.

She'd had enough. She walked over to the human victim. "Sergeant Mulcahaney, Homicide." She showed the patrolman her gold shield.

The dead man was lying supine in front of The Three Little Pigs in a patch of blood and mud—how much of the blood was his and how much theirs would be determined at the lab. He wore a uniform, dark green: the flashlight and ring of keys that had apparently fallen out of his hands were lying beside him. Norah knelt. He appeared to be Hispanic, in his late fifties, with dark, wavy hair turning to gray and in some places already white. He was about five foot six and a hundred and forty pounds. A small, ordinary man, not particularly prepossessing, not a figure to strike fear into a band of young marauders—except for the gun, of course. Where was the gun?

Norah looked around. They could have taken it away. Apparently, he hadn't had time to use it. The reason she thought he hadn't fired any shots himself was the condition of his face: the lower half of his jaw was pulp. To do that much damage the bullet must have hit him from close range. If shots had been exchanged at that range, the perpetrator would also have been grievously wounded, and Norah saw no indications of a bloody trail. The technicians would make a closer examination. She decided to leave it to them; amid the welter of gore and mud, under the piles of dead animals, there was no telling what clues might lie. It would take a team of experts and care to go through it all.

As she got up Norah noted the nameplate pinned to the patrolman's jacket. "What've you got for me, Officer Frasso?"

Notebook open, he was ready to answer, but instead he gasped and pointed. "Sergeant, your skirt!"

Lou Frasso was no rookie. He had been on the force five years, only a little less than Norah Mulcahaney, but he didn't know that. He'd spent three of those years trying to make

17

sergeant and had already taken the exam twice. He'd passed both times, but the first time some candidates had got hold of the questions in advance and the test had been voided: the second time, Frasso's name was halfway down the list, but with budget cutbacks promotions were delayed and time limitations ran out before they got to him. He was now waiting for another try. As a result of his frustrations, Frasso was inordinately impressed with those who had made the grade and eager to please.

Now he sweated under his heavy uniform, too heavy on this mild morning. Had he goofed mentioning her skirt? He'd spoken impulsively, meaning well, but you never knew with women. They were so damn prickly; they made such an issue out of being treated like one of the guys. Women on the force didn't bother Frasso. Before the switch to one-man cars Frasso had actually been riding with a woman. But this was his first experience with a lady sergeant. And no ordinary sergeant, but a detective sergeant, the equal to a captain—in pay anyway.

Norah looked down to where he pointed. She was wearing a knit suit of forest green with a wide beige border and the entire hem of her skirt was soaked in mud and . . . just say it was soaked in mud. "I should have had more sense than to wear my best outfit to work," she observed ruefully. In fact, Norah preferred slacks on the job, not only because they were comfortable and practical, but under slacks she could wear the leg holster with her second or backup gun. She'd worn the suit today to church and then, becoming engrossed with Toni, simply hadn't had the time to change. "I suppose it'll come out," she said, considering the stain.

Frasso relaxed. "My wife washes her knits in cold water with some special stuff. Woolite, I think it's called."

"I'll try it, thanks. So, Frasso, what've you got for me?"

"Yes, ma'am." Frowning in concentration, Frasso now referred to his notebook. "The victim's name is Raul Pelletier, 121a Wellington Street, the Bronx."

"That's the Tremont section."

"It is?"

"I had a case up there once."

"Oh."

"Who called in the complaint?"

"Mrs. Ida Katcoff." Frasso pointed to the woman standing

18

with the two men. Then he turned back to the body. "He must have surprised the gang and they killed him to stop him turning in the alarm."

"Maybe." Norah was carefully noncommittal. She looked up. "This place is like a fortress."

"We had a similar incident about four years ago," Frasso told her. "Nobody was killed. I mean, no person. Anyway, after that, they raised the wall and put up the iron bars to . . ."

To keep the human animals out, Norah finished silently. The children's zoo was at least twenty feet below street level, girded by a low stone parapet. There was a gap from that wall to a second inner wall in which the iron palings were set, a gap which a reasonably athletic person could leap. Norah walked slowly along the perimeter with Frasso accompanying her. They both stopped at the same time.

"Apparently they came prepared," she observed as they regarded the rope ladder.

"Why didn't they pull it up after them when they went?" Frasso wondered.

"Why bother to climb out when they could just walk out through the front?"

Leaving him, Norah went over to the Hansel and Gretel House where the three park employees stood as immobile as the wood and plaster figures around them. The two men were both black, in their midthirties, medium height, lean and fit. The woman between them, whom they seemed to be shielding and supporting, was white—gray might have been a more apt description. She was gray-haired, gray-faced; not really hunchbacked but rather bent and twisted, probably by arthritis. Her hands were gnarled and clawlike. The swelling of her face, however, and the redness of her eyes were because she'd been crying.

"Mrs. Katcoff?" Norah asked at the same time displaying her ID. "I understand you were the one who called the police."

"Yes, ma'am."

"Were you also the one who found Mr. Pelletier?"

"Yes, ma'am."

"I'm sorry. It must have been a shock for you."

"It was. He was such a fine man. He loved the animals, just like we do. I'll bet he was just wild when he saw . . ." The old

19

woman looked around and the tears filled the reddened eyes anew.

One of the men put a hand on her shoulder. "Ida's worked here for fourteen years," he explained. "She knows every one of the animals by name. She knows their history, personality . . ."

"I was here the first time. The first time it happened." Ida Katcoff sniffed back the tears. "I never thought I'd see it again. Never, never."

Norah sighed.

"Why did they have to do it?" she demanded. "Why? My poor Rosie." She pointed inside the stable to the body of a small Shetland pony lying sideways. Behind it, Norah spied another, smaller form. "She gave birth just yesterday. The foal, Clementine, she was so big we thought she was going to be twins. One day old, one day of life she had . . ." Racking sobs convulsed her.

Both men closed in to comfort her.

Norah waited till Ida Katcoff was calmer. "About Raul Pelletier—did he have any enemies? How did he get along with his co-workers?"

Mrs. Katcoff replied promptly and enthusiastically. "Everybody here liked Raul." She turned toward her co-workers with the certainty that they would support her and they nodded decisively. "He was CETA, not civil service, so he didn't get paid as much as the rest of us, but he never griped. He was never resentful; he was just glad to have the work. His poor wife, what this will do to her! They buried the son, Xavier, not six months ago. He died of a drug overdose. They were still mourning. The poor woman. What's going to happen to her? CETA workers don't get pension or death benefits, nothing."

"May I have your names, please?" Norah addressed the men.

"Lewis. Neal Lewis."

"Howard Hoff."

Lewis was the taller, held himself a bit straighter and with more assurance, suggesting seniority in the job. "When did you arrive on the scene, Mr. Lewis?" Norah asked.

"I came with Ida. Actually, I was a few steps behind her. I could see her when she reached the main gate and I took note that she stopped there longer than usual and that Raul wasn't there. Unless it poured rain, Raul was usually stand-

20

ing there waiting to let us in. I don't remember his ever keeping us waiting. So I ran to catch up to Ida, and she told me that she'd found the gate unlocked. Raul would never go off and leave the gate unlocked. Right away I got this funny, sick feeling in the pit of my stomach."

"I see. And how long have you worked here, Mr. Lewis?"

"Six years."

"Did you know Mr. Pelletier well?"

"Yes, ma'am. We're all close. We're a close group here." He paused. Neal Lewis's grave yet pleasant face, light brown skin and neat features, neatly cut hair, neatly trimmed mustache, his freshly laundered uniform suggested a well-ordered life, a man at peace with himself. Suddenly he frowned. "It just struck me—Raul worked at night and we didn't see all that much of him, still he was one of us."

"If he had any enemies outside, would you know?"

"Five minutes ago I would have said yes to that, right off. Now . . ." Lewis's frown deepened. "I'm not so sure."

"How about you, Mr. Hoff?" Norah turned to the other man whose coveralls were rumpled and showed old stains set in the fabric and new ones that would set long before it was washed, whose face bore the look not of peace but of apathy. Nevertheless, Norah thought, there was the same look of sorrow in his eyes as in the eyes of his companions. Like them, Howard Hoff grieved for the dead man and for the animals that he'd fed and cleaned and cared for. "Can you add anything that might be helpful? Anything at all?"

Hoff shook his head.

"Did Raul Pelletier ever talk to you about his troubles?"

"Outside of his kid, he didn't have no troubles," Hoff grunted.

Fishing into her handbag, Norah brought out some cards. She handed one to each of the three. "If you or any of your co-workers think of anything, give me a call. I'll appreciate it."

"Last time it happened, they said it was kids that done it," Ida Katcoff told Norah. "But they never caught them. You'll catch them this time, won't you?"

"We'll do our best."

"You've got to catch them. You can't let this happen again."

21

"Take her outside. Get her some coffee," Norah suggested to Lewis.

"No, no. I have to clean the cages for the others . . . the ones that are left."

"Later," Norah soothed.

"We're behind in the work already," the twisted, nearly crippled woman explained. "You don't understand. I've got to muck out before they can be fed."

"Mrs. Katcoff, nothing can be touched till the experts get here and examine every single body. That's going to take a very long time. You go with your friends."

At her nod, the two men gently led Ida Katcoff away.

The sun grew hotter as it rose in the clear, pale sky. The inevitable menagerie smells were intensified and along with them the odor of death. Too soon, Norah reminded herself, it was too soon for putrefaction; she was allowing emotion to influence her senses. Norah had seen death in many forms over the years and she'd learned to remain objective. On this day, she was troubled because she was more touched by the massacre of the animals than by the death of the man. She understood the reason behind her reaction: the animals had not been merely helpless, they had not understood what was happening to them. Terror, not understood, is more terrible. The night watchman at least had known why the gun was pointed at him. Still, Norah felt guilty for grieving for the animals more keenly and so she promised herself that she would find Raul Pelletier's killer.

It wouldn't be easy. It never was when a stranger killed another stranger. It was not only the saddest of crimes, the most depressing and frustrating, but the most difficult to solve. The crime that every detective dreaded facing and the kind of crime that was becoming most frequent.

On the surface, Officer Frasso's assumption that the break-in had been one of those inexplicable, psychopathic, subhuman acts of senseless violence seemed right. Norah agreed that the torture and murder of the animals had alerted the night watchman, that Pelletier had surprised the perpetrators and had been shot so that he wouldn't turn in the alarm. Both Frasso and Mrs. Katcoff apparently took it for granted that the perpetrators were kids, teenagers. Evidently, there was precedent. Also, they assumed that the raid had been a random impulse which, feeding on itself, had grown into a blood orgy. If so, at this moment those kids must be in the grip of remorse, haunted by nightmares. Unfortunately, all the evidence—the rope ladder as means of entry, the multiple weapons—suggested that the sortie had been planned and well planned. If each member of the gang carried one weapon—gun, club, knife, and the one who used his bare hands—that added up to four. Unless one of them carried the gun in addition to another weapon. Keep the thinking fluid, Norah warned herself; don't reach to conclusions yet, not even tentatively.

"Sergeant Mulcahaney?"

A tall, ascetic figure, so tall that Norah had to tilt her head and squint into the sun to get a good look at him, presented himself. Even for that elongated frame his head was oversized and light brown hair that receded from the bony forehead further emphasized the disproportion. Gray eyes peered out over high cheekbones as though over a ledge. The ridge of a long, aquiline nose separated his face into two parts like a Picasso painting. His voice was soft.

"My name is Arnold Dorrance. I'm the director of the menagerie. They reached me at home and I just got here. I understand that you're in charge. How can I help you?"

"By telling me everything you can about Raul Pelletier. First of all, about his duties. What time would he normally come to work?"

"He worked from midnight to eight A.M. The park closes officially at midnight, but the menagerie closes at five; the public is asked to leave a little sooner. We then lock the access gates and, as I'm sure you've noticed, the children's section is under extra security." He paused. He looked around. "The walls were built because of a previous incident."

"Yes." Norah frowned. "Why didn't the birds—the fowl—the ducks and the geese, why didn't they fly away? Why don't they now?"

"They can't. Their wings have been clipped." Dorrance's soft voice was barely audible.

"Did Pelletier have a regular round and stations at which he clocked in?"

"Yes. He'd just completed his first round."

That would help the Medical Examiner to narrow down the time of death, Norah thought. "I understand Mr. Pelletier was well liked."

23

"Very well liked," Dorrance agreed. "It was unusual because he was a man of superior education and background. Very important in his own country. Held a top government position. He never spoke of it, though, or let it be a barrier." He sighed. "There is one thing; I don't know if it's relevant. His son was into drugs."

Norah nodded. "I was told he died of an overdose."

"Yes." Still Dorrance hesitated.

She could feel the weight of his look probing, measuring, trying to make a decision. "Whatever it is, Mr. Dorrance, you'll feel better if you tell me."

"I suppose so. Well, Pelletier went to the police and positively identified his son's supplier. He brought charges. He insisted on bringing charges. No delays, no postponements, no hours of waiting in courthouse corridors discouraged him. It cost him time at work, but he persevered. Finally, just before trial, the DA dropped the case. After all the hours Pelletier put in, the accused didn't spend so much as a night in jail. Pelletier was beside himself. He came to me; he asked me how such a thing could happen within our judicial system. I couldn't answer."

Dorrance was watching for Norah's reaction. She was careful not to show any.

"He also asked me what he should do next. I couldn't tell him that either."

Any emotion she might show would indicate a judgment on the police, the prosecution, the court, or all of them. "Did Pelletier carry a gun?" she asked.

"None of our people carry guns," the director replied. "We . . . didn't . . . consider them necessary."

On this Norah was not only willing but anxious to show her feelings.

Chapter III

With the drug angle as a lead maybe it wasn't going to be so tough after all, Norah thought as the various crews that rolled on every homicide squeal began to arrive. Men of different personalities, hardened by years of contact with violence, veterans of the unspeakable, each one stopped on the steps stunned by the scene before him.

Clem Everard, photographer, a particular friend of Norah's, turned to her. "I suppose you want shots of everything."

"Everything."

He sighed and began to set up his equipment, his normally florid complexion ashen.

"Don't forget the access route." Norah pointed to the south wall and the rope ladder. "There are a couple of faint prints in the dirt underneath." She made a note for herself to try to trace where the ladder had been bought. Then, while the area was being photographed, measured and sketched, examined and searched, Norah made her own unofficial drawing of the scene. It would be approximate as to dimensions but accurate with regard to the location of the victims in their relation to one another and with specific notes as to the manner of their dying.

"Sergeant!" Dr. Phillip Worgan called curtly. A newcomer to the office of the Medical Examiner and the youngest member of the staff, Worgan consciously patterned himself on his chief. Whereas Osterman's taciturnity based on thirty-one years of high accomplishment was tolerated, even cherished, Worgan's imitation made no friends, not among the police, at any rate. "Sergeant," he repeated the peremptory summons. "Have you been able to establish any time reference?"

Norah was more amused than annoyed. "Arnold Dorrance, the director of the menagerie, states that Pelletier punched in from his first round. He came on at midnight; I haven't checked the time clock yet. I'll do it now."

The station was only a few steps away.

"Twelve thirty-five," she told him when she got back.

"Thank you." Worgan hesitated. He was studious and conscientious but he made a fetish of both qualities that irritated even his colleagues. He frowned behind steel-rimmed glasses, apparently debating with himself as to just how much he should say. "I'll estimate the time of death at between one and three A.M."

Norah nearly laughed. He wasn't telling her anything any detective present couldn't figure for himself; they both knew it. By his lights, however, it was a breach of procedure and Worgan was committing it not out of any particular regard for Norah Mulcahaney but because he sensed the feeling of everyone around him and did not want to seem the only person unaffected and unwilling to bend a little to expedite the solving of the case.

"I can't estimate the caliber of the weapon till the bullet is recovered," he went on, cross at having been forced to relax his standards.

Norah said nothing; she was more careful than ever to show no expression, but he realized himself that he was belaboring the obvious. So then he tried to cover with a pompous display of expertise. "I'd say the bullet will be lodged in that wall over there. Look for it about four feet up and . . ."

"Got it, Doc, right here," Al Krensky, Ballistics, sang out cheerfully. "I'm afraid it's not going to be much use, Norah," he told her as she and Worgan walked over. He pointed to the pocket in the concrete. "Slug's just about flattened out. We'll figure the trajectory and give you the height of the perpetrator, but for comparison purposes . . ." He shook his head.

"Thanks, Al. Everything helps," Norah replied. "Dr. Worgan? Are you going to look at the animals now?"

"What do you want to know about them?"

"Anything you can tell us, Doctor. What kind of club or stick or pipe was used in battering them; the type of knife and length of blade used for the stabbing; how the strangling was done. Anything we wouldn't know without you."

He looked surprised. "Of course, Sergeant . . . uh . . . Mulcahaney." Stiffly, he wheeled around and strode to the first of what was to be a long, minutely detailed round of examinations.

Al Krensky winked. "Sic 'em, kid."

"I meant it, Al."

"I know. That's what makes it work." He grinned at her and went back to his own job.

Having undertaken the task, Phillip Worgan performed it with professional thoroughness. "I can't tell you anything about the weapon used in the battering." He seemed almost apologetic, not quite. "I couldn't find slivers or splinters, so that suggests some kind of metal, a pipe, although it could also have been wood that was strong, well sanded, and varnished . . . say a baseball bat." He hesitated. "I just don't know." He recovered assurance quickly. "There's no difficulty regarding the strangulations. They were done with the bare hands and whoever did them had considerable strength. Those swans put up quite a fight." He pointed.

In death, the wings of the black, mute swans were outspread, their span nearly six feet. It must have taken strength and determination to hang on as they flapped and thrashed.

"We can be quite precise as to the knifings," Worgan continued, and though he didn't smile, there was no mistaking his satisfaction. "The blade was approximately eight inches long; we'll have the exact measurement when we do certain selected autopsies. But I can state at this time that it was the same knife used throughout and by the same person, a right-handed person. I hope that will be useful."

"It's bound to be, Doctor."

"Anything else, Sergeant?"

"Not unless you can think of anything, Doctor."

And he did try. Then he smiled briefly. "We'll move the body."

It took time after that to record the scene and the condition of the animal victims by the photographers and the police artists. Only when that was done could the area be searched for clues. It was slow and tedious and Norah stayed till the very end. She stayed until every cage and every pen and stable, except for those in which the survivors still cringed and whimpered, had been examined—the straw and soil sifted and raked, the drinking troughs scrutinized. Nothing. No threads of fabric caught on a fence, no scrap of paper or matchbook conveniently dropped. Maybe, if one of the animals had scratched at its assailant . . . Nobody complained about the extra time it took to examine the claws, only that it brought no results. Finally, when they could pack it in, when everybody climbed into cars and left, Nora took one last turn for a look at the two possible exit routes—south through the main zoo and toward Fifth Avenue, north through the park branching off into any number of paths. The weather had been unseasonably wet yet there were no conveniently muddy footprints to indicate which way the gang had passed. By the time Norah got back to the squad room seven hours had elapsed. It was three in the afternoon; the temperature had hit seventy. She was hot in her stained wool suit, sticky, tired, and hungry.

She sent out for the usual tuna and coffee; she actually liked it. Sliding low in her chair, Norah munched and thought. She should talk to Pelletier's wife; that was the first thing, but it was already close to the end of her shift. Ordinarily, that wouldn't have been a consideration; when it came to her own time, Norah was prodigal. But now she had Toni to consider. Toni was due home at four-thirty, and Norah didn't like the child coming back to an empty apartment. Furthermore, though Joe was usually home a little after five today he was involved in a meeting at the PC's office that could run past dinner time. In fact, he'd already warned Norah that she might have to go ahead without him. So? She could put the Pelletier interview off till tomorrow—after all it was the drug lead that was of primary importance and a simple call to the Bronx Narco Squad should get the wheels turning on that. The interview with the widow might even be more productive after she had the facts on the pusher. Norah knew

28

she was rationalizing and she didn't pick up the phone. She didn't pick it up because it occurred to her suddenly to wonder whether anyone had noticed Mrs. Pelletier. Surely, Dorrance must have, or Mrs. Katcoff.

The main office of the menagerie was in the Arsenal Building. Norah called and was told by the woman answering that Mr. Dorrance was gone for the day. Norah then asked to be connected to the Children's Zoo and was told they had their own telephone number. Grudgingly, it was given to her. Norah hung up and dialed again. The phone rang and rang. A man answered at last. He'd never heard of Raul Pelletier or Mrs. Katcoff. All he knew was that the place was closed till further notice. He hung up before Norah could ask his name.

Making a ball out of the sandwich paper, she put it into the coffee container and dropped the whole into her wastebasket. She couldn't let the woman hear about the murder of her husband over the six o'clock news!

She wasn't thinking straight! The massacre of those defenseless animals had upset her more than she'd been willing to admit. Raul Pelletier would have been due home from work probably around nine in the morning. When he didn't show as usual, his wife would first have wondered, then worried, then called the menagerie office to find out why he was delayed. And so she would have been told—by telephone. At this point in her reasoning, Norah was in her car and headed uptown. She still had no way of knowing if anybody had bothered to pay the widow a visit, but either way, it might help Mrs. Pelletier to know that someone cared about her husband's death and was working to find his killer.

The Pelletiers lived in one of those squat, eight- to ten-story buildings on the borderline of squalor that could be found in every borough of the city. The narrow front courtyard was clean, the shrubs and trees surviving, if not flourishing, and the soil around them free of weeds. Inside, the whorls of spray paint on the walls and across the mailboxes indicated the building was under attack. Norah consulted the directory and then rang the Pelletier bell. After a brief wait, the buzzer sounded releasing the lock. She found the elevator and rode up to the sixth floor. Here, the walls were washed clean and the floors freshly mopped indicating the tenants were in control, for the time being. She rang the bell of 6E.

She was checked through the peephole, but even after that the door was opened only on the chain. "I'm Sergeant Mulcahaney." Norah held up her ID. "I'm here about Mr. Pelletier."

The door was closed so that the chain could be released. The woman revealed on the threshold when the door was fully open was unexpectedly beautiful with long, jet black hair loose around her shoulders, luminous eyes, and very white skin. She was also young. Surely too young to be the widow. A daughter had not been mentioned. However, she was dressed in black—so, a relative maybe?

"I'm a neighbor, Eva Juvelle," she explained, sensing Norah's uncertainty. "Señora Pelletier cannot speak with anyone at this time." The young neighbor stepped aside so that Norah could see for herself.

She looked into a narrow room that appeared cramped despite the sparse furnishings. At the far end, a small, dumpy woman dressed completely in black sat rigidly on a rigid sofa that was more like a settle. Her face was pasty and without expression. Her hands were clasped loosely in her lap. Across from her, a console table up against the wall was arranged like an altar. At its center, on a small stand, stood a plaster statue of the Virgin Mary. At either end, two votive candles in red glass holders burned steadily. At the feet of the Virgin, between the candles, were two photographs—one, of a young man in graduation robes, very handsome, with fine aristocratic features; the other, of an older man, also handsome, wearing a military uniform. They resembled each other. The woman on the sofa kept her eyes on them. Norah now noted that she held rosary beads, but neither her fingers nor her lips were moving.

"She's been like that for hours," Eva Juvelle whispered.

Norah nodded, then stepping forward placed herself within the widow's line of vision, between her and the altar. "Mrs. Pelletier, I'm from the police. I'm very sorry to intrude, but I would like to ask you a few questions."

There was no indication that the woman heard, nor even that she saw Norah. Her eyes remained fixed as though she could look straight through her at the photographs of her husband and son.

"Have you had a doctor for her?" Norah asked the neighbor.

"Yes. He says not to leave her alone, to watch over her. We are taking turns."

"That's very good of you."

Eva Juvelle shrugged. "We help each other."

"Then perhaps you could answer some questions for me?"

"I'll try." She looked directly at Norah and waited quietly.

"How long have you known Mr. and Mrs. Pelletier?"

"It will be six years in September," she replied promptly. "We all came at about the same time."

"Oh?"

"We came from Chile. We escaped the revolution."

"You were friends of the Pelletiers before you came?"

"Not friends, nor even acquaintances. Señor Pelletier was a very important man in our country. He was in the ministry under Salvador Allende. The rest of us were able to get some money and possessions out when we fled; the señor and señora had all possessions confiscated and gave their money for bribes to get out. They arrived only with the clothes on their backs."

"Did Mr. Pelletier continue to take an interest in the politics of Chile?"

Eva Juvelle smiled at Norah's attempt at diplomatic inference. "You mean are we trying to mount a counterrevolution? That takes money. Would we be living like this if we had money? Would Raul Pelletier have taken the job of night watchman?"

Did she protest too much, Norah wondered. No. The regret, the sense of loss pervaded her words and convinced. Unless . . . Norah put that thought aside for later. She glanced again at the unmoving figure of Marta Pelletier. She appeared oblivious of her surroundings, but you could never tell what word or action might reach her.

"I'm told that the Pelletiers had a son, Xavier, and that he died recently. I'm told the death was due to drugs."

"That is so," Eva Juvelle replied and her gaze shifted, her manner that had been so straightforward became reserved, even defensive.

"He died six months ago?"

"Seven." She indicated the older woman. "The black that Señora Pelletier wears was put on this morning for Xavier."

31

"I've also been told that Mr. Pelletier learned the name of his son's supplier and reported him to the police."

"The boy named him before he died."

"Do you know the name?"

"All I know is 'Stoney.' He is called Stoney."

"That's good enough."

Eva Juvelle hesitated. She seemed to be measuring Norah in much the same way Arnold Dorrance had done. "Señora Pelletier did not want her husband to go to the police. She was fearful of retaliation. But he insisted. He was a brave man, a man of principle. He assured her that it was different in this country. He assured her that here they would find justice, and that the police would protect them. It seems he was wrong in both instances." She spoke softly, with the slight sibilance carried over from her native tongue, and it made the accusation infinitely sadder.

"I'll look into it," Norah said. She wished that she could offer more, that she could give assurance of more than her own effort. "That's a promise."

Though there was no sound, somehow Norah sensed that she had made contact with Marta Pelletier. She had not changed position, apparently still in that catatonic state, yet when Norah looked closely she saw that the stiff fingers caressed the beads and the swollen lips framed the age-old prayers.

The Four-two was on her way as Norah headed back downtown and home, so despite some qualms, she decided to drop in: a personal visit, no matter what the circumstance, was preferable to a phone call.

Heads turned when she walked into Narcotics Division and quickly turned away again, eyes averted. A whisper passed around, a low hiss of hostility. Finally, by a process of silent delegation, one man, Detective First Grade George Berenson, the senior man there, came forward.

"What can we do for you, Sergeant Mulcahaney?"

Three months ago on temporary assignment, Norah had been working with these men. During the course of her investigation she'd uncovered evidence of corruption implicating two undercover cops, two of their buddies. She'd had no choice but to report it to IA. Evidently they hadn't forgotten or forgiven. She sighed; shaking her head, she started for the door of the Commander's office.

Three months ago, Captain Sebastian Honn had been in charge there. Honn was a man of absolute honesty and rectitude, the only narcotics detective to survive the Knapp Committee's probe unscathed. Norah had admired and respected him and come close to falling in love with him. Every woman, no matter how high her standards, how strong her morals, how good her marriage, at one time or another daydreams about another man. Norah was no different. Sometimes the fantasies turn into real temptation. But nothing happened between her and Sebastian. They started as friends and they remained friends. If anything, the interlude served to clarify certain dissatisfactions of which Norah had been only vaguely aware and showed her that what she suffered were the growing pains of maturity and had nothing to do with her marriage. It made her appreciate Joe more and love him more. Nevertheless, there were memories and she cherished them. Though Captain Honn had in no way been involved or had any knowledge of the drug skimming, he had resigned and Norah could not shake off a feeling of responsibility.

There was another name on that office door. Norah turned away. She couldn't face Honn's replacement, not yet.

"I need some information," she announced to the men at large.

"Like what?" Berenson continued as spokesman.

"About a pusher called 'Stoney.' "

The atmosphere changed. She had struck a nerve and she didn't quite understand how or why, but she had made them curious. A detective at the far side of the room raised his hand.

"Over here, Sarge."

Norah remembered Earl Duggan. He personified the public's image of the rugged, experienced, tough cop, the cop who has seen too much to hang on to his ideals. Earl Duggan was exactly what he seemed. Though his creased face, the bitter droop of his mouth, and hair that had turned completely gray made him look at least in his midfifties, he was only forty-three. Norah took the chair beside his desk.

"What's your interest?"

"This Stoney could be a suspect in a murder case."

His unruly eyebrows went up. "Care to give me some details?"

The question was ordinary; the tone, the guarded dislike were hard to take. It was almost as though Duggan were on the pusher's side protecting him against her depredations. Unless, of course, Stoney was Duggan's snitch. Either way, she'd have to make a good case before she got the information she was after. "Early this morning, between one and three A.M., a group of vandals entered the Children's Zoo in Central Park and massacred the animals. Apparently, the night watchman, Raul Pelletier, surprised them and they shot him."

"You think it could be because Raul Pelletier fingered one Harold Stoner also known as Stoney and accused him of supplying the drugs that were the direct cause of his son's death?"

"The charge didn't stick." She couldn't keep the accusation out of her voice.

"You know what it takes to get a drug conviction; you were here long enough."

"Sure, but a direct accusation . . ."

"There was no support for it. None. We couldn't make a case."

"Pelletier got the name from his son when the boy was dying," Norah argued. "It was a dying declaration."

• "So the father said."

She sighed. "While you had Stoner, I hope you scared the hell out of him."

Duggan's worn face hardened; his eyes, heretofore merely unfriendly, regarded her almost with contempt. "If you'd been on the case would you have been satisfied with that?"

"Not satisfied, no, of course not."

"You would have been out to get the guy, right?"

"Sure, but . . ."

"I didn't say I didn't believe what the old man told me, or that the DA didn't believe him. I said we couldn't make a case on his word alone."

She was beginning to understand.

"We'd had our eyes on Stoney for a hell of a long time. He's not much . . . way down on the ladder, but we figured to use him to lead us to somebody higher, say middle-echelon. Then

Mr. Pelletier made his charge. The way we figure it happened was that Stoney got hold of some exceptionally pure junk and sold it to Xavier. He OD'd. We couldn't convict Stoney on that, okay, but if he was so dumb he didn't know what he was pushing, he could be responsible for a whole string of ODs. In that case we couldn't afford to let him go on operating. We decided that we had to take him. We set up the routine buys and on the third we made the bust."

"So where is he now?" Norah asked with the sinking feeling that she already knew the answer.

"Waiting trial."

"In jail."

"You got it. He couldn't make bail. Sorry, Sarge."

She winced. "Well, I knew it couldn't be that easy." She got up. "At least Pelletier knew his son's killer was locked up. He had that much satisfaction before he died."

Duggan looked uncomfortable. "I didn't inform him," he admitted. "I was waiting for Stoner to come up in front of the judge, for the conviction and sentencing. I wanted a pretty package with a big bow on it to present to the old man." He paused. "All right, what the hell! I wanted to look good." His steely eyes narrowed and he dared Norah to make something out of that.

Dusk came early at that time of year, yet Norah was shocked at how dark it was when she came out. She looked at her watch: six-fifteen. She'd just stop and call home to let Toni know she was on her way, Norah decided, and turned back into the station house. She found a booth, dialed her own number, and listened to it ring. She listened with growing anxiety, with totally unwarranted foreboding as it went unanswered. Where was Toni? Maybe she'd dialed incorrectly? She hung up and tried again. The ringing sounded more hollow than before, more ominous. Slamming the receiver back on the hook, Norah ran out of the booth to the street.

She didn't slap the red cherry on the roof of the car, but she drove as though the flashing light were there, running stop signs, swerving in and out of lanes, telling herself all the while that there were at least a dozen reasons why the child had not answered the phone. Of course there were, but she couldn't think of one.

*　*　*

35

She parked in front of a fire hydrant and glanced up to the windows of her apartment. The lights were on. What did that tell her? Too impatient to wait for the small, slow, self-service elevator, Norah ran up to the third floor, down the hall, and rang the bell. Not waiting for an answer, she put her key in the lock. The door opened wide—the chain hadn't been on.

"Toni? Darling? Toni . . ." Norah called and stepped cautiously into the foyer and then to the threshold of her own, brightly lit and empty living room. She had already, instinctively drawn her gun. "Toni . . ."

Striding across the living room she entered the hall leading to the two bedrooms, hers and Joe's, and Antonia's. There was a light coming from under the door of the girl's room. Norah put her hand on the knob and as she did so heard a soft moan.

She burst into the room, gun in firing position.

The child was on the bed, lying on her side, knees drawn up in the fetal position. She was still wearing the school outfit of the morning—plaid jumper and long-sleeved white blouse, brown knee socks and brown oxfords. It took one quick look to assure Norah that there was no one else there. She put the gun down on the bureau and approached the bed.

"Toni?" Norah bent over. Gently, she pushed aside a strand of hair. The child's oval face was swollen and grimy from crying, her dark eyes red-rimmed, but she was not crying now.

"What's the matter, sweetheart? What's happened?"

Antonia kept her head down and her hands clasped between her thighs.

"Please darling, let me see." Norah unclasped the hands and drew them away. They were covered with blood. The plaid skirt was soaked with blood that had partially dried. Was it the child's first period? Surely nowadays the girls were prepared for it, at school if not at home. "Are you sick, sweetheart? Is it your time of the month?"

"No." A tremor shook the slender form on the bed. Straightening her legs, the girl turned over on her back for Norah to see the extent of the stain on her school skirt. "They used a Coke bottle. They put a Coke bottle inside me."

It took every effort of her will to keep Norah from gasping. "Who, sweetheart? Who did it?"

36

"Some girls at school. There were five of them."

Reaching down, Norah raised her niece and hugged her. The girl began to cry again, gentle, healing tears. Norah let her own silent tears mix with them.

Chapter IV

"There's no permanent damage done, and that's the main thing." Softly, Joe Capretto shut the door of Antonia's hospital room behind him and putting an arm around his wife's shoulders guided her down the corridor.

"Physically. How about psychologically?"

"She's a well-balanced, normal child. She's been surrounded by love and will continue to be."

"When will Lena and Jake get here?"

"The best they could do was the gambler's special at four A.M. They'll come straight from the airport."

Norah sighed. "I'll stay with her till then."

"Darling, she's under sedation . . ."

"I'm staying."

Norah's face was pale, her chin clenched. Joe knew there was nothing he or anyone could say that would dissuade her. "I'll stay with you."

"No need."

"I want to."

Each held inside a tumult of emotions; each needed to release anxieties and to seek reassurance and solace, also to offer it. Their eyes met and in one long look everything was said that needed to be. Joe drew Norah close and held her for several moments, feeling her heartbeat against his. Then, hands clasped, they walked together back into Antonia's room.

The night passed neither slowly nor quickly, but uneventfully. Both Norah and Joe had spent many worse nights on stakeouts. They knew how to handle the long hours and how to get their rest while remaining alert. They slept by turn and even then at a level fractionally below consciousness, senses attuned to the slightest sound, the merest deviation from the normal. Norah often thought that in the subliminal state between wakefulness and sleep the subconscious became sentinel, a guardian that she knew from past experience would not fail. So this night, while she rested in a leather chair at the foot of Antonia's bed, with Joe in the other chair beside the door, Norah was aware of the girl's stirrings which, due to the sedation, were few, and she was aroused each time the night nurse looked in on her rounds. The first lessening of darkness registered on her closed lids, caused them to flutter till she opened her eyes and, looking out the window which faced east, saw an aquamarine line low on the horizon.

Joe saw it too. "A couple more hours." He was telling her that she could sleep now at a deeper, more restful level.

When she woke again the sun was streaming into the room and Joe was gone. Instinctively, Norah turned toward the child in the bed. She seemed to be resting comfortably. Tossing her blanket aside, Norah got out of the chair and went over for a closer look. Yes, Toni's face framed by the masses of curly, dark hair was no longer puffed, her color was normal. Thank God! Norah murmured a brief but intense prayer. When she looked again, it seemed that there was a look of strain beneath the calm visage, a sign of emotional imbalance? It would pass, she assured herself, and she asked God to restore Antonia psychologically. Then, in stocking feet, she padded into the bathroom.

She looked terrible, Norah thought, peering into the mirror over the washstand. For Lena's and Jake's sake, she ought to pull herself together and show optimism. Having slept in her clothes, the knit suit turned out to have been a fortunate choice after all because it showed no wrinkles. She splashed cold water on her face and patted it dry with paper towels. Then she ran a comb through her hair, retied it with the green scarf, and applied lipstick. That was a mistake; the bright red only emphasized her pallor. Never mind, forget it. Tiptoeing back into the room, she found her shoes and, with a last look at the sleeping girl, carried them out into the hall.

Joe was just coming around the corner with his sister and her husband.

Elena DeVecchi was the eldest of the seven Capretto girls. She was also the most beautiful, brilliantly beautiful, and exceptionally reserved. Whereas the rest of the family were, like their mother, all extroverts, Elena was shy and withdrawn. She never pushed herself forward; on the contrary, she did everything to avoid attention, remaining on the fringes even at a family gathering. Perhaps she derived that temperament from her father who had died while the children were young and who was remembered vaguely, a shadowy figure. Perhaps she got it because of her disability. For Elena of the lustrous hair and limpid eyes, flawless skin and soft smile, was lame—her left leg an inch shorter than the right. It was a minor flaw in perfection, but Elena was painfully conscious of it. She could have married into money, real money and real society, but she chose Giaccomo DeVecchi instead.

Jake recognized himself for what he was—average, in brains, looks, and status. Five foot ten, about eight pounds over the insurance chart's proscribed weight, and all of it in his belly, he had mild brown eyes and thinning brown hair. He was the head of his own accounting firm with no desire to expand beyond the limits of his own personal supervisory reach. He considered that his greatest good fortune in life had been marrying Lena; he wasn't quite sure how it had happened and he never stopped being grateful. For all his limitations and humility, there was quiet strength in Jake DeVecchi. He was not a man easily pushed around.

Norah quickened her steps to meet them. Impulsively, she embraced her sister-in-law. The two women clung together. When they separated, the tears glistened in both their eyes.

"How is she?" Lena asked.

A glance at Joe told Norah that he'd already reported Toni's physical condition, so what Lena wanted was further assurance. "She's going to be fine," Norah said.

40

But it wasn't enough. She looked straight in Norah's eyes. "I mean, how is she?"

"She'll handle it." Then as proof, Norah added, "She gave me the names of the girls responsible."

Jake stepped between them. "We'll go in now."

"She's sleeping," Norah told him.

"We won't wake her."

Sensing some kind of challenge, Norah stepped back and let them pass.

"I've got coffee." Joe indicated the two containers on top of the counter of the nurses' station. "I was on my way with it when Lena and Jake got out of the elevator." He handed her one and together they went to sit in the visitors' lounge.

It couldn't have been five minutes when the DeVecchis came out, Jake striding forward, an angry scowl on his ordinarily amiable face, and Lena trailing behind looking anxious.

"I wish you'd called our family doctor," DeVecchi complained to Joe.

"It was an emergency. We took her to the nearest facility."

"Not we, I. I did it. I brought her here," Norah corrected. "I made the decision. What's wrong?"

"Nothing. Only . . . she's a child and under the circumstances . . . Well, it would have been better if she'd been examined by someone she knew, somebody sympathetic."

"Do you think I'd let anybody touch her that wasn't sympathetic?" Norah demanded.

"I'm not blaming you. I'm not blaming you, for God's sake. What's done is done. Now, I want to get her out of here. Who do I see?"

Joe's eyes warned Norah not to say any more. She nodded. Jake was simply expressing his anger and frustration and lashing out at the nearest person. It happened to be her.

"The nurse will call the resident for you and he'll sign her out," Joe told his brother-in-law. "We'd better be going," he said to Norah.

"Yes." With uncharacteristic demonstrativeness, Norah kissed Lena on the cheek. "Don't worry. I have the names of the girls. I'm going straight to the school and see the principal, then I'll pick them up. They'll be charged with criminal assault. Of course, the trial will be in family court, but I can't see the judge letting them off. They'll be punished."

41

"Hold it. Just hold it." Jake DeVecchi had started toward the nurses' station, but he now turned back and glared at Norah. "You're not going to do anything. You're not going to do anything at all." He was trembling with the effort to hold in his rage.

Norah was stunned. "Why not?"

"Because I don't want you to."

"But . . ."

"I want this whole thing forgotten. I want it forgotten as though it had never happened. The sooner the better for all of us."

"How about for Toni?"

"Particularly for Toni."

"I don't think so."

"It's not for you to say."

Capretto put a hand on his wife's elbow. "He's right, *cara*."

Norah paid no attention. "You can't let those girls get away with it!" she cried out to Jake.

"I don't give a shit about those girls. I care about my daughter."

"They violated your daughter."

"They did. Yes. And it's going to end there. I'm not causing Antonia any more trauma. I'm not having her relive the experience over and over so that the perverts who did this can get a slap on the wrist."

"Jake . . ." Norah pleaded.

"She's my daughter, and I say no. Period." He turned his back on her deliberately and strode off.

Norah followed. "It's not up to you. The law's been broken. I have to . . ."

"Who's putting in a complaint? I'm not. I'll bet my life the school won't. You stay out of it. It's none of your business."

She stopped arguing. She tried to explain as reasonably as she could. "The principal has to be told. Suppose the girls do it again, to somebody else?"

DeVecchi's face remained closed, antagonism a palpable barricade between them.

It was Lena who broke the impasse. She slipped up to her husband and murmured, "She has to tell the principal, Jake."

"All right. All right. But Antonia is not to be questioned. She's not to be confronted with those girls. She's to be kept out of it."

Norah started to shake her head, then she looked to Joe. He shrugged helplessly.

"Suppose Toni wants to testify?" Norah asked.

"She won't want to, not unless you put it into her head. So you stay away from her. I'm warning you, Norah. Keep away from our child."

Norah was stunned and hurt, deeply hurt.

"He'll get over it. You know that." Joe tried to soothe her.

"Sure." Jake would not bear a grudge for long, she knew that; she knew she'd be seeing Toni maybe in a matter of days. It was the words Jake had used: *Our Child. Keep away from our child.*

She let Joe lead her out of the hospital and home. Joe wanted her to take the day off, but she insisted she'd only brood. While they were arguing, a call from Ferdi Arenas settled the matter.

Fernando Arenas had left his family in San Juan, Puerto Rico, to come to the mainland and find a good job to support them all. He couldn't quite do that, but they were proud of him anyway. He was a police officer. A detective. They considered it a position of honor. So did Ferdi. Just about the time he joined the force, public perception of the police underwent a drastic and pejorative change, but it did not even dent Arenas's dedication. From his earliest days first as an undercover cop, then as a detective, he had worked for Sergeant Mulcahaney on her Senior Citizens Squad and now on Homicide. In essence she had trained him, though the training was more a matter of his following an example he admired than a conscious effort on Norah's part.

"I thought you'd want to know right away, Sergeant." Ferdi rarely disturbed her at home. "We just had a call from Arnold Dorrance. It seems they were doing their regular weekly cleaning inside the concrete structures at the Children's Zoo and they found one more dead animal, a raccoon."

Norah waited. He hadn't called her for that.

"It was wedged up inside one of the turrets of what they call the Raccoon Castle. Along with it, broken off, was the upper portion of a baseball bat. Covered with blood."

"I want to see it. Don't let anybody touch anything till I get there." She hung up.

"They found what is probably one of the weapons in the zoo

43

homicide," she told Joe. "I want to see exactly where they found it. As soon as I'm finished I'll go . . ."

"Why don't I go to Toni's school?" Joe offered. "I can talk to the principal."

"You think you can present the case better than I can."

"I'm less emotionally involved."

Norah frowned. "Are you? Are you really?"

He took a breath. "No," he admitted. "Let's just say I hide my feelings better than you do."

People pitied Jonathan Burrell, but Burrell didn't pity himself; he didn't have time. He was too busy seizing on the positive aspects of his life and developing them. The disease had left him mobility in the upper part of his body. At eighty-two, the paralysis was not the deprivation it might have been when he was younger. Public appearances were behind him anyway, had been when he was stricken, but he could still sit at the concert grand in his living room and play the music he loved; he could listen to the vast collection of his own recordings and those of fellow artists over a stereo of the highest fidelity and be fulfilled to a degree few with full physical capability ever experienced. He could even, in his wheelchair and with the help of his male companion, a euphemism for nurse, get out to concerts and the theater. Lately, he had begun to write short critical pieces and submit them to newspapers and magazines where they were eagerly read and respectfully published. Jonathan Burrell concentrated fiercely on what he was able to do, for if he should permit himself to dwell on what was lost, the precarious structure of this new life would collapse, and if that happened, he knew he would not have the courage to start anew.

"Go ahead, Alvin, go on. I'll be all right," he assured the surly young man who had just checked his watch and glanced at the front door for the fourth time in the past ten minutes.

"I don't like leaving you alone," Alvin Keshen protested while continuing to make it obvious he couldn't wait to get away.

Burrell was just as anxious to see him go as Keshen was to leave. The male nurse was twenty-two, blond, short, muscular, with the kind of overdeveloped torso that could have adorned the cover of a physical-fitness magazine. To Burrell he looked like a pear balanced on its narrow end. Though wasted by the illness, Jonathan Burrell had a massive frame, but Keshen handled him as easily as a mannequin. He massaged the withered legs and taught his charge how to build and strengthen those limbs and muscles he could still use. Unfortunately, Keshen felt no sympathy for his employer, actually regarded him with contempt for his physical disabilities, while Burrell in turn deplored his nurse's insensitivity to matters of the mind and spirit.

Keshen was dressed for his afternoon off. He was wearing velvet jeans, a satin body shirt, and a suede jacket. If clothes were any indication, he had big plans.

"She'll be here any minute. There's no reason for you to wait," Burrell assured him.

"Well . . ." Again the nurse consulted his expensive Piaget watch.

Burrell knew he didn't have any private means. Keshen was not the type to tolerate the restrictions of a live-in job unless he desperately needed the money. The fancy clothes, the watch, a gold bracelet, the inevitable gold chains, all had begun to appear during the past couple of months. They could be gifts, but Burrell suspected that Keshen was stealing— from him. Actually, he hoped it was true. He hoped Keshen was padding the household accounts, was getting kickbacks from the tradespeople, or even worse. He didn't like Keshen, sensed a streak of cruelty in him, didn't want him around anymore. It was his son and daughter-in-law who insisted he keep the nurse. His presence was a sop to their conscience. As long as he had a so-called companion living with him, they didn't have to feel guilty about not bringing him into their home. Not that Burrell had a desire to live with them. God forbid! At least here he was the boss.

"I'm telling you to go, Alvin. Go and enjoy yourself." Burrell couldn't hide his growing irritability.

"I'll put you to bed first."

"I haven't had my lunch. Susan will give me my lunch and help me to bed."

"If you're sure . . ."

"I'm sure."

He wanted to yell, but of course he didn't. Wouldn't the man ever get out? Burrell yearned for some solitude, but his son would never allow him to be left alone. On the nurse's time off, Jason Burrell made it a point either to come to sit with his father or to send his wife, Susan.

"I'm sure," Burrell repeated, and at that moment the sound of a key turning in the lock put an end to the sparring.

"I'm sorry I'm late, Dad. I'm so sorry. I couldn't get a cab and then the traffic was just so terrible. You have no idea!" Susan Burrell made her typical breathless and apologetic entrance.

She lived all of ten blocks away, Burrell thought irritably as he submitted to the ritual peck on the cheek. She had no children, no hobbies, nothing to do, yet she was always late.

"Sorry to hold you up, Alvin," Susan continued her compulsive apologies. "Take an extra half hour, please do; you're entitled to it. Oh." She stopped, stricken. "I'm sorry, Dad; it's up to you, of course."

"Thanks, Mrs. Burrell." Making very much a point of it, Keshen turned to the man in the wheelchair. "Is it all right?"

"Certainly. I'm not going anywhere."

Once the nurse was gone, the constraint between Burrell and his daughter-in-law eased somewhat. She busied herself by taking off her camel's-hair coat, a standard belted style, and hanging it in the closet. Today, Burrell noticed, instead of the usual sweater, skirt, and loafers, Susan was wearing a nice silk dress of a vivid coral shade and pale beige pumps. It was becoming. Come to think of it, she'd been taking more care of her appearance lately. He approved. Susan had been quite a pretty girl when Jason married her. Somehow, her spirit had been quenched. Always shy, she'd become retiring. Burrell hoped that this renewal of interest in herself was an indication that the marriage was improving.

"You look very pretty, my dear."

She blushed. "You don't think the color's too bright?"

"Not at all."

"Oh, I'm glad. Thank you."

Not used to compliments, Burrell thought, and felt sorry for her. "So. How's Jason?"

"Fine. Fine. Sends you his love."

"And Tom and Clare?" They were her parents living in Jersey.

"They send their best. They're looking forward to having you out on Thanksgiving."

"I'm looking forward to going."

46

End of topic.

The next effort was Susan's. "How about lunch? Are you hungry? I'm starving."

So they ate. During lunch the necessity for conversation was minimized and they could deal with the food. Afterward . . .

"Ready for your nap, Dad?"

"All right."

Actually, he did welcome the rest. He let Susan wheel him to his bedroom, hand him the canes by means of which he was able to get himself out of the chair and onto the bed—Keshen had helped him develop the strength to do that. He handed her back the canes which she put across the seat of the wheelchair against the time the process would be reversed. She adjusted his pillows, drew a light blanket over him, pulled the blinds halfway down, and tiptoed out of the room as though he were already asleep.

Soon he'd be able to take care of himself, Burrell thought and stifled his impatience at all the fussing. Meantime, he was collecting evidence against Keshen so that when the time came he could present it to his son and get rid of the creep. To tell the truth, the man was beginning to make him nervous. Well, it wouldn't be long. He closed his eyes and let himself drift off.

Jonathan Burrell awoke with a start.

The room was nearly dark. The lateness and the unexpected heaviness of his sleep caused him to feel disoriented for a few seconds, then he glanced at the bedside clock. Quarter of four. Next, he became aware that the doorbell was ringing. That must be what had awakened him. Hoisting himself to a sitting position, he reached over and turned on the lamp.

The bell rang again, insistently.

"Susan? Susan!" he called out. "Where are you?"

No answer.

Where was she? What had happened to her? Reaching for his canes, Burrell made the difficult shift from bed to chair, then wheeled himself into the living room.

"I'm coming. I'm coming."

He was annoyed. Apparently, Susan had gone out; he had no idea where or why and he didn't care. But apparently she'd also forgotten her keys. Reaching up, he turned on the wall switch. She could have got one of the doormen to let her

47

in with a passkey. Didn't she know better than to disturb him like this? She did know better. Burrell felt a flutter of his heart that the doctor had warned him about. He took a deep breath. Something had happened to Susan. Wasting no more time, he propelled himself to the front door, reached for the knob, and pulled it open.

"You!" He was greatly surprised and relieved. Then exasperated. "What do you want?"

For answer, his chair was grabbed at the back and turned completely around and sent careening through the foyer and across the wide living room. In his attempt to slow it down, Burrell jammed the brake on too hard, causing the chair to stop abruptly and tip over, dumping him on the floor.

He couldn't get up. He saw the bat raised high. He put up his right arm to fend off the blow.

Chapter V

According to the latest statistics there were over 1,731 homicides committed in the city and the year was not over. At that rate, murder had become ordinary. As far as the police were concerned, the ultimate offense of one man against another was reduced to routine. Which is not to say that they had lost respect for human life, or that they were lax in the investigation of murder, only that it required some unusual aspect—say a kinky twist like the two women in the downtown motel whose heads and hands had been cut off and taken away—to trigger an all-out effort. Or, of course, if the victim was a public personality—politician, actor, crook—then the shock waves starting with the homicide cop, usually a "dick three," spread in ever-widening circles till they reached the top brass.

Gus Schmidt was the detective third grade who caught the squeal from Belmonde Towers. A gray man, hair at that uncertain stage between sandy and silver, skin seldom touched by the sun, medium height, slight build, mild eyes peering through black-rimmed glasses, Schmidt looked more like a clerk than a cop. He was thorough and meticulous and also, unfortunately, overly cautious, a man not inclined to "rock the boat," nor ever to call attention to himself. He had looked forward to retiring after the initial twenty years, but with the death of his wife and the absence of another family, Gus had signed on again and then again. Now he had no life outside the job. As a member of the Fourth Homicide, Gus Schmidt had developed into a skilled investigator, he'd gained confidence and learned to accept responsibility. However, he still remained eager to carry out orders but reluctant to give them.

Conditioned instinct told Gus Schmidt that this was going to be one of the big ones. For starters, money was everywhere evident. For starters, there was the cluster of dark, tinted glass towers rising at the edge of the East River spelling luxury. Big money was evident in the manner in which the glass door was held for him by a white-gloved, uniformed doorman; by the marble lobby, lofty, airy, decorated with living plants as discreetly placed as museum sculptures. It was in the respect with which he was passed along by the various employees on his way up to the eighteenth floor, a respect which he derived at secondhand from the victim, Jonathan Burrell. The name meant nothing to Schmidt nor to the patrol officer who had preceded him to the scene and was waiting for him.

Schmidt was first struck by the lights. They gleamed everywhere from lamps on tables and consoles, from spotlights over fine paintings. For a moment all those lights puzzled Gus till he realized they must work off a master switch and that seemed to answer some as yet unformed question in his mind. They created an atmosphere of elegant tranquillity and, for just a moment, almost overcame the chaos. They couldn't for long, of course. The room had been throughly and violently ransacked.

The desk had been rifled; the paintings were askew; the books had been swept from shelves to the floor. The wheelchair had been overturned and the victim lay on the floor beside it at the foot of his grand piano. Gus took a close look at the victim. Blood from a large wound in the chest had soaked into the velvety beige carpet, but there were many other, smaller, wounds, rusty stains on a pristine white shirt. His head was turned sideways revealing an ugly bruise that spread from the jaw to the right eye. The right arm was bent at an unnatural angle, obviously broken.

The woman who had discovered the body and called in the complaint, according to the responding officer, was the dead man's daughter-in-law. She had passed from hysteria into shock and now sat in the farthest corner, eyes averted from the battered body, a soggy rolled-up ball of handkerchief clutched in her hands. When Schmidt spoke to her, she merely moaned.

He left her and went into the bedroom.

The shades were drawn and only the bedside lamp was on. The spread had been removed and the bed was rumpled but the covers had not been turned back. What was of greater import was the wall safe above the head of the bed—wide open. Schmidt scowled. He took off his glasses, massaged the bridge of his nose. This had all the too familiar signs of your "push-in" murder, including the torturing of the victim to find out where the valuables were kept. But this was not your typical "push-in" building. Gus put his glasses back and went to the phone.

"This is Schmidt. Let me speak to the Lieut."

Lieutenant Carlock's son, Tommy, eight years old, had been hit by a car as he crossed the street on an errand to the grocery store for his mother. The Lieutenant had rushed to the hospital and Sergeant Mulcahaney was covering for him. She took Schmidt's call. She told him she'd be right over.

The elegant, luxury apartment was crowded with detectives and technicians by the time Norah arrived. Having completed her own tour of duty, she was by now halfway through Carlock's. Though double tours were not so unusual, Norah was extra tired because of the uneasy night spent at Toni's bedside. Her body dragged, but her mind was alert. In fact, in such situations she'd found that the energy of the mind kept the body going. She began a slow, almost leisurely examination of the scene, listening to Gus's report as they walked together. She was particularly intrigued by the gap in the tightly packed shelves of records and record albums above the stereo equipment. Books had been indiscriminately cleared off their shelves, but the records had not been touched except for this one spot. There were no albums or loose records lying around to account for it and nothing on the turntable.

She looked briefly into the master bedroom: lab men were lifting prints from the wall safe. The bed was pushed aside to give them access, so she assumed photographs had already been taken. She moved on to the second, smaller bedroom. That it belonged to a man and that he was young was obvious from the clothes in the closet. That his circumstances had improved recently she deduced also from his clothes, some of which were worn and cheap to the point of sleaziness, while others were new and snobbishly expensive. She noted a row of medicines along the bureau with a small silver salver covered with a clean, folded napkin.

Next, Norah wandered into the dining room. Whoever had cleared had left crumbs on the highly polished walnut table and in returning the candlesticks had not properly aligned them. The dirty dishes had been left on the pantry counter.

Now she was ready to go back for another look at the victim.

From his position, from the multiple bruises and wounds, Norah drew the same conclusion as Schmidt; however, an inconsistency that he had surely seen but not fully registered intrigued her. The victim was fully dressed and wearing a wristwatch, the crystal of which was smashed. But the watch was on his left wrist, whereas all the damage had been done to his right arm which he'd apparently raised in self-defense. Also, most of the injuries had been inflicted to the right side of his body.

"What do you think?" Norah asked the Medical Examiner who happened on this occasion, by chance or design, to be the Chief, Asa Osterman, himself.

"The watch stopped at three-fifty P.M. That's consistent with my estimate of the time of the assault."

"Could he have smashed it himself to give us a lead?"

"Being the man he was, very possibly."

"The perpetrators could have done it themselves, to throw us off," Norah pointed out, and as soon as she had, realized she'd automatically assumed there'd been more than one— because of the beating and knifing. Osterman didn't contradict her. "How long did they work him over before he died?"

He was a small, dapper man, an aging leprechaun, who had been Chief Medical Examiner of the city of New York for as long as anyone could remember. He was celebrated for his tart tongue, natty attire, and fanatic accuracy. He raised his head and regarded Norah severely through thick pince-nez glasses. "You know I can't answer that."

"I thought the extent of the bruises and the lividity . . ."

"There'd be no point to beating him up after he was dead."

"How about the bleeding?"

"He died slowly." Asa closed his lips as though he had no more to say. Then he pointed to the woman in the corner, the woman Schmidt had said was the victim's daughter-in-law. "Don't ask me how long it took; ask her."

Norah frowned. "Are you saying—"

"Lousy way for any man to die," Asa cut her off. Most uncharacteristically, Norah thought. "It is *that* Jonathan Burrell?" she asked.

"Ayah." Osterman slipped into the dialect of his Maine origin. "Ever hear him play?"

"In a movie, a long time ago."

"Pfui. Tricks on the keyboard, that's all that was. Prestidigitation. I mean, did you ever really hear Jonathan Burrell perform?"

Norah's musical education was limited. Joe had introduced her to grand opera and she'd learned to enjoy it, if not to appreciate it. "I don't think so."

"If you had, you wouldn't forget it," Osterman grunted and got up. "So. How are you, Norah?"

"Okay, thanks, Asa. Fine."

"And Joe?"

"He's fine."

Though he treated her in the same gruff style as everybody else, Osterman had a special predilection for Norah Mulcahaney. He thought he sensed a reservation, but then . . . he shrugged it off. None of his business. His business was finding out the exact cause of death. That would be done in the lab. While he was here, he could consider the why and the who. It was Osterman's contention that forensic medicine and the job of the medical officer should not be limited to the examination of the victim but should include everything at the scene and the final opinion based on all the available evidence. So he looked now at the gap on the record shelf and then at Norah. "It's a very esoteric collection," he remarked. "Mostly Burrell's own recordings and a lot of seventy-eights that are no longer available. It would be interesting to know what was taken."

The phone rang. At Norah's nod, Schmidt picked it up. "Alvin?"

"Who's calling?"

"Is this the Burrell residence?"

"Yes, sir. Who's calling?"

"I'm Jason Burrell. Who are you?"

At that point, Norah took the phone. "This is Sergeant Mulcahaney, Police Department. Are you related to Jonathan Burrell?"

"I'm his son."

"I think you'd better come over here, Mr. Burrell."

"What's happened? What's the matter? Let me speak to my wife. Let me speak to Susan. She is there, isn't she?"

Norah looked over. The woman hadn't moved since Norah's arrival. "She can't come to the phone right now."

"Why not? My God! Why not?"

"She's all right, Mr. Burrell, but she can't speak to you right now. Please come as quickly as you can." Norah hung up.

The officer stationed outside the apartment in the hall now looked in. "There's a Mr. Keshen wants to come in. Says he lives here."

"Okay." Norah nodded and placed herself in such a way that she blocked immediate view of the body.

Keshen came sweeping to the center of the room. "What's going on?" he demanded at large. "Where's Mr. Burrell?"

Norah stepped aside.

Keshen stared down at the battered and bloody body of his employer. "God . . ." he murmured, transfixed in horror. It took several seconds before he looked up. As Norah was the nearest, he spoke to her. "What happened?"

"We're trying to find out. Maybe you can help us."

Under his suntan makeup the nurse went from winter white to ash gray and it showed through. "I don't know anything. It was my afternoon off."

"You worked for Mr. Burrell?"

"Yes, ma'am. Companion and nurse. I take care of him. I took care of him. He was partially paralyzed. He had a degenerative disease of the spine which caused him to lose control of the lower portion of his body. He'd made a good general recovery, but there were certain things he couldn't do for himself."

Norah recalled the medicines lined up on the bureau. "You were responsible for giving him his medication?"

54

"That's right. I acted as his secretary, ran the house, and I was also his friend."

"I see. And where were you at about four this afternoon?"

"I told you; it was my afternoon off."

"Yes. And where were you?"

"Visiting a friend."

"I'm sorry, but that's not good enough. You'll have to give me the name. I'm not interested in your private life, believe me, Mr. Keshen. I just want to know where you were at four o'clock this afternoon."

"Why don't you ask her where she was?" Keshen pointed an accusing finger at Susan Burrell. "She was supposed to be with him, watching out for him. Ask her where she was."

"I'm asking you. What's your friend's name?"

He glared sullenly, but gave in. "Albert Baines—KL-5-6601."

"Thank you." At a look from Norah, Schmidt slipped away to make the call. "Friday was your regular day off?" Norah continued.

"The afternoon. I was supposed to leave at one and get back at eight. While I was gone either Mr. Jason Burrell or Mrs. Burrell was with him. He wasn't supposed to be left alone. But Mrs. Burrell was late getting here; she didn't get here till close to one-thirty. She told me I could take an extra half hour. I took an hour. What was she going to do? Fire me?"

"Do you know of anyone who might have reason to kill Jonathan Burrell?"

"No, ma'am. He led what I call a structured life, everything in a set routine. He couldn't get around except in the wheelchair and even then he needed some help—like if there were steps, or a steep incline, you know? He had a small circle of close friends and he went to their homes or they came here. They were people he'd known for years, important people, most of them pretty old and creaky themselves. They wouldn't need to break in here and steal . . ." He looked around.

"Yes, Mr. Keshen? Steal what? I'd like you to look around and tell me what's missing, if you can. Detective Schmidt will go with you and make a list. But first, I'd like you to take another look at Mr. Burrell and tell me if he's dressed as he was when you left."

Keshen wasn't too eager to look again, but he managed. "He's not wearing his jacket. Probably he took it off before lying down for his nap."

"He took a regular nap?"

"After lunch. Yes, ma'am."

"But he didn't undress?"

Keshen shook his head. "It was too much trouble."

Norah noted Schmidt returning from the bedroom where he had gone to place the call to Keshen's friend. His nod told her the alibi had been confirmed. "Thank you," she said to the nurse and turned to Susan Burrell.

She was about thirty-five, small, slight, and washed-out looking. Her skin was sallow, her dark hair lank and cut in bangs that nearly obscured her eyes. She wore a camel's-hair coat buttoned all the way to the neck and sat huddled in it as though she were chilled through.

"I'm Sergeant Mulcahaney, Mrs. Burrell. How are you feeling? Would you like anything? Coffee? Why don't we go to the kitchen and get ourselves some coffee?"

By an effort, Susan Burrell focused on the woman who stood in front of her and what she was saying. "Coffee. Yes, I'd like some coffee."

"Let's go then."

Norah was patient while she got to her feet so slowly and then looked around as though she'd never been in the place before and didn't know where the kitchen was. It ended with Norah having to nudge her toward the dining room, pull out a chair, and leave her while she went into the pantry to locate the Instant.

"How do you take it?" she called out.

There was a wait, then as Norah was about to ask again the answer floated back. "Milk, no sugar."

When the coffee was ready, Norah brought two cups out to the dining room and sat at the table catercorner from the witness.

"I'm sorry to intrude on your sorrow, Mrs. Burrell."

"You're a policewoman?"

"Yes. Sergeant Mulcahaney. Please call me Norah. I'd just like to go over what you saw when you entered the apartment. For instance, was the front door open or shut?"

"Shut," she replied promptly.

"How did you get in?"

Susan Burrell frowned. "I used my key."

"Good." Norah was starting in the middle of the chronology purposely in order to relax Susan Burrell, to make her feel that she was being called on for facts and that she was not herself under suspicion. Later, she'd double back, later she'd interrogate her about her own movements. "So when you got out of the elevator and came down the hall, you had no idea that anything was wrong?"

"No. Oh, no."

"Tell me what you did, exactly."

"I got out my key and opened the door and walked in. And I saw . . ."

"The lights were on?"

"What? Yes, yes." She was impatient to get the account over with.

"Go ahead."

"Well, actually, now that you mention it, I was surprised that the lights were on because that meant that Jonathan was up. I'd left him in bed, you see, and it was quite difficult for him to transfer from the bed to the wheelchair without help."

"Then the lights were not on when you left?"

"No." She waited for further comment from Norah, but when there was none, went on. "I called to Jonathan from the foyer, but there was no answer. So then I came in here." Her face was contorted by the recollection. "It was terrible."

"What did you do?"

"I . . . I guess I just froze. I didn't know what to do. I couldn't bring myself to touch him." From introspection she went to direct appeal. "It wouldn't have done any good, would it? There was nothing I could have done for him. He was dead, wasn't he?"

Ask her, Asa had said, but Susan Burrell hadn't had the stomach to so much as really look at her father-in-law. Now she wanted assurance that Burrell had been beyond saving. Norah had no interest in making it easy for her.

"We'll never know."

Susan Burrell flinched; her lower lip quivered. Apparently, she wasn't used to facing the blunt truth.

On the other hand, it wasn't up to Norah to pass judgment. Some sort of estimate of the time lapse between Susan Burrell's discovery of the body and her call to 911 would have been helpful, but she wasn't going to get it so she gave up. "I gather that your father-in-law had been partially paralyzed for some time."

57

"Two years."

"And that Alvin Keshen was his nurse-companion and lived with him. On Keshen's afternoon off either you or your husband sat with Mr. Burrell."

"Yes."

"So that he wouldn't be alone."

"Yes." .

"Then why did you leave him alone?"

The witness took a quick, shallow breath and plunged into the prepared answer. "I ran out of cigarettes. He was sleeping, and I thought there was no harm in just running out for a few minutes. Just a few minutes. I'll never forgive myself. Never." She put her hands up over her face.

Norah wasn't sure whether she was crying or hiding. "How long were you gone?"

"A few minutes."

"Try to be more specific, Mrs. Burrell." There was an edge now to Norah's tone; she was beginning to apply the pressure.

"I can't."

"Let's see if we can't work it out. What time did you leave?" The witness shook her head helplessly. "You hadn't turned on the lights, yet it was a dark afternoon. That suggests you went out early."

"No, no. It was getting dark. I remember now. I was watching television. I didn't need the lights."

Norah could have asked what show she'd been watching—some instinct told her not to, not now. "All right. It would take you two to three minutes to wait for the elevator and ride down. How long to get to . . . where did you go for your cigarettes?"

"First Avenue. There's a stationer's on the corner."

"That's a long block. I suppose you were walking briskly, still . . . shall we say five minutes over and five minutes back? To be on the safe side let's say five minutes in the store. Would you say you were away twenty to twenty-five minutes?"

"I guess so."

"Mr. Burrell's watch was smashed during the assault, it shows three-fifty. Using that as a guide you were gone anywhere from three-thirty to the time the call was received by 911. We can check that. The lobby attendants probably saw you and can narrow it down considerably."

58

"If you know what time he was killed . . ." She licked her lips nervously but didn't finish. "May I go home now?"

"Your husband is on his way over," Norah told her as a man's voice, loud, authoritative reached them through the closed double doors. "Apparently, he's here," she said as the doors were flung open.

Jason Burrell was a big man about six three, with the same strong build as his father, but his face lacked the open, noble look of the artist. The son's features were smaller, set closer, giving him a secretive look, even mean. Maybe he looked that way because he was so angry. Ignoring Norah, he strode right up to his wife.

Trembling, Susan offered her apology and defense before he demanded either. "It's my fault, Jason. It's all my fault. I left him alone for a few minutes. Just a few minutes, that's all. I'm so sorry. I'll never forgive myself."

"One afternoon a week, that's all I asked you to give up. Was that too much? Where the hell were you?"

She flinched.

"I asked you a question." Jason Burrell's voice dropped threateningly and he took a step forward, his face close to his wife's. "Where the hell were you while punks broke in and beat up my father and robbed him and left him to die?"

"Oh, Jason . . ." Tears, real tears, streamed down her cheeks.

"Well, speak up. Tell me!"

He raised his hand; his wife cringed in anticipation, but the blow never fell. Norah stepped between them.

"That's enough, Mr. Burrell."

"Who the hell are you?"

"Sergeant Mulcahaney, Fourth Homicide. I'm in charge." She displayed her gold shield.

"Is that so?" His handsome face was white, shriveled with anger.

"It is. Now I understand that you're upset, but it's not going to help. I want you to calm down and answer some questions. To start with, where were you between three-thirty and four-thirty this afternoon?"

He looked at her with dismay, then he guffawed. "You think I killed my father?"

"Just answer the question, please."

"Okay. I was in my office. That's at 658 Madison, Swanson,

59

Ludlow, and Dorp, members of the New York Stock Exchange. Trading went through the roof this afternoon; the ticker ran over an hour late. I never left my desk, not even to go to the john. I can verify that."

Norah nodded. "See how easy it is?"

"Where was she?" He jerked his head toward his wife. "Have you asked her? Has she answered?"

"I went out for cigarettes," Susan Burrell murmured.

"You did get them?" Norah wanted to know.

Susan Burrell reached for the purse she had placed on the dining-room table. She opened it and silently proffered the pack for Norah to see. It was a Parliament's soft pack, much crushed, with about four or five cigarettes left. Norah had not seen her smoke one, not before, nor during, nor after the interrogation.

Chapter VI

"I'd like you to take a look around and see what valuables, if any, are missing," Norah told Jason Burrell.

"If any!"

"I can see that there are plenty of valuables the robber or robbers could have taken and didn't," she pointed out. "Maybe they just didn't appreciate their worth, or weren't prepared to fence this kind of merchandise. On the other hand, much time and effort was expended in getting the combination of the safe from your father. Was he in the habit of keeping large amounts of cash on hand?"

"He usually had several hundred dollars in there."

"It's also possible that murder was the prime purpose and the rest—" she gestured around the room—"all of it a cover."

"Why would anyone want to kill my father?"

"I was going to ask you that."

Jason Burrell scowled. "If you're thinking of Alvin . . . first of all, I don't see why he should. Then, he could have done it in so many other more subtle ways. I mean, the two of them were together most of the time. He had all kinds of chances."

"All of which would probably have pointed directly to him."

Burrell shrugged.

"Who hired Keshen?" Norah wanted to know.

"My father, of course. Well, I did the initial interviewing to weed out the obvious incompetents, and, of course, I checked out Alvin's references. He's okay. He's gay, but what difference does that make? This was a good job for him and he was damned glad to get it." Nevertheless, Burrell paused to consider the possibility of Keshen's guilt. "No," he answered his own doubts. "He would have had to know that Susan was going to go out and leave Dad alone. There was no way he could have known that. Nobody could. It had to be a coincidence. Some punk loitering in the hall saw her come out and took the opportunity. There's just no other way to explain it."

Relief that her husband's anger had abated flooded Susan Burrell. Timidly, she assayed a step toward him. He opened his arms to her and in silence they made their peace.

After they were gone, Norah checked the ashtrays in the rest of the apartment. There were plenty of butts left by the police but none was a Parliament filter. The pack Susan Burrell had shown her was an old pack. Whatever she had gone out for, it hadn't been cigarettes.

Norah got home shortly after midnight. Joe was reading in bed. He got up when he heard her coming in. She looked worn out—why not after more than sixteen hours on the job? He took her in his arms and held her for several moments. She didn't respond with much enthusiasm. He let her go.

"So what was it?"

"Could be a push-in robbery and murder, but that involves a lot of coincidence. I'll know more when I talk to the building staff tomorrow. How about you? Did you talk to Toni's principal?"

"I did. Want something to eat? A beer?"

"A beer."

She preceded him into the kitchen. She was tired, Joe reminded himself, just tired. Norah waited while he opened a couple of cans and poured.

"So?" she prompted.

"The principal's name is Garfield. Robert Garfield. He was shocked, naturally. He'll investigate."

"He'll investigate?"

"He needs more than just my word."

"Toni's word," Norah corrected. She was angry and disappointed. She tried to hold both feelings in check. "What did you do? Did you take a look in the washroom? Did you look for blood, for fingerprints . . . I don't know . . . for something just to prove it happened?"

"To start with, I had no right. Besides, the place had been cleaned."

Norah smiled bleakly. "I'm sorry. I'm sorry, darling. I don't mean to take it out on you, but everybody is just sloughing off this thing. And it's not fair. Those girls are going to deny everything Toni says and they're going to get away with it."

"Garfield doesn't strike me as a stupid man. I'm sure he'll know if the girls are lying."

"Then what? What will he do? Expel them?"

"We have to wait and see."

"Forgive me, but I think you're taking this thing much too calmly."

"And you're getting too excited."

"I don't think so. I should have gone myself. I would have demanded that he expel those girls. That's the least, the very least . . ."

"Norah," Joe sounded a warning. "You're trying and convicting those girls. Let's just take it one step at a time."

She glared, but she knew that he was right. "Okay." She sighed and then took a long swallow of the beer. "How is Toni? How's she doing?"

"Good. I called Lena. They're going to keep Toni home for a few days."

"I should think so."

"Darling? Knock it off."

"I know. Sorry."

They sat at the kitchen table in silence for a few minutes. Then Joe cleared his throat. "About the Burrell case—Jonathan Burrell was a very famous man. There's going to be a lot of pressure from a lot of sources for a quick solution. Maybe you could use some help?"

"You?" Her blue eyes brightened; she smiled with pleasure. "You're going to take over? That's terrific. Oh, Joe, I'm glad."

"No, not me, not directly." He took a breath then told her straight out. "The Chief is assigning the task force. He called about an hour ago, asked if I thought you'd welcome assistance."

"That was fast." She scowled, then shrugged. "What could you say?"

"You'll still be carrying."

"Not me. Gus. It's his case. He's not going to argue."

"Gus is a good officer."

"And I'm not."

"Oh, come on! What's got into you lately, sweetheart? What is bugging you? Your attitude toward the task force ... every time it's mentioned you get so—negative and resistant. I don't understand."

"I think it's superfluous."

"The task force? You don't mean that."

"Yes, I do."

"Then that has to mean you're turning down the offer, right? Okay, if that's the reason you're going to give, I don't advise your doing it by telephone or letter. You'd better get yourself down to Jim Felix's office and tell him to his face that the elite squad of the city is expendable, part of the fat to be sliced off the budget ..."

"I'll do that." She turned her head away.

He assumed her chin was stubbornly set, but as he didn't look he couldn't see that it was quivering.

Joe drank the rest of his beer. "I give up," he said. "Let's go to bed."

Norah's first stop the next morning was the stationer's on First Avenue, which was small and so cluttered with merchandise and people she could hardly make her way through the aisles. Most of the customers were from the neighborhood, down to the aged couple that ran the place and also to the graying son and daughter who along with their respective spouses worked there. Quips and pleasantries were exchanged with the regulars; strangers were barely acknowledged. No one remembered a petite, dark woman in a camel's-hair coat who had come in the previous afternoon to buy Parliament cigarettes in the soft pack.

From the stationer's Norah went on to Belmonde Towers to interview the day staff. There was no lack of witnesses to Susan Burrell's arrival shortly after one P.M. on the Friday. The doorman had opened the cab door for her. The desk man had called out to her and handed her Jonathan Burrell's mail. But no one had seen her later in the afternoon on her alleged trip out for cigarettes. It was possible that they had missed seeing her once, but both times—going and coming?

Using the service elevator, Norah went down to the basement. She looked into a large, well-kept laundry room. The machines were churning cheerfully; the women chatting contentedly, most of them in uniform—the maids, of course, for the ladies of these buildings would not dream of venturing into a laundry room, would not know where it was or how to operate a machine. Norah passed by the open door slowly; not one head turned to look at her. Presumably, Susan Burrell could have walked by unnoticed. But could she have got out of the building?

"Can I help you, madam?"

Nicholas Kosloff sat at the desk in an office whose walls were metal mesh so that he had a clear view of the rear door and the corridors. He wore a gray, fatigue-type uniform. He was in his fifties, neat, clean, and he took his job seriously. As soon as Norah approached, he was on his feet, polite, but blocking her way. When he found out who she was, he was more friendly but less respectful.

"My job is to check every delivery," he told her. "I make sure the delivery is expected and the person genuine before I let anybody go up. Then I make sure that whoever does go up comes back down in a reasonable time. If it looks like anybody's been in the building too long, I call the tenant and make sure that everything's all right. If the tenant doesn't answer, or if she sounds . . . funny . . . you know . . . I send one of my handymen right up there."

"I'd like to have you in my building," Norah said.

He accepted the compliment as his due. "I come on at eight and leave at five. The door is locked the rest of the time."

"Do any of the tenants use this entrance?"

"Why would they want to?"

"You'd know if they did?"

"You bet." He pulled back his shoulders and thrust out his chest.

"Did any tenant or visitor use this door yesterday afternoon between four and five P.M.?"

"Absolutely not."

"All right, thanks." She was just about to leave. "How about the maids?"

"Them? They come in the front." There was no mistaking his disapproval.

Back up in the lobby, Norah took another look around the airy, open space. Glass walls extended the vista to the inner patio where trees were still in leaf, and roses, sheltered by the four towers of the complex, still bloomed. The patio was completely enclosed, but Susan Burrell might have used it to enter one of the other buildings and so reach the street. Patiently, Norah questioned the different sets of doormen and deskmen. None of them remembered Susan Burrell.

So she had lied about leaving the building. Why? Was she an accomplice in the murder of her father-in-law? If so, wouldn't she have made a point of being seen? Wouldn't she have made sure not only to leave the building but to be seen leaving? Wouldn't she in some way have called attention to herself both leaving and returning? Did that indicate that she was not merely an accomplice but a participant in the crime?

Returning to Tower A by way of the patio, Norah lingered in the unseasonably warm November sunshine. She raised her face to it, looking up into a rectangle of cloudless sky.

"What do you see up there?"

She jumped. "David! You startled me."

"Sorry. How are you, Norah?"

"Fine. And you?"

"Fine."

He smiled, but he didn't look fine. The sun was harshly revealing. It showed the pouches under bloodshot eyes and the blue sag of his jowls; it emphasized an unhealthy pallor. With slick black hair and regular features, David Link was still handsome, but he looked—dissipated. Norah hadn't seen him in a very long time and the change saddened her.

"And Marie and the boys?" she asked.

"Well, actually . . . we're separated."

"Oh. I'm sorry. I didn't know."

A spasm of distress passed over his face, not for the first time, for it fitted into the tracks that Norah saw there. "What can you do?" He shrugged. "She couldn't take the life style, you know? The routine, or rather, the lack of it."

"I'm very sorry."

66

Norah meant it sincerely. She and David Link had joined Homicide North within months of each other. Both were idealists and being the newest and youngest members of that prestigious squad had immediately joined forces. As time passed, however, a competition developed, friendly at first, then less so. Norah thought that David Link was becoming dangerously pragmatic; David thought she remained foolishly idealistic. He also thought that Joe Capretto had thoroughly quashed Norah's initiative, that through his influence she was mired in routine, stodgy with procedure, and had lost all individuality. Link's theory was that procedure was the crutch of the incompetent, that a good detective knew when to take a shortcut. Norah now saw David as shallow, all flair and no substance. As both, by their respective styles, got results, they began to resent each other. Yet Norah and Joe had double-dated with David and Marie DeWitt. They had been guests at the wedding. However, as the friendship was based on professional contact and as their attitudes continued to clash, they saw less and less of each other outside the job.

"Is it final?" Norah asked. "Is there any chance you might get together again?"

He took a deep breath. "I don't know. I keep trying. I keep trying every way I know to get her back."

There was a long moment of awkward silence as they faced each other in the sunshine.

David spoke. "So. What've we got here? How does it look to you?" Seeing that Norah hesitated, he asked, "Didn't they tell you? Weren't you advised the task force was coming into the case?"

"Yes, I've been advised. I just didn't expect you. I didn't know you were on the force."

He smiled that nice, deprecating smile that she remembered. "I got lucky; I was one of the first picked. But, what the hell, I hear you're up for the assignment yourself."

Suddenly, Norah made up her mind. "I'm not interested. I'm going to study for the lieutenants' exam." Up to now, that had been merely a vague option.

"You're willing to go back into uniform?"

"It wouldn't be for long, I hope."

"You never know. Of course, in your case . . ."

"What do you mean, in my case?"

67

"You've got a built-in rabbi, haven't you? With Joe as Felix's assistant to push for you . . ."

"I don't rise to that bait anymore, David," she retorted. "Everybody needs help. I'm lucky to have Joe, yes. But no matter how hard he pushes for me, in the end I have to deliver. And I know that I can."

"I know it too. Sure. I never questioned your ability."

"Nor I yours."

With that uneasy truce, they got to work. Norah filled him in, but David had already familiarized himself with the basics. While she had been looking for an exit that Susan Burrell might have used, he had been upstairs examining the scene and interrogating Alvin Keshen.

"They didn't get along, those two," David commented, referring to the nurse and his employer. "I got it from several members of the staff and from the handyman who was up there installing a new set of shelves for Burrell. He spent a lot of time, and according to him, the antagonism was thick."

"Why didn't Keshen quit or Burrell fire him?"

Link shrugged.

"Keshen has an alibi," Norah pointed out.

"Alibis can be broken." David produced a tight smile. "I noticed that all of Burrell's private papers have been cleared out of his desk. Keshen said you ordered it."

"Yes. You can come over to the precinct and look at them, or I'll have them sent."

"I'll come over. What are you looking for?"

"I don't know. With Keshen staying on in the apartment, I didn't think they should be left lying around."

"Aha!"

"No *aha*, David, just routine."

"All right, so if you don't like Keshen, how about the Burrells, either or both? Could be Jason Burrell needs money and if he's mentioned in his father's will, as he must be . . . we'll have this wrapped up in no time."

Norah said nothing. The Burrells were certainly the logical, even obvious suspects. What disturbed her was that David should be so ready to settle for the obvious.

The first thing Norah Mulcahaney did when she got back to the squad room was to talk to Gus Schmidt.

"Find anything in Burrell's papers?"

"Maybe." Gus looked up from the hours of close work, took off his glasses, and rubbed the bridge of his nose. "Burrell lived high. Spent a lot of money on groceries for one person— two, including the companion. Even so, the last four monthly bills were way out of line compared to the earlier ones. Apparently, Keshen did the buying and it looks as though Burrell had started to check up on him. There are notes in his handwriting on the margin of Keshen's accounts."

"Good. Go talk to the merchants. Go in as a customer and price the merchandise. Let's see if there was a kickback."

"Right."

Elbows on the desk, Norah cupped her chin in her hands. If Keshen was ripping off his employer and Burrell found out and confronted him, would that be motive for murder? Would Keshen both beat and stab the old man in the wheelchair? And would it all happen in twenty minutes during which Susan Burrell claimed she was away? Norah closed her eyes for a moment and when she opened them again found Ferdi Arenas standing in front of her.

"Got a couple of minutes, Sergeant?"

She waved him to the chair.

"I was just over to the FBI. You know how they are; first they pumped me, then they 'cooperated' by telling me what we already know."

Norah grimaced. "They had heard of Raul Pelletier?"

"Oh, sure. They knew who he was, his position in Chile, his escape along with his wife and son to this country. They knew where he lived and worked. According to them, he took no political action of any kind since coming over. They don't see his death as an assassination. They think that if it had been politically motivated his car would have been bombed, or a knife stuck into his face, or a poisoned needle in his thigh, something like that. Also, it would have been done long ago. I must say, I agree," Arenas concluded.

So did she. "How about the baseball bat?"

"No identifiable prints."

She sighed. "The bat itself? The wood, the quality, so on?"

"It's no cheap toy. It's a real professional model."

"Get on it. Find out who sells it in New York. How about the knife? Doc Worgan get more specific?"

"It's a hunting knife with an eight-inch blade."

She mused aloud. "Who needs a hunting knife in the middle of Manhattan—beside hunters?"

"Criminals," Ferdi answered. "And kids."

"I saw an ad . . ." Norah began.

"I cut this out of the Sunday paper."

Their eyes met.

Ferdi Arenas held a quarter-page mail-order ad from the pages of the *New York Times* extolling the excellence of precisely such a knife.

"The warehouse is over in Jersey. I thought if you didn't have anything else for me, I'd go over this afternoon and get a list of the customers to whom they sent this particular item within the past . . . three months?"

"Make it six," Norah told him.

Chapter VII

Detectives work around the clock and police stations are open on weekends, but the Stock Exchange and the banks are not. So the investigation into Jason Burrell's finances had to wait till Monday. David Link was impatient. Up to now his assignments on the task force had been ancillary and he'd worked in the shadow of his immediate superiors. With Norah, though she was higher in rank, he felt on an equal footing and saw this case as his chance to make a showing, to make points, maybe even with the Chief himself. So, he was out for a quick solution. He rejected the theory that the murder of Jonathan Burrell had been a push-in crime. An attempt had been made to look like it, but that's all it was—an attempt. Security at Belmonde Towers was tops; strangers just didn't get in. If, somehow, someone had slipped by on the particular afternoon, he would have had to pick the particular apartment of a helpless invalid at the particular time—a twenty-minute span—when he was left alone and unattended. No way. Too much coincidence. Motive was what counted in this one. David was sure that once he examined Jason Burrell's bank accounts and inquired into his Wall Street manipulations he'd have enough for the victim's son to squirm. If it turned out that he was wrong and Jason was clean, well, there was the male nurse to fall back on. Maybe Keshen and his close friend, Baines, were in it together? Why not? A case against the two wouldn't be hard to make.

Restless, with time on his hands, David paced the furnished studio apartment he'd sublet after the separation from Marie. It was cramped and expensive; the rent was more than the monthly mortgage on the three-bedroom house in Kew Gardens. "Damn," he muttered, wincing as he stubbed his toe on the brass-cornered campaign chest in the middle of the room that served for cocktail table and provided storage for the bedclothes during the daytime. "Damn!" he repeated and glared into the empty eyes of an African tribal mask on the wall. He ought to sweep the whole stinking collection out! He took a deep breath. Why bother? He didn't intend to be living here for long. He sure wasn't going to spend a rare weekend off-duty cooped up here. No way. He was going out to the house to visit his wife and children.

David did some shopping first and arrived with gifts for all—skates, the new kind with the soundless urethane wheels attached to supple leather boots, for the boys; and for Marie, a dark ranch mink hat, all full female skins.

Expensive gifts, which he could ill afford, Marie pointed out. "It's only money." David shrugged off her protestations. She looked wonderful, he thought, eyes devouring her. She was beginning to put on some of the weight she'd lost during their last, combative months together, filling out. The lines of strain between her eyes and across her brow had eased. She looked younger, David acknowledged, certainly happier. It filled him with resentment. Marie claimed there was nobody else, but there had to be.

"Let me come back, darling. Please. I'll give you anything you want, anything in the world, if you'll just let me come back. Just name it; I'll find a way to get it for you. I swear. Anything."

"You know what I want."

He groaned. "Other jobs are just as demanding. Doctors, lawyers, restaurant people, hotel people—they don't work nine to five."

"It's not the hours; it's the uncertainty. It's not knowing what's going to happen to you once you walk out the door.

72

You've been wounded twice. I couldn't take a third time. I couldn't."

"There's not going to be a third time. Most cops don't even get hit once, so I've already beaten the odds." He pulled her to him roughly. "Marie . . ."

She resisted. "No, David. That's not going to solve anything."

"It would, if you'd give it a chance. It's all that counts, babe."

She looked into his eyes and shook her head sadly. "Two years ago, one year ago even, you wouldn't have said that. You wouldn't have thought it. You used to be a gentle, loving man."

"You used to be . . ." He hesitated, than spat it out. "You used to be an obedient wife."

"Let's say we've both changed and let it go."

Her coolness infuriated him. He was filled with rage at it. He shook with frustration. He wanted to hit her, to get some kind of reaction out of her. The need was close to overwhelming. He took his hands off her arms and backed away for fear that he might do something neither of them could forget. "I want you back. I'll do anything, anything . . ." His voice was hoarse from the strain.

"Except resign."

"That's right. I'm a cop. I don't know how to do anything else."

"You could learn." Her face was pinched, her eyes entreating. Then the moment passed. Her face relaxed, her eyes became blank. "You don't want to. So that's that. The subject is closed. Let's not start again, David. Please."

Norah didn't take the weekend off. While David Link concerned himself with motive, she concentrated on opportunity. To that, Susan Burrell was the key. She was certainly lying about having left Belmonde Towers. The only way to find out why was to ask.

The Burrells lived on East Seventy-ninth in one of the newest and most prestigious condominiums. It flaunted a magnificent lobby. It featured a health club with sauna and swimming pool; offered maid service, catering service, valet, telephone answering. What it amounted to was an apartment hotel in which all the apartments were individually owned. As she rode up to the forty-fourth floor, Norah appreciated the hushed silence where lesser buildings would have inflicted Muzak. She acknowledged that she was impressed. This was living refined of minor daily irritations. She thought of the petty concerns of her own life—getting the laundry picked up and delivered before she left for work, the TV fixed in time for the big game, making an appointment with the window washer only to have it rain—and felt at least a twinge of envy.

On entering the Burrell apartment, however, she was surprised at its smallness. If not for the view, which was an impressive sweep of mid-Manhattan, the room in which she stood would have been claustrophobic. It was elegantly furnished; everything new and not a speck of dust anywhere—the maid service, of course. In contrast, Susan Burrell appeared unkempt.

Though it was eleven, she was still in nightgown and robe. She didn't even look rested. In fact, she didn't look any better than she had immediately after her father-in-law's murder. She waved Norah to a seat, but remained herself standing uncertainly, a displaced object in her own rigidly ordered living room. Norah had a sudden intuition that the place and the life style were not of Susan Burrell's choosing, that she would have preferred to have some responsibility in running her home, to be in a place where the cooking and cleaning and washing would fill some of the hours. She knew the Burrells had no children. Children wouldn't have fitted in here, she thought, and wondered if Susan Burrell wanted children.

"How long have you lived here?" It was not a question Norah had intended asking.

"Two years. Jason likes it."

"Where did you live before?"

"On the Island. Near Stony Brook. It was a very long commute for Jason. And, of course, here we're close . . . that is, we were close to his father."

"But you liked it better out there?"

"Well, we had a big old house and a garden. I was on the library board. I did community work." For a moment her eyes and face came alive.

"What do you do here?"

"There are so many things to do. I mean, we're right in the center of everything—theaters, museums, stores."

74

Norah felt sorry for her and at the same time impatient: there were things one could do; there were ways to occupy one's time usefully if one had the spirit and initiative to find them. "Do you want the killer of your father-in-law apprehended?"

"Of course, I do. What kind of question is that?"

"Then tell me where you went on Friday afternoon."

"I did tell you. I went out for cigarettes."

"Nobody saw you go out or come back in."

"I can't help that."

"Nobody remembers you at the stationer's. The pack you showed me was not a fresh pack."

"Yes, it was."

"Susan, look at me. Susan?" Norah waited till the woman reluctantly did as she was asked. She put the question gently. "Were you present when Jonathan Burrell was killed? Did you see it done?"

Susan Burrell gasped. "No. Oh, no. My God, how can you think such a thing?"

"What else can I think?"

"I had nothing to do with it. I swear to you. Nothing."

"You have no alibi," Norah pointed out.

"Alibi?"

"That's right."

Apparently the fact that she needed an alibi hadn't occurred to her. She seemed confused rather than frightened.

"I don't think the timing was pure chance. I think somebody knew in advance that you would be gone and for how long and that it would be more than twenty minutes."

Susan Burrell said nothing.

"You left Jonathan Burrell in his bedroom napping. When you got back he was on the floor of the living room beside his overturned wheelchair. He had been beaten and then knifed. For his sake, I wish the ordeal had lasted only twenty minutes."

The young woman shivered, drew the drab robe closer, seeming to shrink within herself. She took a step back from Norah and looked around as though for escape. Suddenly, she turned and in a few paces was at the window.

Norah sprang after her reaching with both hands to grab her, but it wasn't necessary. The wall-to-ceiling window was not designed to be opened and Susan Burrell was not so

75

desperate that she would hurl herself through the thick glass.

"Where I went and what I did had nothing to do with Jonathan's murder," she murmured.

"It had everything to do with," Norah replied. "It was the basis for it. How long were you gone?"

No answer.

"All right, then, I'm going to tell you what I think you did. You had lunch with your father-in-law as you usually did on Fridays. After lunch, you helped him to his bed and settled him for his afternoon's nap, also as usual. You waited till you were sure he was asleep, then you left. You went to another apartment in Belmonde Towers."

She paused. Norah, schooled in detecting reaction, had caught the straining of the neck cords, the hiding of shaking hands in the pockets of the robe. She knew she'd got through.

"As usual, you returned before your father-in-law was likely to wake up, except that on this particular occasion something went wrong. Somebody broke in and I doubt that it was by chance. Now, I don't really care where you were or with whom," Norah went on. "Ordinarily, that would be strictly your business, but it's my business to solve this case, and if you won't tell me, then I'll have to start ringing doorbells and asking questions. Belmonde Towers is large and I can't do it singlehanded. That means I'll have to outline the situation to four, maybe six other detectives who will in turn have to explain to the tenants what and why they want to know. The tenants will certainly discuss it among themselves."

"Oh, God . . ."

"So why don't you just tell me now? I can't promise you absolute confidentiality, but I'll do my best to see to it that no one will know that doesn't have to know. And"—she paused for emphasis—"you may find an alibi useful." Apparently that idea still hadn't penetrated. "We have only your word that you left the apartment. Why should we assume that anyone else came in?"

She got it now, all right, Norah thought, watching her swallow nervously over and over as though she were trying to keep down a disagreeable mouthful. "I was visiting a friend," she offered finally. "There was nothing wrong." Another swallow. "He's just a friend."

"Where does your friend live?"

A couple more beats, a token resistance, then Susan Burrell gave up. "Tower D. Apartment 1507."

"Thank you."

"Sergeant . . ." Susan Burrell called after her. "If Jason ever finds out, he'll . . . he'll divorce me."

Norah thought back to the scene Jason Burrell had enacted on the night of his father's death, the way he had treated his wife.

Could be he already knows, she thought.

Despite assurances by the management and the police that the security of Belmonde Towers had not been breached, the tenants were understandably nervous. There had never been so much as a burglary in the complex; now suddenly there had been a break-in, robbery, and violent murder. The brutality of the crime and the slow death of the victim were particularly frightening. Like most New Yorkers, the residents of the Belmonde Towers ignored each other; next-door neighbors remained strangers by choice. Now shock brought them together. Warily, they appraised each other, and reassured by an almost mirror image, they spoke in guarded whispers exchanging rumors. Jonathan Burrell had undoubtedly been the most famous personage in the complex, but there were others who, though less well known, were wealthier and more influential. They demanded and got a twenty-four-hour armed guard in each of the four lobbies. The guard was required to keep a log of the comings and goings. At first it was merely an inconvenience, for the guard didn't know the residents and one of the staff had to be summoned each time to make the identification. Passes were issued and frequently forgotten or mislaid. Inconvenience gave way to annoyance and finally indignation. After a week all guards were removed. Everyone was edgy for a couple of days, but tension can be sustained just so long and then the psyche adjusts. Belmonde Towers returned to normal.

On the ninth floor of Tower D Sylive Guthrie blinked back the tears and tried to concentrate on her homework. She was a vapid, gangling girl of fourteen with straight blond hair and braces on her teeth. She was the proverbial ugly duckling. But Sylive Guthrie didn't know that time would produce a transformation. She could only compare herself with the young swans at school—Anita Thatcher who at fourteen was

77

already gloriously filled out, bursting both front and rear, who was always in a corner of the corridor giggling with some red-faced boy; Helen Khour, already dubbed a tease but chased anyway. When Sylive looked at her *maman*—Françoise Guthrie was French and preferred to be so addressed—she could only shed tears of frustration, for *maman* was an authentic beauty, exquisite, forever young. Where other women struggled for careers, Mrs. Guthrie made a career out of her beauty. She basked in male admiration and thrived on female envy. A superb hostess for her husband, Roland Guthrie, an oil executive, she was much in demand as a guest and lent distinction to any party she attended. She was constantly surrounded by an entourage of men vying for her favors, all of whom she kept dangling with consummate skill.

Sylive was relegated to the background. If her mother was entertaining in the afternoon, she was not permitted to show herself in the salon. In the evening, if there were guests, Sylive dined in her own room by herself. Rather than being an incentive, a goal for which to strive, her mother's beauty and charm hurled the child into despair. She neglected herself, was dirty and unkempt. Which in turn caused Françoise Guthrie to rail at her child with Gallic excess and made Sylive more certain than ever that her mother was ashamed of her.

Roland Guthrie sensed his daughter's distress but did not fully understand its depth. He tried to explain to her that there was another set of values, the values of the inner self, but she was too young to grasp the concept. And Guthrie had his own troubles. Lately, however, he had noticed a change for the better in his daughter. She kept herself clean and neat; she fixed her hair this way and that; she was cheerful, most of the time. He was relieved. Being a sensible and modest man, Guthrie didn't take the credit but attributed it to nature: the child was maturing and discovering herself. He was partly right. Sylive had attracted the attention of a boy. Not just any boy, but the handsomest and smartest boy in the whole school. It had started with his asking her questions about the homework assignment. She was surprised because he was a scholarship student and got better grades than she did. Then one day as she came out of school he was waiting and asked if he could walk her home. Just remembering set her blood coursing.

Peter Tomasiello continued to seek Sylive out. The other girls took note. They made sly implications that caused her to feel a strange warmth, a tingling throughout her whole body. She never invited Peter up to the apartment though he suggested they do their homework together many times. She was afraid of what *maman* would say. The innuendos of the girls were flattering, but if *maman* should even suggest . . . Sylive would die of embarrassment. So she continued to resist Peter's urging that he come upstairs. But he was getting angry at her refusals. This afternoon he had stalked off without even saying good-bye.

Had she lost him? Sylive asked herself for the hundredth time as she sat in her room crouched over her desk. If Peter had invited her to his house or anywhere, Sylive would have gone. But he had not even hinted at that.

The doorbell rang.

Wiping her tears, sniffing, Sylive got up and went out to answer it. As she crossed the salon, Françoise Guthrie called out to her in her light, airy, company voice.

"If that's Uncle Alfonse, show him in and ask him to wait, will you, *chérie*?"

All of *maman*'s friends became uncles automatically. Sylive went to the door and checked the peephole as she was constantly being cautioned to do. "Peter!" she gasped and opened immediately. "What are you doing here? How did you get up here?" she whispered.

"Sylive, I have to talk to you. Please."

The coquettish voice floated out to them. "Alfonse, darling! Is that you? I'm in the bath. I'll be out in a few moments."

Sylive stood there confused and embarrassed. She didn't know what to do or say. Turning, she called over her shoulder. "No, *Maman*, it's not Uncle Alfonse. It's . . ."

She didn't get any further. She was seized from behind, a hand clasped over her mouth, and she was shoved backward into the apartment. She had no way of knowing who had grabbed her, that there were two of them who had entered with Peter. All she knew was that he stood there doing nothing to help her.

"Sylive, *chérie*, who is it?" The voice had changed slightly, become less gay, less flirtatious.

Sylive struggled. She kicked. Reaching up she grabbed a tuft of her assailant's hair in each small fist and tugged.

"Ow!" he screeched, but he didn't let go. While he held her, someone stuffed a towel into her mouth, hard and deep.

"Sylive! Answer me."

Now the one who had been holding the girl let her go and she sank slowly and silently to the floor. Without a backward look, he followed the voice down a corridor to the bathroom. He opened the door and walked in. He looked down and smiled at the beautiful woman, her naked flesh shimmering in the blue-tinted and perfumed water. He leaned over, the refraction striking his glasses and blinding him a moment. Then he reached inside the sleeve of his dark green blazer and pulled out a knife.

Chapter VIII

The bodies were not discovered till well after eleven that night. The scene in the apartment in Tower D was essentially the same as the one in the Burrell apartment in Tower A twelve days before. The place had been turned upside down, but apparently only cash taken. This time, however, there were two victims—a mother and her daughter. The reaction of the residents was different. They openly expressed their outrage and their fear. No longer did they lurk behind their doors and peer through peepholes. They came out to demand what was being done for their protection. They milled in the lobbies and halls, they met in each other's apartments. Though it was past one A.M. by the time the word of the crime spread, calls were made to contacts, and as a result police cars, marked and unmarked, converged on Belmonde Towers, and cops swept the lobbies and the halls. Chief of Detectives Louis Deland was awakened and sent a personal representative, Captain Joseph Capretto.

Joe wasn't concerned with protocol; he let the regulars, Detective Link of the task force and Sergeant Mulcahaney from the Fourth Division, get on with the job.

They approached the Medical Examiner who had also been

personally requested to take charge. "What do you think, Asa?" Norah asked.

"I think it's a damn shame." Osterman was examining Sylive Guthrie. "Violence for kicks. Violence as a high. This child choked on her own vomit."

For a moment Norah could see only her niece Antonia in the victim's place. She shook the image away. "How about Mrs. Guthrie?"

"I'm going to have to examine her lungs," he snapped.

"I'm looking for a connection," she half explained and half apologized. She referred, as they both understood, to the two deaths here and the murder of Jonathan Burrell. "Neither apartment showed any signs of forcible entry. Both were thoroughly and savagely ransacked, but nothing was taken except cash. A knife was used each time."

"I'll make a very close comparison of the wound; you can count on it." Osterman's sarcasm had more than its usual bite. He got up, brushed off the pants of his chocolate-brown flannel suit, tugged at the tattersall vest. Unexpectedly, he looked directly at Norah, then at David, then at Capretto who stood slightly behind them. "Find out what time the girl had lunch. She died about four hours after." Lifting the crushed Irish-tweed hat in salute to all, the Chief Medical Examiner strode out.

The three detectives stared at each other. For Osterman to offer such an estimate at the scene was unprecedented. To do it without being asked . . . they could only shake their heads in disbelief.

"Let's go talk to Guthrie," Joe suggested.

The study was lit by a single lamp on the desk. Roland Guthrie sat motionless in its light. Spread before him were the contents of his wife's jewel box and a large metal cash and document case. He had been asked to go through his valuables and make a list of what was missing. Evidently he was taking infinite pains over the task, drawing it out, using it as a buffer against the reality of tragedy. Once it was done . . . Norah had a feeling he would collapse. A man on his way to the top of the corporate world, Guthrie had surely presided over the disaster of others, yet he was now unprepared to deal with his own.

He looked up when they came in and leaned back in his

chair, thus finding the protection of darkness for everything but his hands—strong, sinewy, and shaking.

"I'm Captain Capretto, Mr. Guthrie. You've already met Sergeant Mulcahaney and Detective Link." Joe was courteous as he would have been without the Chief's admonition. "I know it's very late, but I would appreciate it if you could talk to us. The sooner we start, the better chance we have of apprehending the perpetrators."

Guthrie nodded. They could just make it out.

"May we have some light?" At Joe's signal, Link found the switch and flipped it.

The switch controlled various table lamps which were softly shaded in cream silk, yet Roland Guthrie blinked. Older than his wife by at least ten years, he was, despite badly scarred skin, an attractive man. His face was square, strong; eyebrows and hair coarse and thick; lips full, the upper curve sensuously sharp in outline. By contrast his eyes were small and deep-set but gleamed with intelligence. Even now, in his distress, Guthrie was sizing up his interrogators. He was a man of impressive presence, a man accustomed to authority; therefore, Norah asked herself, were those shaking hands an indication of shock and grief or something else?

"As a matter of routine, Mr. Guthrie, we have to know where you were and what you were doing from, say, about three this afternoon till the time you came home," Joe said.

"I was attending an executive meeting."

"Which began?"

"At precisely three," he replied with a bleak, bitter smile. "We broke for dinner, which was served in our own private dining room, and then we resumed till just short of eleven P.M."

"You came directly home?"

"Yes." Guthrie sighed.

There was no need to review what had confronted him when he walked in, not now, at any rate. "So Mrs. Guthrie was not expecting you home for dinner?"

"No."

"Did she have any plans of her own for the evening?" Norah now asked. Mrs. Guthrie had been taking a bath; satin evening pants and a diaphanous top had been laid out on the bed along with a jeweled purse and long white gloves.

83

Guthrie turned to Norah with courteous deference. "I believe she planned to attend the theater."

"Alone?"

"Hardly. Françoise would have had one of her escorts on tap. I can't tell you which one." He didn't appear to care.

No one commented.

"Is there any way we can find out?" Joe asked. "An appointment book? A diary?"

"Françoise was a most efficient hostess. She kept lists for everything pertaining to her parties and entertainments. However, she did not commit her personal life to paper." He paused. "She'd had the pantry partitioned off into a small office. You're welcome to examine it. Or anything else, of course. Of course, you don't need my permission, do you?" He smiled again ruefully, and seemed more at ease, yet the hands continued to tremble as though they were a separate entity. He didn't appear aware of their betrayal.

"Assuming that your wife's escort arrived, rang the doorbell, and got no answer . . . would he have just gone away? Shouldn't he have tried to contact you?"

"That would have been difficult. I left orders that I wasn't to be disturbed."

"Shouldn't he at least have gone down to the desk man? Got him to use his passkey?"

"I don't know."

Now the three detectives did finally exchange glances. Perhaps Guthrie didn't understand the thrust of the question, Norah thought.

Joe proceeded to clarify. "That he didn't do either of these things suggests he might be involved in your wife's and your daughter's deaths."

"I will give you some names, if you wish, but I would not have suspected that any of Françoise's young men cared deeply enough to . . . kill."

There was a moment's silence. Norah spoke. "Your daughter, Sylive, what would she have done tonight with both you and Mrs. Guthrie out for the evening? Was there someone who would have stayed with her?"

At last anguish cracked the executive's reserve. Whatever accommodation he had reached with his wife, Roland Guthrie had cared deeply for his child. Tears sprang into his eyes, his face grimaced with pain. He gripped the edges of the desk so

84

tightly that the desk shook. Norah got up, went to a small drinks cart, and poured some water out of a thermos jug for him. His hands were frozen; she had to wait till he disengaged them almost finger by finger and could take the glass from her and sip.

"Thank you." He collected himself. "Sylive was old enough to stay by herself. On the occasions when neither my wife nor I were to be at home, Sylive would go downstairs to the restaurant in the building for her dinner. It was perfectly safe. We thought the building was absolutely safe. Then she would come back and do her homework. She was a very good student. She would be in bed and asleep by the time we returned."

"What school did she attend?" It was an automatic question.

"The Dowd Academy. Many foreign children go there; language is a specialty. Sylive, of course, was born here, but her mother was born in France and she was anxious that Sylive not only be fluent in French but that she should understand the French ethic."

"How about servants?" Link put in. "Does your maid have a key to the apartment?"

"We use the housekeeping service of the building. You'll have to speak to them."

"One more thing, Mr. Guthrie, and we can leave you to get some rest." Joe pointed to the boxes on the desk. "Were you able to discover what's missing?"

"Only cash. I kept a few hundred in the house. That's gone. There were so many other things they could have had—jewels, paintings, silver." He stopped and asked as though it had just occurred to him, "How many were there?"

"We don't know," Joe replied. If he had known he wouldn't have divulged it; it would only have added to the man's pain.

"Why? Why did they do it?" Guthrie demanded in his anguish. "My wife was in the bath; she couldn't interfere. And Sylive . . . she was not a strong child. What could she have done against them? There was no need to kill. They could have taken anything they wanted. There was no need to kill my girl."

Norah spent the first half of the next morning sitting quietly among the lush potted palms and dieffenbachia in the lobby of Tower D, watching as the residents and the maids

85

and the occasional early visitor passed in and out. She could detect no loopholes in security: those who were known were passed through without question; others were stopped while a call was placed to the resident he claimed to be visiting and their legitimacy confirmed. There might well be laxity on occasion, but Norah reasoned that after the first murder security had been tighter rather than looser.

Just as Susan Burrell had not got out of the complex, it appeared that no one had gone in.

So it got down to the ringing of doorbells after all. Having extracted a list of the residents of Tower D from a reluctant management, Norah called on Schmidt and Arenas to assist her. Starting on the fifteenth floor, because it was there that Susan Burrell visited, they spent the rest of the day canvassing. The questions were simple:

"Are you usually at home on Friday afternoons?"

"Is any member of your family at home on Friday afternoons?"

"Do you know your neighbors on the floor? Have you ever encountered visitors? On a regular basis?"

The results were not helpful. Of the hundred and seventy residents, eighty either did not answer their doors or else the door was answered by a maid. A check of the rental applications showed most of these to be working couples. Of those who did answer, forty-two were housewives who were in and out on different days and at varying hours, women with no set schedule. Twenty-five were retired, people who went out in the morning on busy work and came home for lunch and a nap. Twelve were women with children of school age who came home at varying times depending on whether the child attended a public school with split shifts or a private school with a standard school day. The rest were men who either worked nights or worked at home: artists, writers, one PR man who couldn't afford a separate office, and, of course, the occupant of 1507.

Norah rang Mr. Carson's bell herself, but he didn't answer. She wasn't surprised: Carson was a salesman. He could without difficulty have adjusted his schedule to accommodate Susan, and his office wouldn't have the slightest suspicion that he wasn't out with a client. She'd get hold of him later.

Norah wasn't discouraged. She intended to canvass Tower A. It was as likely that Susan had been spotted leaving the

Burrell apartment as entering that of Carson. But the job didn't warrant overtime, so Norah told Gus and Ferdi to go home with the intention of having them resume in the morning.

For herself, she was in no hurry to quit. Joe was working late again and with Toni gone there was no urgency to get home. The child had been with them a mere two weeks, thirteen days exactly, but she'd made a place for herself in their lives. Norah had packed her things and closed the door of her room, yet the presence remained. Maybe when the bags were gone, when Lena or Jake got around to picking them up, Norah could forget about her. Why not take the bags around herself? Right now. She had the time. She might even get to see Toni. At least she'd find out what was happening to the girls who had assaulted her. No. Norah sighed inwardly. She'd promised Joe to keep out of it. She wasn't Toni's mother; her opinion didn't count. As for Jake, he'd reacted emotionally in ordering Norah to stay away. She knew he'd get over it, in time, and if she didn't aggravate him.

So Norah went back to the building's management office to spend what was left of the afternoon in preparation for the next morning by studying the rental applications of the occupants of Tower A.

The next morning before she, Schmidt, and Arenas had even left the precinct, Norah's phone rang.

"It's me, darling."

"Joe!"

"Can you come over, please? Right away?"

"What's up?"

"I'll tell you when you get here."

"Okay."

"And hold Gus and Ferdi off the Belmonde job for a while."

"Why?"

"I'll explain when you get here."

"What do you mean we're invading their privacy?" Norah flushed as she faced Joe across his desk in his private office. "They knew when they filled out those application forms that the information would be checked."

"Not by the police," he pointed out.

"I didn't sneak behind anybody's back," she proclaimed

righteously. There had been occasions, as they both knew, when she might not have been able to be so righteous. "I went straightforwardly to the management and requested permission to examine their files and they gave it."

"They didn't know they had an option," he replied mildly.

She shrugged. "So then we could have got a court order. What's the difference?"

"I'm on your side, believe me," Joe assured her with a conciliatory smile. "We can still get an order if necessary."

"If necessary?" She didn't like the inference. "I don't understand the problem. They've been screaming for protection over there, demanding beefed-up security. What better security than to have the perpetrators caught? All we've been doing is asking some innocuous questions. Politely, believe me, with kid gloves on."

"What questions?"

"If the tenant is normally home Friday afternoons and if he or she had heard or seen anything suspicious with regard to either crime."

"Wouldn't such a person already have come forward of his own accord?"

"Well, that's the lead-in," she admitted. "What we're really after is someone who's normally home on Friday afternoons and might have observed the regularity of Susan Burrell's visits to her lover."

"Would that person admit it?"

"He'd admit being home, I think. It would be risky to lie."

Joe didn't argue. "The complaint is that you're treating the residents like suspects."

Her blue eyes blazed at that. She inflated her cheeks and then blew out a small gust of frustration. "No. Absolutely not. I specifically warned Gus and Ferdi to be polite and I'm sure they were." She paused. Considered. Made up her mind. "This is the way I see it. I've prowled all over those buildings, front and rear, patio, underground service areas, and the security is about as good as it can be. I'm convinced the perpetrator is a resident."

She'd expected it to be a bombshell. She'd tensed in anticipation of Joe's shock and resistance. She sat on the edge of her chair, chin thrust forward, ready to do battle to defend her theory.

Joe remained relaxed and unperturbed.

"It has to be," she reiterated.

"According to you, both crimes were committed by the same perpetrator or perpetrators."

"Yes. Don't forget, Asa leans in that direction."

"Let's let Asa speak for himself, which he'll do as soon as he's completed the autopsies." Joe leaned back, folded his arms, his dark, handsome face thoughtful as he regarded Norah. He was puzzled that she should commit herself this early in the investigation. "I'm not convinced. It's just as likely that the two crimes are separate and have no link whatsoever."

"Explain the perpetrator's access."

"Each one was a legitimate guest." Joe waved her into silence as she made to contradict. "Isn't it possible that each killer was a legitimate guest of his victim? Jonathan Burrell could have had a guest and okayed his entry, and we know that Mrs. Guthrie was, in fact, expecting her escort for the evening."

"That's a lot of coincidence."

"Coincidences do happen."

"Mrs. Guthrie was in the bath," Norah reminded him.

"All right, when the doorman rang, Sylive gave the okay. Sylive knew her mother was expecting a guest. In the Burrell case, his son was known and wouldn't even have needed an okay. If Keshen had come back unexpectedly—well, he was a resident himself and would have got through without challenge."

"I suppose so. All right, yes."

Joe smiled at her. "By your own examination of Burrell's papers we know that he was becoming suspicious of the nurse. According to David, Jason Burrell had been juggling the funds of his clients' accounts. He'd also lost considerable amounts on personal market speculation. So far, it all balances out and there doesn't appear to be any money missing, but they're not through looking. If, in addition, it turns out that Jason knew about his wife's affair, knew that she'd been sneaking out every Friday afternoon, then we've got opportunity along with possible motive. So why don't we see where that leads us and leave the canvass for the time being? We can always resume if we need to."

"You're the boss." Norah bit her lip. "Sorry, I realize it's not your decision."

"As a matter of fact, I'm in agreement with it." He looked hard at her for a moment. Then he spoke into the intercom. "Reach out for Detective Link, please. I want him as soon as possible."

"I really don't know why you need me when you've got the task force on this case."

"You object to working with David?"

"No, of course not. What gave you that idea?"

"The look on your face. Come on, *cara*, don't you think it's about time we straightened out this task force thing? You don't want the appointment? Okay. Fine. But fish or cut bait. I don't care what you tell Jim Felix, but I want to know the real reason you're turning it down. And I want to know it now."

Norah sighed. She got up. She walked around the small office looking at the pictures on the walls. There was Joe, very young and lean in a new uniform that seemed at least a couple of sizes too big, sitting in the second row of his policy-academy graduating class, his dark face set and earnest. There he was again, four years later, with his teammates after the Police Department's big victory over the Fire Department for the city uniformed services softball championship held in the Great Meadow of Central Park. He'd filled out, looked very macho in the ballplayer's uniform that to Norah always looked like long johns. In the picture that hung directly behind his desk, then-Lieutenant Joseph Capretto was posed with his fellow officers at the completion of the course given by the FBI for specially selected lawmen. In this, his expression was a combination of that in the earlier photos, plus a hint of determination which had not appeared before. That look was the precursor of the man today. Even to have been considered for the course, Joe had needed the recommendation of a superior. Jim Felix had given it unstintingly. It had been the push Joe had needed and afterward his rise in the department had been, not dramatic, but satisfyingly steady. For a while the paths of the two men had diverged, but now Deputy Inspector James Felix was head of Homicide detectives with the Manhattan task force under his specific control, and Captain Joseph Capretto was his executive officer. Norah was grateful to Felix on Joe's behalf and on her own, for he had helped her too at a time when women officers were barely tolerated by the brass. She respected Jim Felix, and that's what made it so hard now.

"Norah?" Joe prompted. "It can't be so bad that you can't tell me about it."

This was the moment she'd been dreading. No way she could put it off anymore. "The word is going around that the guys on the task force are living high. Parties, dinners, tickets to the shows and sporting events for them and their wives . . ."

"So? The force is very close to the Chief's heart. You know that. He believes in rewarding his people. It comes out of his own pocket."

"If you say so."

"My God!" Joe stared. "You're not impugning Chief Deland's honesty?"

"No." She looked at him trying to convey the message without speaking the words.

"Whose, then? Come on, Norah, let's have it . . ." He stopped. "Not Jim's? Not Jim Felix's? Never. You ought to know better."

His dark face was livid, his eyes blazed with indignation. Joe was loyal to Deland, but his feeling for Felix went beyond loyalty: it was unequivocal trust. It was why she'd been so reluctant to mention the rumors, though of course she'd known that sooner or later she'd have to speak. She was relieved that it was done and that he finally understood her reluctance to accept the appointment.

"It's not Deland nor Felix they're talking about, it's the men. The word is the men are taking payoffs."

"And I'm telling you there's nothing to it. If you don't want to take my word, the easiest thing is for you to accept the job, join us, and find out for yourself."

Instinctively, Norah drew back. Her recent visit uptown to the Narcotics Squad had revived all kinds of memories and guilt feelings. She'd told herself over and over that she was not responsible for Sebastian Honn's leaving the force, that he'd had other problems, but there was no denying that her discovery of the corruption in his department had tipped the balance. She didn't want anything like that to happen to Jim Felix.

Or to Joe.

Looking at her husband, Norah saw not only his dear face

91

but all the qualities of which she alone was fully aware and for which she loved him, saw all the shared joys and the sorrows. As second in command of the task force, Joe would have to answer for any irregularities along with Felix. His career would be on the line too.

Three months ago at Narco, Norah had done what she'd had to do. She'd had no choice. She did have a choice now.

"That's a job for Internal Affairs," she said. "Let them do it. Let them get one of their 'field officers' assigned to the squad. I'm not interested in being a snitch. Not ever again."

Chapter IX

Alfonse Lamont was very, very nervous, but he did not deviate from his story. He'd had an engagement to take Madame Guthrie to dinner and then the opera. *Traviata*, he specified as though that would serve as confirmation. He was to pick her up at six. He arrived promptly. As he was well known to both the doorman and the deskman, he was simply passed on without a call upstairs. He rode up alone in the elevator and saw no one in the corridor on the nineteenth floor. He rang the doorbell of the Guthrie apartment but got no answer. So he went away.

David Link stared incredulously at him. "Just like that? You just left?"

"Yes."

Norah made no comment.

The three were wedged together in Lamont's cubbyhole office on the twenty-second floor of the UN building. The lack of space indicated Lamont's status; the fact that he had a window suggested he might hope for advancement. However, it was a dark day and the mists swirled and thickened and hung like a dirty curtain behind the glass and increased the sense of claustrophobia.

"It didn't occur to you to try to call her on the telephone? To inquire for a message at the desk?" David marveled. "You just rang the bell, she didn't answer, you walked away. It didn't occur to you to wonder why the child, Sylive, didn't come to the door, for instance?"

"Sylive usually took her dinner in the restaurant downstairs at about that hour," Lamont explained.

"Ah!" David threw a quick look at Norah. He might as well blow a trumpet, she thought and groaned inwardly as he added, "So you were familiar with the habits of the family."

Lamont would have to be really dumb not to realize that he'd goofed. In his late twenties, slim, poetically pale, with dark brown hair which he wore just short of touching his shoulders, and dark, doleful eyes, Alfonse Lamont was the scion of an aristocratic family that traced its heritage to the time of Louis XVI. He carried himself with a touch of arrogance, usually. At this moment, all self-confidence had deserted him, not out of fear of the police, for Lamont had diplomatic immunity; what young Lamont dreaded was the displeasure of the elder Lamont, of *Papa* back in Paris. He flushed.

"I had been Madame Guthrie's escort on several previous occasions when her husband was not available."

Link nodded. "My question, Mr. Lamont, is why you didn't notify anyone that there was no answer to your ring?"

"Because I was not alarmed. There was no reason for me to be. I assumed Madame Guthrie had simply changed her mind about going out."

"In other words, she'd stood you up."

He raised one shoulder and thrust out his lower lip in a Gallic version of a shrug.

"Had she ever done that before?" Norah asked.

He hesitated. "No."

"Then why should you think she'd done it this time?"

Lamont was restless. He yearned to get up, pace, work off his anxieties, but there was no room for it. The two detectives blocked passage to the door so that he was literally pinned behind his desk. He was also pinned to telling the truth. He raised both hands in resignation. "We had quarreled."

"Ah!" Link grunted his satisfaction.

This time it was Norah who threw him a look, a warning look, too late.

"You were her lover."

"Her current lover."

Link pounced. "So she'd found somebody new; you were jealous and you killed her."

"No, no. I was the one who wanted to break it off. I was the one who wished to put an end to the affair."

"And she threatened to tell her husband and ruin your career. So you killed her."

"Hardly." The young diplomat managed a smile. "Mr. Guthrie was well aware of Madame's propinquities. I was not the first of her friends, nor would I be the last."

"Correction, Mr. Lamont, you were the last."

Lamont's smile disappeared.

While Norah didn't subscribe to David's style of interrogation, he appeared to be getting results, so she kept quiet.

"I think you'd better tell us the whole story."

"I have already told you everything."

"You haven't told us why you wanted to break off with Mrs. Guthrie."

"That is my business."

"Not anymore."

Lamont groaned. "Very well. There is a young lady, one whom I truly love and wish to marry."

"And Mrs. Guthrie threatened to tell your young lady, so you had to kill her."

"*Mon Dieu!* No matter what I say you twist it."

"You had a date with Françoise Guthrie that evening, but you came early to have it out with her. Sylive answered the door. Once she'd admitted you, she retired to her own room as she was accustomed to doing. Her mother was in the bath and called to you. You went in to talk to her. A quarrel ensued. She threatened to tell your girl; you threatened her with a knife. She screamed and rose up in the tub. You stabbed her. She tried to get out. You pushed her back down and under the water. You held her there till she was dead. When you turned there was Sylive standing in the doorway. She'd heard her mother's screams and had seen you kill her. She tried to get away. You caught her in the foyer. You had no choice but to kill her too."

At first glance it wasn't a bad reconstruction; on closer examination there were plenty of holes. Norah knew it, but apparently Lamont did not. Stricken into speechlessness, he could only shake his head.

Link went on. "You ransacked the place to make it look like an ordinary robbery. You took cash but nothing else, no jewelry or art objects because getting rid of them would have been a problem."

"No, no, no." The Frenchman groaned. He realized he must present a defense. "Françoise and I had quarreled, that is true." Having admitted that much, he clasped his hands on the desk in front of him and appeared to gain some composure. "I called her yesterday morning to tell her that I would not be escorting her to dinner and the opera and that she had better get someone else if she intended to go. She was, surprisingly, quite reasonable. She said she wouldn't be able to get anyone suitable at such a late hour and asked me to reconsider and keep the commitment. She promised it would be the last time. She wanted us to part friends. Under the circumstances, what could I say? I agreed. After all, I didn't hate Françoise—to the contrary, I admired her. I had never considered the liaison anything other than temporary, nor, I'm sure, had she. So. I arrived punctually at six and rang the bell. At first I was taken aback that there was no answer. I was anxious," he admitted, "at first. Then it occurred to me that she might very well be . . . as you say, standing me up . . . purposely humiliating me, that she had got herself another escort for the evening and was punishing me by not being there. Except that it wasn't a punishment because I didn't care. I was relieved. In fact, I was so relieved that I ran back to the elevator quickly just in case she might change her mind and answer the door after all." He groaned. "And that, childish as it appears, is the truth." He looked from David to Norah. "Surely, the doorman will remember that I was upstairs a very short time, not long enough to do . . . the things that were done."

"Sorry, but he doesn't," Link told him. "He remembers your arriving because you spoke to him. Evidently, you did not speak on your way out."

"I don't know how to convince you."

"You might tell us the name of the man who preceded you as Mrs. Guthrie's escort," David suggested.

"Jacques Tuffet."

"We'll speak with him."

Lamont winced. "You can't. Tuffet was reassigned four months ago. He is now at our consulate in Buenos Aires."

Link shook his head portentously.

Why did he keep doing that? Norah wondered. Why did he keep underscoring every point that went against Lamont? He'd done the same with Jason Burrell, though to a somewhat lesser degree. As a technique, Norah thought it should be used with caution for it was just as likely to strengthen the witness's resistance as to break it down.

"What were you doing yesterday afternoon before you called for Mrs. Guthrie?" Norah asked. "Were you working between—three-thirty and six?"

"No, madame. No, Sergeant. I did not come back here after lunch. I took a walk along the esplanade." With a nod over his shoulder toward the fog-blocked window, he indicated the area along the East River. "Afterward, I went to my home to change."

"Can anyone vouch for your movements?"

"I was alone."

"No one called you at your apartment? Your doorman doesn't remember?"

"No one telephoned, and my building does not have a doorman."

This time there was no need for David to punctuate.

"He's the logical suspect. Hell, he's the only suspect. Plus, he's got no alibi. But I don't think he did it. I believe his cockamamie story," David blurted out when he and Norah were alone and riding down in the elevator.

"You certainly didn't act like you believed him."

"Of course not. I wanted to shake him up, get everything out of him I could."

She didn't answer. They rode to the accompaniment of a Muzak medley of Christmas carols and it wasn't even Thanksgiving yet, Norah thought, recalling that she'd seen Christmas decorations in some stores and had not thought them particularly inappropriate. Christmas had lost religious significance; it had become a retail promotion.

"If we scratch Lamont, we've got nobody left but the husband," David went on. "And Guthrie's got a damn good alibi. Sitting in on a board meeting of Trans-World Oil is as good as you can get."

"I thought you said any alibi could be broken."

He grinned ruefully. "This one might just be the exception that proves the rule."

"I don't think you need to worry," Norah assured him. "However Roland Guthrie may have felt about his wife and her affairs, he loved his child. He cherished Sylive. It's plain to see. Assuming he wanted to kill his wife, he would never have done it while the child was at home. Certainly, he would never have harmed her."

"I'll go with that. So then where are we?"

Back to the theory of a common denominator, she thought, back to a perpetrator or perpetrators, still unknown, who had committed both the Burrell and Guthrie felony-murders. She didn't say anything, however; David wouldn't be interested. Once they would have argued the pros and cons back and forth heatedly. Anyone who didn't know them would have thought that they were hopelessly alienated, but in fact, those sessions had been the cement of their friendship. Whether from laziness or lack of caring, now David looked only for the easy solution. The elevator stopped; the door opened, and the music was cut off in the middle of a measure.

Norah stepped out and David trailed after her across the lobby.

"How about lunch?" He glanced at his watch. "It's a little early, but . . . what do you say?"

She started to say no. Then she thought that they had to work together so they should try to get along. David was showing his willingness; it would be churlish to turn him down.

"That would be nice," she said.

Leaving their cars where they were parked, they strolled over to First Avenue and found a restaurant with a glass-enclosed sidewalk café. Hardly the lunch-counter kind of place where Norah usually grabbed a sandwich and coffee.

David would not be dissuaded. "It's on me."

Again, it would have been ungracious to refuse.

The expense-account crowd had not yet arrived, so they got a good table and were expeditiously served. They sought ease in talking about the old days, and Norah was surprised at her own nostalgia. Evidently, David shared it, for when the meal was finished and he was waiting for his change, he leaned across the table.

"I envy you and Joe. You get along so well. You understand each other."

"We've got a lot in common."

"You mean the job?"

"That's part of it."

"To tell you the truth, I don't go for this equality bit. I mean, women truck drivers, soldiers, wrestlers, football players . . . policewomen. What's the point? But when I look at you, I think I'm beginning to change my mind. Maybe if I could find myself a policewoman like you the next time around I might make a go of marriage."

Impulsively, Norah reached out and put her hand on his. "Would you like me to talk to Marie?"

He looked surprised at the offer. "I'd be grateful, Norah. I'd be very grateful." When they got up, he kissed her cheek.

Warmed by the revival of rapport, Norah and David strolled back to their respective cars. With a friendly wave they drove off, each ostensibly heading back to his own squad room to turn out his own batch of reports. Actually, David Link returned to the UN. Norah called on Duane Carson in the Continental Products Building on Third Avenue.

In his midforties at least, overweight and balding, Duane Carson was not at all what Norah had expected. Certainly, Jason Burrell was much better-looking, but then looks weren't everything. His office was small but attractive, with wall-to-wall carpeting, comfortable leather-upholstered chairs, and the inevitable, undistinguished but beautifully framed prints on grass cloth covered walls.

Having offered her a drink either alcoholic or nonalcoholic and been refused, Carson leaned back and regarded the detective with concern. "Sergeant Mulcahaney. What can I do for you? What's this all about?"

"The Burrell murder."

He sighed. "I was hoping . . . well, I was hoping I wouldn't get involved."

"You haven't spoken to Mrs. Burrell since it happened?"

He frowned. Obviously he was deciding whether or not to admit the affair, wondering how much Susan Burrell had told the police.

Norah decided to spare him the uncertainty and to get on

with it. "I'll be straight with you, Mr. Carson, and I hope that you'll be straight with me. I'm not interested in your relationship with Mrs. Burrell, but I am very much interested in the timetable of your meetings and who was likely to know about it. I believe that has a direct bearing on the crime."

He didn't like not being allowed to make his own decision. "I don't see . . ."

"Of course, you do, Mr. Carson. It was while Susan Burrell was with you that her father-in-law was murdered."

Her directness worked, though he grimaced at it. "What do you want to know?"

"I take it that you and Mrs. Burrell met on a regular basis."

"Right. Once a week. Every Friday. In my apartment."

"Always at the same time?"

"More or less. She had lunch with the old man, settled him in for his nap, then when she was sure he'd dropped off, she'd slip away."

"That would be about . . . ?"

"Two-thirty."

"And she went back . . . ?"

"Say, four-thirty. Never later than five."

"So that he never knew she was gone?"

"Apparently not."

"Someone knew and made use of her absence."

Carson's rather small eyes narrowed. "You mean Jason?"

"I don't know. That's what I want you to help me find out."

"Me? I don't know the Burrells or their friends. I swear to God, Sergeant Mulcahaney, I don't know anything about any of them. Look, I met Susan and Jason Burrell at a party of about fifty people. I didn't think much of her at the time. She seemed colorless. Jason dominated what there was of our conversation. I spent the obligatory couple of minutes with them and moved on as soon as I could—I don't go to parties to discuss the stock market and that's all Jason seemed inclined toward or capable of—take your choice. Anyway, less than a week later I was in the lobby of Tower A trying to trace a parcel I was expecting and Susan and I ran into each other. She told me she was visiting her father-in-law, and I told her that I lived in Tower D. She was like another person—peppy, bright. I invited her up for a drink. She said she couldn't leave till the male nurse got back and that wouldn't be till around eight. I said I'd be waiting."

"When did all this happen? Can you give me a date?"

He had to stop and think. "The party was right after Labor Day; make it five days after that. Look, Sergeant, Susan and I see each other once a week for a couple of hours. I know that they have no kids, that Jason's a workaholic, that she hates living in the city—like that. She's told me about Jonathan, how he was recovering from the paralysis and how he was trying to get rid of the male nurse, which Jason wouldn't hear of. But the real talk between us was crazy, happy stuff, lovers' nonsense. We laughed a lot. You know what I mean? Susan's a great gal. We laughed together. We were happy." His fat, middle-aged face was transformed. "I wish . . ." He didn't finish and his face became wistful.

"Susan never suggested that her husband might be getting suspicious?"

"No."

"Nor that Keshen, the nurse, might be?"

He shook his head.

"Did anyone ever see Susan entering or leaving your apartment?"

"She was careful not to be seen."

"She could have run into someone in the hall or elevator."

"You'll have to ask her . . . oh, wait. Sure. There was an incident, unpleasant, with the kid next door. He brings a couple of his friends home from school most days. Susan ran into them playing ball in the halls a couple of times and it made her nervous. I told her not to worry, to them she was just another visitor. Then one of them made an obscene remark to her. She came in crying. By the time I calmed her down and went looking for the little bastards, they weren't in the hall anymore. I went to the Stucke apartment and found them and told the three of them off. I also complained to the management about their ballplaying and running up and down the halls and generally causing a nuisance."

"Three boys . . ." Norah's heartbeat quickened.

"Teenagers," Carson clarified. "Bud Stucke, the one who lives next door, is just a runt about fourteen or fifteen, the kind that wants to be one of the gang, but can't quite make it, you know? It's his buddies, the other two, that are the troublemakers. There's one tall, good-looking macho—I figure him to be older and the leader. He's the one that made the crack to Susan."

"What happened after you complained to the management?"

"Nothing. No more trouble. That was the end of it."

"No more unpleasantness for Susan?"

"No."

"Did Bud continue to bring his friends home after school?"

Carson shrugged. "If he did, they stayed inside his apartment and kept quiet. That's all I cared about."

Norah got up. "Thank you for your cooperation, Mr. Carson."

He accompanied her to the door. "The reason I didn't want to tell you about Susan and me . . . It wasn't to cover myself, Sergeant. Why the hell should I care who knows? She's a terrific gal, really terrific. I don't want to make trouble for her. You get me?"

Norah was already thinking ahead, but the salesman's tone, the look of real concern in his bulging eyes, the film of sweat on his brow that reached up well over his bald pate aroused her sympathy and brought her attention back to him and Susan Burrell. "I'm not sure I do get you, Mr. Carson."

"Well, what I mean is . . . I'd really appreciate it if you could keep her husband from finding out. She loves that cold, self-centered, mean son-of-a-bitch."

"Oh? What makes you think so?" Norah asked. "Did she tell you?"

"No."

"Have you ever asked her?"

A boy bringing his friends home after school to play, to do homework; regularly and approximately at the same hour, waving to the doorman and passing through till it became part of the building routine, unremarkable, Norah thought. Kids, teenagers, one of whom was smart enough to notice the pattern of Susan Burrell's comings and goings and mature enough to interpret them; one of whom resented Carson's dressing down and his complaint to the management and was looking for a way to pay him and his girl friend off. Could Susan Burrell's illicit visits to her lover have provided not only the opportunity but the motive for the murder of Jonathan Burrell?

Her thoughts tumbled one after the other, too fast, too fast. Slow down, Norah cautioned herself. This was treacherous ground. She sat in the gray Honda, key in the ignition, motor running, but not moving.

She'd have to talk to Bud Stucke and his friends. It was possible that they weren't involved at all, that Carson's complaint had in fact ended the incident. But Norah could not get rid of her qualms. Then another possibility occurred to her—sickening, but it had to be dealt with sooner or later. Sooner was better. She got out of the car and found a phone booth. After looking up the number, she put in a call to the Dowd School. That was the school at which her father had said Sylive Guthrie had been a pupil.

At the Dowd School the principal was dubbed the headmaster. The headmaster's tone was reserved, his consonants clipped in pseudo-British style. "I'm very sorry, but I can't give that information."

"Why not?"

"School policy. I don't know who you are or why you want it."

"I've just told you that I'm a police officer, Sergeant Mulcahaney, Fourth Homicide Division."

"Ah, well, anyone can say that on the telephone, can't they?"

"All right. What is your name, sir?"

"Willard Dowd."

"Okay, Mr. Dowd. I'll be right over."

She didn't go back to the car; she walked; it was near enough. She was more anxious than annoyed; she wanted to be told that she was wrong. As Norah walked briskly up Third Avenue with her long, athletic stride, she let her annoyance grow to smother the fear that she might have guessed right. On Sixty-ninth, she turned. It was a block of elegant townhouses, tree-lined, cleanly swept, one of the few where garbage and refuse were kept decently hidden till pickup time.

The Dowd School occupied two adjacent buildings. As Norah approached, the students were just getting out—girls from one door, boys from the other. All wore uniforms: the girls plaid skirts and green blazers; the boys, gray flannel trousers and green blazers. There was little mixing, almost no loitering. Some were picked up by chauffeured cars; others headed on their way toward the bus stop on Lexington Avenue. All were nice-looking, neat, apparently well-bred

103

children of junior-high or high-school ages. According to Roland Guthrie, they came not merely from affluent families but from families of high social status.

Norah found the administration office easily enough and was, after some resistance, passed through to Willard Dowd. He took his time scrutinizing her credentials closely, letting her know where the authority lay. He was a man acting out a mental self-image, Norah thought, observing the manner in which he removed the briarwood pipe from his clenched jaw and rested it on a heavy crystal ashtray, the way he leaned back in his chair adjusting the set of his tweed jacket and stretching out his arms to show the leather elbow patches. Settled finally in what he considered the appropriate pose, Dowd peered at Norah from behind black-framed glasses with the genial yet formal manner he might adopt interviewing the parents of a prospective pupil. "I'm sorry to have to put you to this inconvenience, Sergeant Mulcahaney, but I'm certain that you understand the reason for my caution. We have the children of some very important people here."

"And if that weren't so?"

"Then they'd be attending a public school, wouldn't they?"

"I haven't a lot of time, Mr. Dowd, so if you'd just answer my question: Is Bud Stucke one of your pupils?"

"Why do you want to know?"

Norah maintained a significant silence.

Working his fleshy lips back and forth, the headmaster gave in. "Yes, Bud Stucke is enrolled."

Chapter X

The door was opened on the chain. Pale gray eyes magnified by thick lenses of a pair of steel-rimmed spectacles peered sullenly through the crack.

"Nobody's home," the boy announced flatly and moved to shove the door shut.

"Wait." Norah found herself in the hackneyed situation of having to stop it with her foot. "You're home. You're the one I came to see, Bud."

He was startled that she knew his name and it made him more wary. "What do you want? Who are you?"

"My name is Norah Mulcahaney. I'm a police officer."

That frightened him. She could see it, but she didn't give it too much significance; it wasn't unusual for innocent people to feel a vague sense of guilt when confronted by the police—and he was only a boy.

He pulled himself together quickly enough, though. "Do you have a warrant?" he challenged.

She decided to treat that lightly. She chuckled. "Of course not. I'm not here to arrest anyone. I just want to talk to you, Bud, that's all. Ask you a few questions about the murders upstairs."

"I don't know anything about any murders."

"You've heard about them. You've heard what happened?"

"I've heard . . . sure."

"I've already talked to most of the residents in the building. When I came around the first time you weren't home." He didn't respond to her smile. "I came back because I was hoping, really hoping you could help me."

"Why me?"

She made a point of looking up and down the hall. "Do you want to talk out here?"

"I'm in the middle of homework," he mumbled, but when he closed the door it was to release the chain and let her in.

Bud Stucke was around fourteen. Carson had called him a runt; he was perhaps small for his age, but not unusually so—he would probably shoot up and get all of his height overnight, Norah thought. His face was sallow, had not started to break out, and he was very thin. He had blond hair cut in an unbecoming Prince Valiant style. He looked a bookish boy, certainly not athletic. Carson had further characterized Bud as the last kid to be picked when sides were chosen up—if he didn't get left out altogether. A follower. Such a boy should be thrilled at being consulted by the police. The appeal for help should be grist to his ego. He should at this very moment be visualizing the effect the encounter would have on his friends—how he would tell them about it, how he would embellish it making himself the confidant of the detectives, the star witness in their case. Yet Bud Stucke was showing no such normal, adolescent reaction.

Maybe the boy wasn't too smart, but what he lacked in mental quickness he surely made up for in doggedness.

"Why me?" he repeated as he ushered Norah Mulcahaney into a large living room dominated by a picture window that overlooked the central patio of the complex.

"Because you and Sylive Guthrie went to the same school."

"We did?"

The counter came too quickly. A chill passed through Norah: he'd been primed. "You do know that I'm talking about the girl upstairs? The one who was killed?"

"Yes."

She decided to give him one more chance. "And you didn't know that she went to the same school as you?"

"We don't pay any attention to the girls."

She noted the pronoun. "That's a shame. I'm really disappointed." Norah sighed. "What with you and Sylive going to the same school and living in the same building, I thought I'd hit it lucky. I was just positive that you knew her and would be able to tell me about her."

He shook his head.

"That's it, then, I guess." Norah looked around. "How do you like living here? I mean, it's a great building and all that, but it can't be much fun for kids." She glanced out the window and down into the patio. "I don't suppose the management encourages playing down there. So where do you go? Does the school have any kind of athletic program?"

"They take us to the park. We play soccer in the winter, baseball in the spring."

"What position do you play?"

"I pinch-hit."

Figures, she thought. She didn't want to confuse him into incriminating himself, but she was convinced that he knew more than he was admitting. "Bud, I have to be honest with you. I've spoken with Mr. Carson next door." His face darkened, became even more closed and sullen. "He told me about the run-in you and your friends had with him over Mrs. Burrell. Is it possible that you all went over to the Burrell apartment in Tower A intending to play a prank and get back at Mrs. Burrell and Mr. Carson?"

"What kind of prank?"

It could have started out as a prank, she told herself, no more than that in intent. "I don't know, just a prank. Did your friends come home with you after school two Fridays ago?"

He had two choices: he could say that he hadn't brought them home with him that particular day, or he could say that he had but that they had spent the entire afternoon in his apartment.

"I don't remember."

He was shrewd enough not to commit himself to either. "I thought that if you or they had gone over to the Burrell place you might have happened to see someone coming or going, or heard something, anything." She sighed. "All right. Never mind. I'll talk to the boys myself. What are their names?" She got out her notebook and pen.

"I can't give you their names."

"Why not? What's wrong with giving me their names?"

His thin lips were set tight. His sallow face almost sickly. He didn't answer.

"You know what you're making it look like? You're making it look like you and your friends did something really bad that afternoon."

The words had no effect.

"Bud, this is silly. I can find out who they are. You can save me some time and trouble." She waited. "I'm not going to tell them where I got my information, if that's what's worrying you."

He turned away. During the impasse, the front door opened and a woman's voice called out.

"Buddy, darling. I'm home."

The boy stayed where he was, stony-faced, as his mother walked into the room. She was an elegant lady in a dark ranch mink coat, her auburn hair newly set, her skin with the healthy glow of recent exercise, or an expensive facial. As she was not likely to have been jogging in the park in her mink, it had to be the facial. She was a youthful forty and holding—by all possible means. She stopped short when she saw Norah. She fluttered long false lashes that had been individually glued over her own short, real ones. She smiled carefully so as to cause the minimal number of wrinkles.

"Buddy, darling!" She went over and kissed her son. He winced in embarrassment, but she didn't appear to notice. "Is this one of your teachers, darling? Aren't you going to introduce us?" She held out her hand. "I'm Isabel Stucke."

"How do you do?" Norah shook hands. "I'm not one of Bud's teachers, though. I'm a police officer. Sergeant Mulcahaney. I'm investigating the recent crimes in the buildings and talking to all the residents."

"I see." Isabel Stucke pulled back her hand in a manner that suggested Norah had misrepresented herself. "I'm sorry that I wasn't at home, but there's really nothing I can tell you. I didn't know either the Guthries or Mr. Burrell."

"It was Bud I wanted to talk to. Sylive Guthrie attended the Dowd School."

"I've already said I didn't know her and never noticed her," Bud complained to his mother.

"He hasn't discovered girls yet," the mother offered but her accompanying smile was no more than a parting of the lips this time. "So it appears that neither one of us can be of assistance, Sergeant ... uh ... Sergeant."

"I thought perhaps Bud's friends, the boys that come home with him after school so frequently, might have known Sylive."

Mrs. Stucke managed a questioning look without raising her eyebrows more than a fraction. "Why don't you ask them?"

"Bud won't give me their names."

"I'm not going to snitch on my friends. I'm not!"

"Snitch?"

"Betray," he corrected himself.

The lady now turned her full displeasure on Norah. "You had no right to interrogate my son in my absence. You had no right to talk to him without me or his father present. He's only a child. You had no right to harass him or to try to trick him into involving himself or his friends."

"I made no such attempt, Mrs. Stucke, I assure you. I asked Bud some routine questions."

"I want you to leave."

"Mrs. Stucke ..."

"I intend to lodge a formal complaint against you, Sergeant ..."

Not registering the name was a classic putdown. Norah gritted her teeth. "Mulcahaney. Sergeant Norah Mulcahaney. Fourth Homicide Division. There was no harassment. I asked Bud some questions."

"You're not dealing with ghetto children here, Sergeant. Bud is a well-brought-up boy from a good family and his friends are the same. They attend one of the finest private schools in the city. They have an honor code. Bud is quite right not to divulge the names of his friends. I'm proud that he upholds the code."

"There have been two break-ins in these buildings in the course of which three people were brutally murdered," Norah reminded her.

"Well, I don't know anything about Jonathan Burrell, but I can tell you that Françoise Guthrie had a string of lovers," Isabel Stucke informed Norah. "Everybody knows it, including Mr. Guthrie. Why don't you talk to them and to him? What in the world do you expect to learn from a child?"

109

"Bud and his friends had a run-in with your neighbor, Duane Carson."

"That's none of your business."

"I think it is."

"Really, Sergeant." She still refused to dignify Norah by remembering her name. "All that amounted to was a group of schoolboys running up and down the halls playing catch. They happened to disturb Mr. Carson's ... siesta," she finished with the glint of a leer.

"One of the boys made an offensive remark to Mr. Carson's visitor."

Isabel Stucke laughed. "Boys pick up words and use them without fully knowing what they mean."

Norah didn't bother to comment on that one. "It appears the boys were aware of the regularity of the lady's visits. I want to know whether they passed that information on, perhaps accidentally." She paused. "Or used it themselves."

"My God! What are you suggesting?"

"I'm asking, Mrs. Stucke. Just asking."

"Bud doesn't know anything."

"All I want is the names of the boys that came home with him and ran up and down the halls in innocent high spirits. What can be wrong with giving me their names? Do you know them?"

"I do not."

"I can get a warrant and arrest Bud as a material witness."

"Then he'll be represented by our lawyer."

"If that's the way you want it, Mrs. Stucke."

Isabel Stucke's pretty, well-cared-for face was distorted by malice. "If that happens you'll be off the case. So the choice is yours, Sergeant Mulcahaney."

No matter how spurious, a civilian complaint against a police officer meant trouble. Though she was absolutely certain she'd be able to defend herself successfully, Norah waited with anxiety for the call from Captain Childs, her commanding officer. It would take a while, of course, for the complaint to filter down through the chain of command, depending on how high Mrs. Stucke had started. As the days passed, however, and nothing happened, Norah began to breathe more easily. Finally, she convinced herself that

Isabel Stucke had thought better of it and had decided to leave well enough alone.

The problem of who Bud's friends were remained. According to Mrs. Stucke, her son's silence was honorable; Norah considered it adolescent, at best. But then how about her own attitude about the job on the task force? Wasn't she avoiding her responsibility by turning it down? Yes, but she was motivated by her friendship with Inspector Felix and love for her husband. Why attribute less worthy motives to Bud? Actually, by refusing the job on the task force, wasn't she proclaiming that she believed the Inspector and Joe had something to hide, that she doubted their leadership? That she thought, at the least, that they didn't know what was going on under their noses?

She requested an appointment with Inspector Felix. "If the job is still open, I'm ready," she told him.

Green eyes under high, perfectly arched brows regarded her steadily. "Good," James Felix replied.

He had aged well. Nearing fifty, Felix still had the lean, raw-boned look of his youth; if anything, he was thinner, tougher. His long, narrow, lantern-jawed face showed only a fine tracery of lines. However, the thick roan hair had gone completely gray and the bony shoulders seemed more hunched; in fact, he sat bent in an attitude of perpetual attention. Jim Felix had been one of the youngest men to make detective lieutenant. He was a fine investigator, an efficient administrator, but his forte was dealing with people. Despite a period of turmoil within the department, a rebellion against discipline, a flouting of authority, demand for rights and money, Felix had been promoted up through the civil-service ranks and above to those positions where men served at the pleasure of the Police Commissioner. His rise was due to his feeling for the men and women under his command.

"Good," Felix repeated. "You'll continue on the Belmonde case, of course, but you're to conduct all future interrogations accompanied by another officer. That way, whatever happens, there'll be corroboration."

Norah flushed; she was aware of it; she could feel the burning all over her body. "Mrs. Stucke did lodge the complaint?"

"She most certainly did. She went right up to the PC."

Norah groaned. "I thought . . . when I didn't hear . . . I hoped . . ."

"You were in the wrong, you know, Sergeant," Felix admonished. "You'd been issued a direct order to cease canvassing the Belmonde residents." He held up his hand when she tried to speak. "I understand that you had new evidence which you felt required interrogation of that specific witness. No argument. I'm also certain that you neither browbeat nor attempted to trick Bud Stucke. But it would have helped if you'd had someone with you to confirm it all." He laughed. "I really shouldn't need to tell you all this, Norah."

"No, sir."

"Under the circumstances we'll set up a meeting with the boy and his parents and his lawyer here, in my office."

"Yes, sir." The interview was over, but she hesitated. "Inspector, when did Mrs. Stucke lodge the complaint?"

"It reached me four days ago."

It should immediately have been handed down to Captain Childs at the Fourth. Instead Felix had sat on it waiting for her to come in. Trusting that she would.

"Thank you, Inspector." It was good to be back.

The appointment with the Stuckes was set for the next morning, but it didn't take place. That night, as Norah was preparing to leave the precinct for the day, she received a frantic telephone call from Isabel Stucke. She was sobbing in broken, convulsive gasps.

"Sergeant Mulcahaney, you've got to come over here right away. It's Bud. He's been beaten. Horribly, horribly beaten up."

"Have you called an ambulance?"

"Yes, yes. I'm at the hospital now. Lenox Hill. They're operating. Oh, my God, I've got to talk to you. Can you come over? Please."

"I'm on my way."

Bud Stucke lay unconscious in the hospital bed. Bandages covered his head down to his eyebrows and wound under his chin. What could be seen of his face was bruised and swollen. His lips were cut. According to the resident, his jaw had been broken.

"You've got to get the bastards who did this!"

The expensive work done by Isabel Stucke's masseuse had been destroyed. Her face was ravaged, stained with tears and twisted with anger. Her voice throbbed with intensity but she kept it low; not that it mattered—she could have yelled and not disturbed the boy in the bed.

"You've got to get them and make them pay, Sergeant Mulcahaney!"

Bernard Stucke, a stolid man in a gray pin-striped suit heavily padded at the shoulders and tapered at the hips, reached over and soothingly patted his wife's hand. "Don't upset yourself, Belle. Don't upset yourself."

She ignored him. Her dark eyes glittering with fierce determination were fixed on Norah. "We'll offer a reward. We'll do anything, everything. Name it, just name it, Sergeant Mulcahaney."

"First, I need to know exactly what happened in as much detail as you can manage to give me."

With a rasping noise, Isabel Stucke sucked in a lungful of air and exhaled it in a rush. It took several such gasps before she was able to breathe normally. Her husband poured her a glass of water and put it in her hand. When she spoke again it was, if not calmly, at least with an effort to be rational. "I got home from shopping at about five this afternoon. I walked into the living room and found Bud." Her eyes filled with tears; she caught her breath.

"Easy, Mrs. Stucke, easy. Was there any damage done to the apartment? Anything stolen?"

"My God, who cares? I didn't notice. I didn't look. All I could see was my child, what they had done to my child."

"All right, Mrs. Stucke, all right. Did you notify the police?" she asked quickly as the woman started once more to hyperventilate.

"I called my doctor." Isabel Stucke looked at Norah as though she were an imbecile.

"Yes, of course. And he called the ambulance? Good, good. And then when you got here you called me. So, I'll go back to your place and take a look around and make a report."

"What for? I don't care what they took! If they took anything. This was no ordinary robbery or break-in. Don't you understand? It's why I called you. My God, it's obvious enough. They broke his jaw!" she shrilled, and then remembering, threw a quick, penitent look at her unconscious son.

113

She lowered her voice. She hissed. "What could be plainer than that?"

Bernard Stucke made to take her into his arms, but she pulled away.

"They broke his jaw so he couldn't talk."

"Who?" Norah asked.

"Who else? Those boys, of course. Those lousy, rotten boys."

"I need their names, Mrs. Stucke."

"I don't know their names." She groaned.

"You don't know the names of Bud's friends?" Bernard Stucke asked. "You don't know who the boys are that he brings home day after day?"

"I thought . . . since they were from the school . . . I thought that was all the reference I needed. I thought any boy from the school had to be all right."

"You couldn't take the time to stay home one afternoon, just one, to meet your son's friends?"

She was saved from further castigation by a low moan from the bed. They all heard it and were galvanized by it. Isabel Stucke ran to the head of the bed and bent anxiously over Bud; his father stood beside her. Norah went to the foot of the bed. Bud moaned a second time. His eyelids fluttered. He opened his eyes.

"Mmm . . ." He couldn't speak, of course; his jaw was wired shut. But his eyes moved. They moved to his mother, and she took his hand and kissed it; to his father, who smiled encouragement; to Norah. When he saw her he shut his eyes and turned his head aside on the pillow.

She went around to that side and stood opposite Mrs. Stucke. "You can't talk, Bud, but you can write. I'm going to raise your bed so that you'll be sitting up. I'm going to give you pen and paper. I want you to write down the names of those boys."

His eyes remained tightly shut. He gave no indication of even having heard.

"You've got to tell her, darling," his mother pleaded. "You can't let them get away with this."

Reaching to the side of the pillow, Norah located the box that electrically controlled the various positions of the hospital bed. She pressed the *raise* button. A hum indicated the mechanism was working and the upper section began to lift. When it reached what she judged to be a comfortable height,

114

Norah stopped it. She took her notebook out of her handbag, tore a page from it, put it and her pen on Bud's lap.

"Who did this to you?"

Bud opened his eyes. He looked at Norah and then down at the paper and pen, but he made no move to write.

"How many were there?"

Nothing.

"Why did they do it?"

No longer able to contain herself, Isabel Stucke broke in. "That's obvious. My God, I told you . . ."

Norah silenced her with a wave of the hand, while keeping her eyes firmly on the boy. "I know it was a terrible experience for you, Bud. You're frightened. Anyone would be. You're afraid they might come after you again. The one way to make sure they don't is to give me their names. Once you tell me who they are there won't be any reason for them to hurt you. In fact, they'll be the ones who'll be afraid." She waited. He needed time to think it through. Slow though he sometimes appeared, it should make sense to him. Unless . . . unless there was something else bothering him. What? What? Norah asked herself. The answer had to be that he was involved with them in something he didn't want to tell. It couldn't amount to much, she reasoned, or they could have counted on his guilt to keep him quiet.

"If you're mixed up with them in anything, Bud, anything you're sorry for, this is your chance to make it right. What is it that they don't want you to talk about?" She took the pen and placed it in his hand, wrapped his limp fingers around it. "Why did they beat you and break your jaw?"

He looked quickly at her, then away again.

"Whatever you've done, your mother and father will stand by you. I'll do everything I can to help, but you've got to help me. Why did they beat you up like this?"

Now the fingers tightened around the pen. He lowered his eyes to the paper. He scrawled one word: *Secret.*

Norah frowned. "Secret? I don't understand. I know it's a secret, but . . . You mean, a secret pact?"

He nodded.

"You boys are bound together in some kind of secret . . . society?"

Again, the nod.

A boys' secret society. What came to mind was Tom Sawyer

and Huck Finn pricking their fingers to swear a blood oath. Blood, she thought; there had been blood spilled here too. "What's the purpose of your society?"

No sign. No movement.

"What kind of secret society?"

He remained stolid and still.

"What is its purpose?"

Bernard Stucke broke in. "That's enough, I think, Sergeant. You're upsetting the boy. Later, perhaps . . ."

"No, Bernard, now!" Isabel Stucke cried out. "He's got to tell it now. All of it. Whatever it is. If he'd done it last week when she wanted him to, none of this would have happened. It's my fault he didn't. Bud, sweetheart, I told you then not to give the names of your friends. I was wrong. They're not your friends. They're hoodlums. They're monsters. I want you to tell Sergeant Mulcahaney now, right now. I'm begging you to tell her everything you know."

"Write down their names," Norah urged. "The purpose of your group. What you did, yourself, that you're sorry for now."

His glasses had, of course, been removed, and without them his gray eyes looked vulnerable. Tears filled them and then spilled down the swollen, lacerated cheeks. The hand moved across the paper. *Killed . . . animals . . .*

Somehow, Norah managed to hide her shock. "You mean the animals in the zoo? On Halloween?"

"What? What animals?" Isabel Stucke demanded.

"Is that what you mean?" Norah pressed. "The animals that were massacred? You and your friends were responsible for that?"

He dropped his head.

She felt sad, unutterably sad. "Why? Why did you do it?"

The hand wrote as though by its own, independent volition. Finished, the pen fell from Bud Stucke's fingers and the paper fluttered off his lap. He closed his eyes.

Norah picked the paper off the floor and read the single word: *Initiation.*

Chapter XI

Bud Stucke had been prevailed upon to write once more. He had put down a name, one: Peter Tomasiello. No entreaties, no threats had served to get anything else, not even the number of boys who had participated in that gory, brutal, and debauched ritual at the zoo.

With that name, Norah returned to the Dowd School. David Link went with her.

Their reception was quite different from Norah's the first time she'd called on the headmaster. As soon as he saw the two detectives, Willard Dowd set aside his pipe and got up and went to greet them. He was particularly attentive to Norah. He reached for her hand and held it as he led her to the visitors' chair, hovering to make sure she was comfortable. When there was nothing more to fuss over, when both his callers were settled, Dowd reluctantly returned to his desk, shoulders sagging and ruddy face haggard. It didn't take Norah long to find out what had caused his distress.

"Mrs. Stucke is demanding that I expel Peter Tomasiello. She's been on the phone haranguing me all morning."

She hadn't wasted any time, Norah mused. She certainly sympathized with Bud's mother. She'd felt the same way exactly about the girls who had assaulted Toni, yet now Norah found herself in the position of defending Tomasiello's rights. "Have you spoken to Peter or his parents?"

Dowd shook his head. "This is extremely difficult for the school. What I find particularly distressing is that Peter is one of our scholarship students. It is the policy of the Dowd School to provide a certain number of grants to the disadvantaged and the minorities. In this manner talented boys who would not otherwise have the opportunity get a high-quality education. Our regular students benefit as well, of course, as they have contact with boys outside their own economic and ethnic world. Peter is one of a select and carefully chosen group. I cannot believe that the governing board and I could have been so wrong about Peter."

The regret struck a false note as though the headmaster was more concerned over an error of judgment than the boy or what he might or might not have done. David cast a glance at Norah, but said nothing. He was sitting this one out.

"The whole business has been a dreadful shock for me, Sergeant," Dowd continued. "Staggering. Bewildering. As far as Bud Stucke is concerned—well, I'm sure that you've noted for yourself that he's not particularly bright, a boy easily led. In spite of that, I can't believe he would take part in . . ."

"Massacre? Butchery? Wanton killing?" Norah suggested.

Dowd winced. "I can't believe that any of my boys would take part. Of course, we don't know that there were others." He paused, considering that possibility hopefully.

Norah lost no time in disavowing him of it. "There were others," she told him firmly. She thought of the methods by which the animals had been tortured and killed. "At least one other."

Dowd sighed, but he was relaxed enough to reach for his pipe. He put it in his mouth and sucked.

"I want to talk to the students in Bud's class."

"Why?"

"I need to know who his friends are, get some kind of feeling for how the boys spend their time after school. Look, Mr. Dowd, if you're hoping to keep what's happened from the parents, you're deluding yourself. Children have an uncanny way of ferreting out scandal. They'll talk among themselves whether I question them or not. Either way they're going to carry home rumors, magnified for the worse if left to their

118

imaginations. And then, of course, there's Mrs. Stucke," she reminded him.

He groaned and bit down hard on the pipe stem.

"She might take it on herself to notify the other parents."

He took the pipe out of his mouth. "God!" Evidently, that terrible eventuality hadn't occurred to him.

"You might placate her by telling her that the police are talking to Bud's friends and want the whole thing kept quiet while they do so. Actually, we don't know exactly of what Bud accuses Tomasiello—the beating, the raid in the park, or both."

"Yes, I see. All right, Sergeant. Do what you have to do."

"Thank you. Detective Link and I will be around when school lets out."

"The two of you? I would like to keep this as restricted as . . ."

"Standard procedure, Mr. Dowd. You can be present if you like to make sure the children's rights aren't violated."

He waved that off. "There is one courtesy I would ask in return." He included both in his look.

Here it comes, Norah thought. David leaned forward slightly.

"I'd be grateful if you could keep the name of the school out of the papers."

"I don't like dealing with juveniles," David complained looking distinctly unhappy. "It's a thankless, frustrating job."

"How thankless?"

"To start with, everybody's on the kid's side. I mean, everybody. It's bad enough if you're after the kid for a misdemeanor: that's all the business in the park amounts to. They'll call it a prank, admittedly gruesome, but a prank. They'll fob off the shooting of the night watchman as a regrettable result of the prank's getting out of hand. Which is exactly right, Norah. What you're trying to do, what you apparently want to do, is tie that prank to two felony murders."

He was finished. He indicated it was her turn.

Norah lashed out indignantly. "No. I don't *want* to, David. It's the last thing in the world I *want*. There are just too many signposts to ignore." She ticked them off. "Opportunity: through Bud, Peter and any other of his schoolmates could come and go in and out of the Belmonde without attracting special

119

attention. We know and it's been admitted that while playing in the halls they had seen Susan Burrell on her regular visits to Carson. They made a lewd remark to her, and Carson reported them to the management. They decided to pay him back: they'd break into the Burrell place while Carson and Susan were together. Sooner or later, Carson and Susan would be found out. A perfect revenge with considerable side benefits. They knew exactly when to go over and they knew how long they could stay."

What she meant was that they knew how long they would have to ransack the place, or, as it turned out, to torture the helpless invalid till he told them how to get at the cash.

"It's positively Machiavellian," David derided. "How do you figure it ties in with the Guthrie homicides? What's the motive there?"

"Money; they didn't get all that much from Burrell," Norah answered instantly. "I don't know whether the Burrell robbery whetted their appetites or whether there were incidents prior to it. I do think that they tried to follow a similar pattern and strike at a time when Sylive Guthrie would be home alone."

"How do you get that?"

"You remember what Sylive's classmates said—that Peter Tomasiello had taken a shine to her? He started waiting around after school for her and walking her home. She was not only a plain girl, but very shy, and he's handsome, intelligent, popular. They couldn't figure it. I think he was trying to get a line on her family's routine. Maybe even get her to invite him up."

"With the intent to rob?" Link shook his head. "They're only kids, remember."

"I can't forget it," she assured him. "Kids do a lot worse out on the street every day and we both know it."

"You don't realize what you're letting us in for." He groaned. "The juvenile people aren't going to help. To the contrary. Where a youthful offender is concerned their first instinct is to say no. Okay. So, assuming we manage somehow to build a case on our own, the trial is going to be in family court and the attitude is exactly the same—in favor of the youthful offender."

"Under the new law a juvenile accused of a violent crime is

120

tried in the regular criminal part as an adult," she reminded him.

"Right. Sure he is, but the jury still sees a child. I tell you, the jury won't convict a child of murder. Look what happened to that kid who was thirteen when he committed murder. It took two years to get him to trial. Then he was found guilty all right and he didn't even pretend he was sorry, but the court reduced the charge to manslaughter, so back to family court he went. He got a three-year sentence, and we both know he'll be out in one. God knows what he'll do afterward."

"So you figure it's not worth bothering."

"I want you to know the odds. In this particular case, they're really stacked against us. We're dealing with kids from middle- and upper-echelon families. Kids with all the advantages. Why should they be running around committing push-in robberies and murders?"

"Tomasiello isn't rich." Norah didn't like putting the onus on the disadvantaged boy, making him the scapegoat as Dowd was so anxious yet fearful of doing. "He gets his tuition free, but he has to buy books and he sees that the other kids have things he doesn't—clothes, pocket money, cameras, records . . ." Records. She'd have to get Gus to find out exactly which of Jonathan Burrell's records were missing. Either Susan or Jason Burrell should be able to tell him.

"How about the other kids? Why should they go along?"

Norah was locked into her thoughts. If those special records of Jonathan Burrell's should turn up in Peter Tomasiello's possession . . . They'd have to have the artist's fingerprints on them to make them count as evidence. Could she get a search warrant? Did she have enough probable cause?

"Norah? How about the rich kids?" David recalled her to the problem in hand. "What did they get out of it?"

"Kicks," Norah answered and shivered involuntarily as she thought of Toni huddled on the bed, her skirt soaked with blood, sobbing with humiliation and pain. How else explain the gang rape by her schoolmates? "Rich kids are out for kicks same as poor kids."

David put a hand on Norah's shoulder. "I heard what happened to your niece. I'm sorry."

"So what should we do?" Norah's blue eyes flashed a challenge. "Turn our backs on four brutal, coldblooded homi-

121

cides because they might have been committed by juveniles? Is that what *you* want?"

He kissed her on the cheek. "What I want is for us to make damn sure of the facts before we stick our necks out."

Peter Tomasiello, Sr., was a bus driver. He got off work at four and usually made it home by four-thirty. Nastasia Tomasiello was a private nurse. She worked nights from seven P.M. to seven A.M. So the late-afternoon dinner was the only time the family were likely to be together. In fairness to the boy, and as this was to be an exploratory session, both Norah and David had agreed that Peter should be interviewed along with both parents. Norah parked in front of the project on the block between Columbus and Amsterdam avenues and waited for David to join her before going up. She considered that Felix's explicit order to work with a partner referred to interrogation of residents of the Belmonde, yet, in honesty, she knew it wasn't limited to that and he would consider the coming interview too sensitive to be handled by any officer alone. So where was David? She got out of the Honda and looked up and down the street; no sign of him. She looked at her watch: ten after five. Mrs. Tomasiello was working downtown at the New York Infirmary that week; to get there for her shift she'd surely have to leave by a little after six. Norah was getting anxious.

Whatever reservations she might have about David's methods, he was reliable. Norah was well aware that since his appointment to the task force David had handled the most plodding kinds of jobs and that this was his first real opportunity to show initiative. Naturally, he was anxious to take advantage of it not only to prove himself to Inspector Felix who after all knew David from the old days as well as he did Norah, but to Chief Deland who did not. She was also perfectly aware that he was competing with her and she didn't mind. The point was that if David was late it was for good reason, and that being so, there was no telling how late he would be. Norah decided not to wait any longer. He would realize that she had gone ahead and would catch up with her.

Standing in front of apartment 5A, Norah felt the familiar queasiness in her stomach which despite the years of experience still bothered her before an important interrogation. It was, she imagined, what stage fright must be like.

As the apartment door was opened a cascade of piano music, limpid, delicate yet strong, spilled from somewhere inside. It seemed an appropriate background for the young man who stood on the threshold. She'd been told over and over that he was handsome but she had not been prepared for the clarity of his dark eyes, the openness of his brow, for the look of—innocence. He wore an open-necked, white shirt that looked as if his mother had just got through washing and pressing it, with dark slacks. His black hair was cut short in the traditional way. He was tall for his age, a growth that must have been sudden for he didn't deal with it comfortably. He could pass for eighteen or nineteen, Norah thought. He could also have taken the part of the eldest son in one of those wholesome television families.

She showed her ID. "I'd like to talk to you and your parents."

The only change in his expression was a slight narrowing of his eyes and a general stillness.

"May I come in?"

He stepped back immediately.

The room which she entered was unexpectedly spacious and tastefully furnished. The furniture was old-fashioned and of good quality, probably inherited or bought in the early days of the marriage. Everything was well cared for. The Tomasiellos lived in comfort and some grace.

"Mama!" Peter called.

Nastasia Tomasiello bustled out of the kitchen. She was a short, sturdy woman in her late thirties and Norah saw immediately where her son got his eyes. Except that Nastasia Tomasiello had shadows under hers so dark they looked like permanent discolorations. They made her seem congenitally tired. She also seemed harassed. Norah could understand why—trying to serve dinner, wash up, change into her whites, and get herself downtown for a twelve-hour shift. In spite of all that there were traces of the pretty girl she had once been—skin that was white and flawless, the hair, though severely pulled back, was black and glossy. Peter had got his looks from his mother and his height from his father, Norah noted as the elder Tomasiello rose politely from his chair. He was at least six foot four with a large hook nose and an old man's scraggly eyebrows. The stooped shoulders indicated the same weariness as his wife's. Norah recognized it as the result of the constant struggle to provide a life style just

123

beyond reach. The look of defeat was the realization the struggle would never end.

Again Norah showed her ID and introduced herself. "I'm sorry to disturb your meal, but I wanted to talk to Peter and to have you both present." There was the inevitable anxious look exchanged between the parents. "I assume you've heard that one of the students at the Dowd School was murdered and another, more recently, beaten."

"A dreadful thing," Tomasiello senior murmured, but he relaxed and the look he and his wife shared this time was one of relief; the policewoman wasn't there about their son.

"My partner and I were at the school this afternoon to talk to the students and somehow we missed Peter."

"Pietro, the music—turn it off," the father ordered.

"It's very beautiful," Norah commented. "Chopin?"

He nodded.

"A nocturne? Which one?" He could hardly deny knowing.

"It's the Piano Concerto in E Minor."

A gut feeling stopped her from asking who the artist was, though it was not one of the recordings Gus had determined was missing from the Burrell collection. "Marvelous recording," she said. "Of course, the recording is only as good as the system it's played on." She looked around: speakers and turntable must be in his bedroom. "Do you mind telling me the manufacturer? I'm thinking of buying a stereo for my husband for his birthday."

"I assembled the components myself from various makes."

"That's the best way, I guess, and the most expensive, and of course you have to know what you're doing." It was not the moment to ask to look at the system.

"Peter earns his own spending money by tutoring," his mother informed Norah proudly, a pride shared by the father.

"Is that so?" Not only was he tall for his age, but his manner was so reserved that Norah had to remind herself that she was dealing with a fifteen-year-old. "Whom do you tutor?"

"Nobody regularly. Just, like, when a test is coming up, then I help whoever asks me."

"Bud Stucke?"

"Sometimes."

"Sylive Guthrie. Did you ever tutor Sylive?"

"No. She was a very good student. She didn't need tutoring. Sylive and I were friends."

He was certainly straightforward. "Did you visit Sylive in her home?"

"No."

"But you did visit Bud?"

"Oh, sure, lots of times."

"There were other boys along too? Three, four, five?"

"It varied depending on who needed help with homework or who needed to cram for an exam."

Norah got out her notebook and pen. "What are their names?"

He scowled, shuffled his feet, very much the youngster. "Gee, Sergeant, I'm not supposed to tell. Their parents don't know they're being tutored."

"So how do they pay you?"

"They get big allowances and they don't have to account for what they do with their money."

More than a hint of envy, but it was only human and Norah couldn't help sympathizing. He was playing out of his league.

But the parents were shamed. "I asked you to turn off the music," his father reminded the boy tersely and this time Peter went instantly to obey. When he was gone, Tomasiello turned to Norah. "Just what is it you want from my son?"

"I explained . . ."

"No. You were not honest. You have been asking Pietro about himself, not about the others. Unless you tell me what you really want I will forbid further questions."

"Your son is a friend of both victims."

"So are others at the school." The bus driver displayed considerable dignity in the defense of his son.

Norah had to make a decision. She clenched her jaw. David had warned her to test every foot of the ground before taking a step. She wished he were here with her. Faced with these two decent people and their clean-cut, well-mannered, intelligent son, her suspicions were monstrous. David had reminded her that what had happened in the park was a misdemeanor. Norah decided that for now she would limit herself to that incident.

"Your son's friend, Bud Stucke, the one who was beaten?

He says that a group of the students at the school formed a secret society. He says that Peter is a member."

"I don't understand." There was no exchange between parents. Tomasiello kept his gaze firmly on the policewoman.

Peter returned from his room in time to hear the last of what Norah had said. "It's a lie!"

"Taci!" The father stopped him.

Peter ignored the order. "How could Bud say anything? His jaw is broken."

"He can't speak," Norah agreed. "But he can write."

The fight oozed out of Peter.

"What kind of secret society?" His father demanded. "What is she talking about?"

"It's a joke, Papa. We called the study group a secret society so the parents wouldn't find out."

"And to make sure that nobody would tell, the boys got together on Halloween and went down to the Central Park Children's Zoo and joined in the slaughter of every domestic animal that wasn't inside a cage. It seems excessive."

The stolid nurse made a whimpering sound and abruptly sank into the nearest chair.

"You did such a thing?" The father whispered.

"No, Papa, no. I swear. I don't know what she's talking about."

"Some of the animals were strangled, some clubbed to death, some knifed. Which method did you use?"

"Enough! That's enough! The boy says he didn't do it." Tomasiello senior stepped between Norah and his son.

"Bud Stucke was beaten and his jaw broken to keep him quiet."

"Are you accusing my boy?"

"I'm suggesting that one of the boys in the 'secret society' did it, and I'm asking Peter for their names."

"According to the newspapers, the boy was beaten in the course of a robbery like the other robberies in that same building."

"Nothing was stolen from the Stuckes." Norah paused, tried again. "Bud was too frightened to accuse anyone directly of beating him, but he did tell about the secret society and he admitted that they were responsible for the massacre of those poor animals. When I pressed him for names, he gave one only: Peter's. If Bud is lying and Peter is not involved with anything but a study group why shouldn't he tell me who the other boys were?"

Tomasiello's scraggy eyebrows knotted. "She's right," he decided. "Tell her."

"They'll never trust me again."

"Tell her." The order was sharp and brooked no denial. "Tell her," he repeated.

Before anyone knew what he was up to, before anyone could stop him, Peter Tomasiello, Jr., ran past his father, out of the room, and out the front door.

"Pietro! Vieni qui! Pietro!" His father shouted after him.

In reply, the front door slammed shut. Tomasiello, red with fury at his command being flouted, lunged past the two women and after his son. It was several minutes before he returned, the color of his anger faded into concern. "He's gone. Out of the building. I don't know where."

"He'll be back," Norah assured them. "He needs a little time to himself." Or to consult with his buddies, she thought, to warn them the story wasn't holding up.

"He's a good boy, a good boy." Nastasia Tomasiello moaned. "He could never have done . . . what you said . . . to those animals. Not my Pietro."

"Children can be cruel, Stasia." Her husband put an arm around her. "They have little understanding for animals as living creatures of God." He was preparing her and himself for what he now feared was the inevitable. "If Pietro did those terrible things, he will confess." He looked at Norah. "I promise you that he will."

Now! Norah thought, and took a deep breath. "There's more to it, I'm afraid. During the raid, the night watchman was killed."

"No! Madre di Dio, no!" The mother groaned.

What was left of his anger was drained and the father was left a defeated man.

She didn't like it, but she had to seize the advantage. "May I look at Peter's room?" Norah asked.

"What for?" Tomasiello resisted out of instinct.

"I want to look at that recording on the turntable and I want to see if he has a gun. You don't have to give your permission. I can get a search warrant."

Nastasia Tomasiello kept faith. "Look all you want, Sergeant."

127

She held her head high, the dark bruises under her eyes looking as though they'd been freshly inflicted. "Look all you want. There's no gun. My boy is a good boy."

Silently, they filed down the hall.

It was a typical boy's room with scarred maple furniture and cheerful, inexpensive, bright Indian throws for the bedspread and drapes. The usual accumulation of possessions was neatly stored on a system of adjustable shelves which covered the entire wall above the desk. The shelves held plenty of books, plenty of records, and the stereo equipment. Norah made a note of the various manufacturers, then she gave the room a professional toss while the parents stood watching with growing unease. Norah searched drawers and closet, under cushions; she felt every inch of the mattress, looked behind drapes and under the lid of the toilet tank. Not a word was spoken till she finished.

"Nothing!" Nastasia Tomasiello was triumphant—and relieved. Not that Norah had expected to find a weapon—not a baseball bat, nor a knife, much less a gun. If he'd ever possessed any, Peter wouldn't leave them lying around his room where his mother might find them at any time. He might have a hiding place outside. What she'd wanted was exactly what she'd said—to have a look at Peter's room, at his expensive stereo components, at his record collection. She could tell that his parents, who had taken their son's hobby for granted as Peter brought the various items home one by one, seeing it all in the aggregate were dismayed at the money represented.

"Now what are you looking for?" Tomasiello demanded as Norah lingered over the stereo and the record collection.

Both parents had grown increasingly jumpy as the search dragged on. During the past few minutes, Tomasiello senior, head tilted toward the front door, had been listening for sounds of his son's return. For all her avowed confidence, Mrs. Tomasiello, the sturdy, self-contained nurse, was casting anxious glances in the same direction. Neither one was anxious to be caught standing by while a police officer went through their son's belongings. If he walked in now, protesting they'd allowed the search as an act of faith in his innocence wouldn't cut it with Peter, Norah thought. He'd see it as a violation of his privacy and his parents knew it. They were not likely to mention that she had even been in his room, yet she didn't want to draw their attention to what might turn out to be damning evidence against the boy.

"Nothing," she replied and turned away.

"You were looking for a gun. There is no gun. So why don't you go?" Tomasiello asked.

For once, Norah didn't know what to answer. She didn't have the heart to thank them for cooperation which they would be bound to regret. She could in no way reassure them that the troubles for their son were over. So she merely nodded and walked out of the room and out of the apartment.

She walked down the hall and rang for the elevator.

The interview had been inconclusive, but the search had not. She'd found what she'd almost been hoping not to find. The album of Chopin nocturnes recorded by Jonathan Burrell, the missing album. Though it was a rarity, hard to come by, there was no proof that Peter hadn't bought and paid for it. The proof would be the artist's fingerprints on it, but there was no way she could have taken the album with her. She'd already stretched the legalities. She could only hope that she hadn't drawn attention to it and that it would stay where it was for a while.

She jabbed at the elevator button and looked up at the indicator over the door. It stood at B for basement. Somebody was holding the elevator, to load probably. Norah gave the button a couple more long, hard rings mostly to vent her pent-up frustrations. She was generally depressed over the case, tired of interrogating children and their parents, trying to trip the one and avoid inflicting pain and sorrow on the other. What she wanted was to get home to Joe, have a nice dinner, maybe go to a movie. What Norah wanted most at that particular moment was to be an ordinary housewife with an ordinary housewife's concerns. Only the other night she'd seen a television commercial in which a young, attractive matron had stood in the middle of an impossibly perfect kitchen beaming on her shining kitchen floor with a look of complete self-fulfillment. Usually, Norah pitied such women, if there really were any such, but right then she envied them.

Again she looked up at the indicator; the elevator still hadn't budged. Must be stuck. Damn. She looked around; apparently it was the only elevator in that wing. So? She could use the stairs; it was only five flights. The red exit light was visible at the other end of the hall. Briskly, Norah headed toward it, leaned on the cross bar of the heavy metal fire door, and pushed to step through to the landing. The door hadn't finished hissing shut behind her when an arm was thrown around her neck and she was jerked back and nearly off her feet. A knife, its blade glistening, was held for a moment out where she could see it, then lowered till its sharp tip tickled her exposed throat.

Norah knew a couple of tricks herself. First, she went still; completely, limply still. She wanted to give her assailant confidence that she would not resist and herself the best opportunity for a sudden move. Cautiously, but not wasting time, she edged her right leg back till she felt her assailant's leg. A couple of seconds was all it took, then, flexing her knee, she brought her heel down hard on his instep. He yelled and let her go. She ran—up the stairs because he was blocking the way down and because it would give her a favored position as she drew her gun and turned on him.

"Peter!"

She should have been surprised, yet somehow she wasn't. "Drop the knife."

He didn't comply. He didn't move; he didn't speak.

"I don't want to hurt you, Peter. Drop the knife. What you're doing is foolish. It won't help. Let's talk."

Face set, knife still raised, he answered by taking a step up toward her.

And instinctively, Norah drew back. "You're making a big mistake," she warned, continuing to back up the stairs. On reaching the next landing, she turned sideways, still keeping an eye on the stair, and moved quickly to the corridor door. She grasped the knob and pulled hard. It wouldn't budge. She had to turn her back, stick the gun in her belt, and use both hands. No use. The door was locked.

Damn, she thought, damn. She wanted at all costs to avoid a confrontation with the boy; she didn't want to be forced to use the gun.

She could hear his footsteps coming up after her, slow, halting, uneven as though he were limping, but relentless. If only she'd been wearing spiked heels instead of the sensible, comfortable oxfords, she thought, the injury would have been severe, might even have incapacitated him. Forget it. She ran up the next flight. The door there was locked too. The grim reality hit her—all the doors were locked on this side; it

130

had become standard procedure to lock doors on the outside in order to prevent access by prowlers. She was trapped. And he knew it.

He knew she couldn't get out. He could afford to take his time, to stalk her deliberately till he cornered her and used that same eight-inch hunting knife he had used to slaughter pigs and maybe an invalid old man and a woman naked in her bath.

For a long moment time was suspended, and Norah Mulcahaney forgot who and what she was and let primordial fear take over. What could she do? Where could she run? She could run the rest of the way up to the roof, and then what? Cross to the next roof? If that was possible. Her training and conditioned reflexes took over once more. She had her gun and she had the advantage of being above him. She must forget his youth and deal with him as she would with any would-be assailant. Raising the .38 with both hands, looking directly down on him she assumed the combat stance.

He stopped where he was, halfway up the flight.

"Throw the knife down into the stairwell," she ordered. "Now."

As before, he didn't obey. This time his dark eyes were unblinkingly fixed on her, however, and there was the indication of a sneer on his lips. Was he high on something? His pupils appeared normal.

"Do it," she snapped, a cold command.

It was most definitely a sneer. "You won't shoot," he said.

"Don't fool yourself. I'll shoot if I have to." She held her stance.

"No, you won't. You won't shoot. You can't afford to. I'm only fifteen years old."

Norah gasped, not only because for those brief moments she had forgotten, but because he was using his youth, because he knew enough to use it deliberately and ruthlessly as a license for violence! It made her flounder. "You look a lot older."

"But I'm not." Now he grinned openly, enjoying himself. He took a step up toward her, then another.

At the first, Norah held steady; at the second, feeling for the step above and behind her, she moved away. "It doesn't matter how old you are."

"Yes, it does."

He was right. She couldn't believe that she was standing

there holding a gun on a child. She was at that moment sharply reminded of the troubles of other cops who had tangled with juveniles. They'd overreacted. She was not going to make that mistake. "And you're not going to stick a knife into a police officer," she countered. "What would be the use? So, you get rid of me, but somebody else will take over the case. He'll go through my notes and he'll know what I know. When he comes after you it won't be for slaughtering a few animals, but for killing a cop. It's a standoff."

Keeping her gun steady and her eyes on him, Norah went on. "You claim you're innocent, but you're acting guilty. If you didn't kill the night watchman, if you had nothing to do with the murders at the Belmonde, what are you afraid of?" She gave him a few moments to consider, then quietly urged, "Drop the knife, Peter."

His hand quivered.

"All I want is the names of the boys."

She'd spoken too soon, she knew it instantly as the hand that held the knife stopped shaking and his arm jerked back, raising the knife high, ready to strike.

"No, Peter, no! You're making a bad mistake."

His answer was to resume climbing, step by deliberate step matching hers as she backed away. Soon he would be on the landing with her, and unless she could continue feeling her way around the landing to the next flight without turning her back . . .

"Drop the knife."

"Shoot. Go ahead and shoot, I dare you."

She didn't realize she had reached the next landing. Probing behind her for the step, she met emptiness and stumbled, and fell. As he pounced on her, she fired.

The shot reverberated within the stairwell. It was a ricochet of sound bouncing off the walls on every floor. Momentarily deafened, Norah watched Peter Tomasiello finally drop the gleaming knife to clutch at his left thigh from which blood spurted. Oh, God! She prayed she hadn't hit an artery. The boy's face was contorted. He grasped the railing to support himself, but the pain dragged him slowly to his knees.

Norah was talking to him—babbling would be more accurate. She didn't know what she was saying, for her head was still filled with the sound of the gunshot. After the echo had finally faded, the voice she heard was Peter's.

"Are you just going to stand there?" he groaned. "Are you just going to stand there and watch me bleed to death?"

She ran down past him, down the five flights. At the bottom, in reverse to all the others, the door opened out. Norah stepped into the dark street.

Chapter XII

Norah was lucky on two counts: the ambulance from Mount Sinai arrived in record time and a couple of squad cars were close behind.

She'd used the street phone on the corner to make her call but then had to reenter the building from the front, and as the elevator was still down in the basement, go out to the back stairs and climb the six flights to where she'd left Peter. She arrived panting to find him sitting where she'd left him, pretty much in the same condition and alone. Loud as the shot had seemed to Norah, either it hadn't penetrated the inner corridors and apartments, or if it had the tenants of this project had heard enough gunshots to learn to ignore them. Just as well, she thought. All that she needed was a bunch of agitated, well-intentioned neighbors.

"The ambulance is on its way," she told Peter. The upper part of his left leg was covered with blood. He'd tried to stanch the flow with a handkerchief which was now a useless rag. Reaching into her purse for the packet of tissue she carried, Norah leaned down to him. "Let me . . ."

"Don't touch me," he barked.

The wound had stopped bleeding. She could see that. In

fact, she could see that the bullet had merely grazed his thigh and scanning the walls she saw where it had lodged. Probably he was perfectly capable of getting to his feet and walking down, Norah thought. But let the paramedics take that determination when they got there. She was relieved to hear the siren's pulsating wail.

What her shot had not done, the siren accomplished—it brought the project's tenants running from every wing and annex into the street. By the time Peter Tomasiello, strapped to the gurney, had been carried down the six flights and was wheeled to the waiting ambulance, a throng had gathered that included residents from other buildings. As she hovered alongside, Norah heard the menacing grumble begin and grow.

"She's the one who shot him."

"She's a cop."

"He's just a kid."

"Peter Tomasiello. You know the family. Live in the project. Right there. Building I. His mother works nights. Somebody ought to go get his father."

The word was passed along, but nobody wanted to miss anything and Peter Tomasiello, Sr., must either not have known what was going on or not be in the building, for he didn't appear. The crowd closed in on Norah.

As the gurney was lifted, the wheel assembly underneath folded, and the stretcher slid into the rear of the van. One of the medics murmured to Norah, "You better ride with us."

The crowd was spilling off the sidewalk and into the street. Once the doors of the van closed and it pulled away, Norah would be alone. She glanced toward her own car, half a block ahead, and she realized that she'd never make it. She was about to accept the medic's offer when a pair of patrol cars came skidding around the corner. Behind them, she spotted David Link's bright blue Chrysler Cordoba. The police parted what was turning into a mob and escorted Norah to her car. She got in with reasonable dignity.

However, the mob did not disperse.

"Fucking woman cop shot a kid in cold blood. Trapped him in the stairwell."

"Why? What did he do?"

"Nothing. He's only a kid. Fourteen."

"Thirteen, I heard."

"Why doesn't she pick on somebody her own age?"

"Pig."

"Sow," somebody corrected, and the laughter was raucous and ugly.

Felix's long, bony jaw was set, his face dour.

It was ten that same night. A strategy session was being held in the Inspector's office. Present were his aide, Captain Capretto, and Sergeant Mulcahaney with Detective Link.

Norah tried to explain why she'd gone up and conducted the interrogation of the Tomasiellos on her own. "Mrs. Tomasiello was due to leave for work and I thought it was important to talk to the boy in the presence of both parents." She didn't add that she'd been expecting that David would join her at any moment.

"You could have waited till tomorrow," Joe said. "What was wrong with waiting till tomorrow?"

She had no answer to that. She could have waited a day, two days. There hadn't been any real urgency. She cast a glance at her partner. Wasn't he going to say anything? David hadn't offered any explanation for his lateness, and nobody had asked for one. He wasn't on trial; she was—literally. Norah realized that and she also knew that she'd brought it on herself. Correction: she'd brought it on all of them. It was less than four hours since her escape from the hostile mob and already the storm had broken. The familiar outcry against police brutality had already been raised. It had reached Chief Deland. This meeting was intended to formulate the account which the Chief would offer the press in the morning.

"Doesn't anybody believe me?" Norah cried out in frustration.

"Of course, we all believe you," Felix told her, his green eyes assuring her of it. "Every man and woman in the department believes you. It's the public we have to convince."

"I know. I'm sorry."

"It would help if we had the knife."

Norah groaned. How could she have been so dumb as to forget the knife? She had forgotten it—completely. She'd panicked—like a civilian. She'd been justified shooting: she'd stand by that forever, but then she'd lost her head. When she saw all that blood ... dear Lord, how he'd bled ... She should have picked up the knife right then. At least, when she got back and realized that the injury wasn't serious, she should have remembered to pick up the knife. She'd been distracted by the arrival of the paramedics. It didn't excuse a critical oversight.

"It's got to be there," she insisted.

"It isn't," Felix replied. "The boy claims he never had a knife. He claims your charges upset him and he ran out of the apartment and out of the house to be by himself. He says that after walking around for a while he realized that running away wouldn't do any good, so he went back. The elevator was stuck, so he took the stairs. As he was going up, he met you coming down. You said you were going to arrest him, and he panicked and tried to get away."

"Again."

"All right, again," Felix agreed. "He ran, you pulled a gun and you fired."

"No knife, no threat, no daring me to shoot, no nothing."

"Nothing."

"So how come he got shot in front in the thigh and not in the back?"

"He says he tried to run up the stairs past you."

"That doesn't make much sense. All right, all right. He lives on the fifth floor. If I was coming down from there, how come the shooting took place on the sixth? If I was coming down and he was going up, shouldn't it have happened on a lower floor, not a higher?"

Felix nodded. It was evident that he, along with the others, was impressed with the reasoning. "He panicked," Felix repeated, spreading out his hands in a gesture of helplessness. "That's his story, and as long as we can't find the knife, we're stuck with it. Believe me, a very thorough search has been conducted for that knife."

She was sure of it. Norah had followed the ambulance to Mount Sinai hospital emergency, waited till the doctors had examined Peter. Only when they had confirmed her opinion of the superficial nature of the wound did she even think about the knife. First, she checked with the medics to see if they might have picked it up. Her next thought was that one of the patrol officers who had rescued her had found it during an examination of the scene. But there had been no such examination. There had been no apparent need to climb up six flights—and that was her fault too because she hadn't given the order. She'd been distracted . . . yes, intimidated

. . . by the crowd. So she'd had to call Joe and he'd sent a man over there. Too late.

"There's no way he could have got rid of it," she repeated as though if she said it often enough it would change the fact. "I wasn't gone long and when I returned he was in exactly the same spot and the same position as I'd left him. There are no windows in that stairwell; there are no receptacles, no trash chute. The doors were all locked from the inner corridor sides. And that's a point! Did he explain how he expected to get from the fire stairs into the building?"

"No. He didn't mention it and we didn't ask."

"Ask," Norah said.

"Maybe there's a trick to opening the doors."

"Maybe, but I don't think so. Let's say for the sake of argument that there is—the way he was bleeding he would have left a trail of blood if he'd moved so much as a foot. Everything around him was clean."

"There's only one possible answer then." Joe entered the discussion. "Somebody in the building used the stairwell, found the knife, and took it away."

"To make it look bad for me," Norah concluded. "It would have happened before I came back from calling the ambulance because after that I stayed with Peter till the medics came and carried him out. How could anyone have known about the knife?"

The full gravity of the situation washed over Norah in a hot wave of anxiety. It passed but left her queasy and flushed. Investigation by Internal Affairs was mandatory in any shooting of a civilian by a police officer. A lot more than a reprimand or even loss of rank was at stake. Unless she could prove that Peter Tomasiello had held a knife on her, that he had actually lunged at her with it and that she'd fired in self-defense, she could lose her job. She could be thrown off the force. She could even face criminal charges.

They all sat staring glumly at each other.

"An accomplice?" Norah offered without conviction. "An accomplice," she repeated, fixing each one in turn with a look that demanded consideration. "It has to be." She was warming to the idea. None of the crimes had been committed solo. An accomplice fitted the pattern. "The whole thing was planned: the elevator was purposely stalled in the basement so that I'd be forced to use the stairs. Peter was standing

138

there waiting for me as I came through the door. Why not an accomplice waiting downstairs till I came running out to find a phone and call for help so that he could run in and pick up the knife?"

Felix made the characteristic pass of his hand over his mouth. "We'll pass it on to IA and see what they can do with it. Meantime, you'll have to stick to desk duty, Norah." He got up, signaling the end of the conference.

Norah was dismayed. "But he set me up! He jumped me as soon as I stepped through the fire-escape door. He could have killed me right then and there, but he didn't. He never intended to kill me." She paused, taking a moment to look to Joe for support, then again appealing to Felix. "He dared me to shoot him. He wanted me to shoot. To get me thrown off the case. Or at least to discredit me so that whatever evidence I might present would be dismissed as pure vindictiveness."

"It's a little involved for a kid, don't you think?" David asked.

Norah looked him straight in the eyes. "No."

"He took a big risk," Joe pointed out. "He could himself have been killed or seriously injured."

"Children see guns shot off on television a dozen times a night and then they see the actor get up and walk away. They don't grasp the reality, the irrevocability of death."

The men sighed. Joe took a breath. "Jim, if we take Norah off the case, won't that imply that we don't believe her story or support her?"

Felix pursed his lips, frowned. From a PR point of view, restricting Mulcahaney to desk duty would be perceived as a gesture to placate the public but would satisfy no one. To keep her active would enrage the public but would assure every officer on the force that if his veracity should be on the line he too would receive the full support of his commanding officer and of the department. "Okay," he decided. "But keep away from the Tomasiello boy and his parents. If you see them walking down the street, you cross over to the other side. I won't even listen to alibis or excuses on this. Understood?"

"Yes, sir."

"And you." Now Felix turned on David Link. "What happened to you? Why didn't you meet Mulcahaney when you were supposed to? Where the hell were you?"

David was embarrassed. "I'm sorry, Inspector. It was one of those damned things. I had a flat."

The next morning, Friday the seventeenth, the residents of the project in which the Tomasiellos lived along with their neighbors from nearby project and nonproject buildings formed at Ninety-seventh Street and Columbus Avenue. Over three hundred and fifty men, women, and children; white, black, brown; poor and middle income were all aroused and feeding off each other's indignation so that they grew bolder and angrier as they marched downtown to the precinct. Picking up adherents all along the route, most of whom didn't know or care what cause they were ostensibly supporting, by the time they reached Eighty-second Street they had lost any semblance of order and had become rabble. Warned that they were coming, the men of the Two-oh had set up wooden barriers across the street from the station house and stood behind them in a grim and nervous line.

Crude, hand-lettered placards were pumped up and down by the mob; hate slogans shouted:

Death to the killers of our children

Down with the police state

Cops have a license to kill

Captain Donald Petrie came out to reason with them, to get them to disperse and go home. Being a black man, he hoped that he would have some additional credibility. They weren't interested in him, or his color, or his empathy for them. They wanted the woman. They wanted Mulcahaney.

She wasn't there.

Norah was already working out of her new command, but she knew what was going on. The news spread throughout the city in minutes: It was communicated by phone, over patrol-car radios, from cop to cop by walkie-talkie. The moment she heard it, Norah went to Joe and asked to be allowed to go to her old precinct and face the people. Permission was denied.

Crowd Control was dispatched and eventually broke up the demonstration.

As it turned out, that demonstration was only the beginning. The newspapers played it up. For the first time in her career, Norah Mulcahaney was depicted unfavorably. For the first time, she found herself on the unpopular side of a controversy. Though she'd always dismissed her publicity when it was complimentary, it wasn't so easy to do that now. Though she knew that she was in the right, the criticisms hurt. She was surprised at how much. She was surprised at how much she cared what others thought of her.

What hurt most was that even her fellow officers were divided. Those who knew Norah well stood staunchly at her side; the others were careful to be noncommittal. That included some of the women.

The Deputy Commissioner for Public Relations put out the usual official statement: *Both Chief Louis Deland and Inspector James Felix, commander of the Manhattan Homicide Task Force, are satisfied that Sergeant Norah Mulcahaney acted in self-defense. Nevertheless, the Internal Affairs Division will conduct its own independent investigation to assure that the rights of all parties are protected.* It was the best that could be done for her.

The strength of the first part was vitiated by the second part. The only one who openly and unequivocally supported Norah was Mrs. Isabel Stucke, Bud's mother.

Of course, she was prejudiced, so all her statements and exhortations were dismissed. Though her son's injuries were serious, they too were written off as a result of a fight between two boys. In that light, Bud's accusation of his schoolmate was deprecated.

Isabel Stucke was pitied because she was a mother. She was forgiven her vicious verbal attacks on the teenager Peter Tomasiello because her own teenage son was a victim. Much was made of the fact that Norah and Joe Capretto had no children. Somebody dug up the story of their adoption four years previously of a three-and-a-half year-old boy and their subsequent turning him back. It was cited as proof that Sergeant Mulcahaney had no feeling as far as children were concerned. She lacked empathy. The facts were correct, but not the conclusion. The reporter hadn't bothered to find out why Norah and Joe had given up their adopted son. He didn't know the pain it had caused them both. He couldn't know. No one outside the family could ever know for neither Norah nor Joe ever talked about Mark.

Somehow, that same reporter discovered the recent assault on Antonia DeVecchi. He learned that no charges had been brought against the girls allegedly responsible. He suggested

141

that in shooting Peter Tomasiello Sergeant Mulcahaney was subconsciously avenging the rape of her cherished niece.

"One minute they accuse me of having no maternal feelings, of lacking womanly compassion, and the next they say that I'm overly sensitive about Toni and that I'm out to get the first teenager I can turn my gun on," she complained to Joe. "They can't have it both ways."

"Don't expect to be treated fairly when you're in the public eye," he told her.

It got worse. She was accused of shooting out of panic. The implication being that a woman was not stable in a crisis situation. That male cops had used their guns in situations equally, if not more, questionable was conveniently forgotten. It was a long time since Norah had had to defend herself for being female and she seethed.

The storm raged through the weekend. Then on Monday morning, she was summoned by Internal Affairs for the second time.

Scanning the early editions as she and Joe rode downtown, Norah erupted. "If Tomasiello were sixteen instead of fifteen, nobody would give a damn!"

"Age shouldn't be a factor," he cautioned.

"Don't tell me," she snapped. "I know that. That's my point."

She was irritable because of the coming interview, Joe knew. He answered soothingly. "My point is that you should go on as you would with any investigation." Once again she started to interrupt but he wouldn't let her. "Don't let yourself get hung up on the age factor. Don't let yourself get emotionally involved because you're dealing with juveniles."

"That's easy to say."

"I know. Forget the kid for a while. Examine every other possible alternative."

"First I have to clear myself of his charges." The indignation she'd been striving so hard to swallow now erupted. "I have to defend myself against a child's lies!"

"IA will do it."

"I wish I could count on that." She sighed. "I get the feeling lately that . . . we don't protect our own anymore. I'm not saying IA isn't fair, just that everybody, from the CP on down

142

seems to be scared of public opinion. They're more interested in public relations than in supporting the officer."

Joe agreed but he didn't say so: it wasn't the time. Both Felix and the Chief had tried, but in the end had had to defer to the demands of Internal Affairs. The fact that Norah was being called down for a second interrogation was not a good sign. To offer empty encouragement would make it worse. He pulled over to the curb.

"Are you sure you don't want me to go up with you?"

"Positive."

"At least let me wait for you."

"Please, darling, we've been through all this. I'd rather you didn't."

He sighed. He leaned over and kissed her. "Good luck, *cara.*"

The cold formality of the IA's team toward her was disturbing. Norah realized that she'd become accustomed to a certain preferential treatment. She got it, she supposed, on a variety of counts: rank, reputation, and yes, her sex. All right, she was spoiled. These men were not interested in anything about her, only in the facts of this particular charge and those remained against her. They didn't tell her so, but she didn't need to be told. Nor did she need to be told that Inspector Felix was getting plenty of flak on her account. For his sake, she kept her cool during the exacting interrogation which covered every detail of the incident on the back stairs, an interrogation that stopped just short of intimidation.

Finally, it was over.

She picked up her coat and took her time putting it on. She slung her handbag over her shoulder and drew on her gloves, letting her questioners wait while she did it. Then she walked to the door. She opened it, but before going out she turned, head high, chin thrust forward.

"When you find the knife, please inform me immediately. It may be evidence in the Burrell and Guthrie homicides."

It was her way of reminding them that despite all their efforts she was still on the case.

"How'd it go?"

David approached Norah as soon as she entered the squad room. She shrugged and made to pass, but he wouldn't let her.

143

"I'm sorry. I just want you to know that I'm sorry for the mess you're in."

"Okay." She wasn't interested in his self-recrimination, which was too late or his explanation which should have been addressed to Joe or to the Inspector. Once again she tried to get by.

"Norah . . ."

"Why didn't you show up when you were supposed to?" she burst out. "Where were you? What happened to you?"

"I got a flat. I explained. Didn't you hear me?"

"Oh, I heard. How long does it take to change a tire? Twenty minutes? Half an hour? You didn't show up till the ambulance was taking the boy away. That was more than an hour after we were supposed to meet. So where were you? What were you doing?"

"Okay, okay." David groaned. "I had a meet with an informant about another case. Look, I got the call at the last minute. I couldn't get hold of you. What was I supposed to do, turn him down? Tell him to wait? You know how it is with a snitch, how nervous he can get. I'm sorry. I'm real sorry. I had no idea what would happen. I feel terrible about it." With a sudden movement he reached into his jacket pocket and brought out a small, oblong package. "Here."

"What's this?"

"Open it."

Tearing off the paper, Norah uncovered a velvet jeweler's box. After a quick look at David who responded with an encouraging nod, she opened it. She gasped. Then she picked up the slim gold chain and held it to the light. "David, it's beautiful." It was thin yet substantial, exquisitely crafted, with the rose sheen of eighteen-karat gold: not merely an expensive, but an extravagant gift. "I do thank you, David, but I can't accept it."

"Please, please, don't say no. You've got to take it, Norah. I feel so lousy about the trouble you're in. I feel responsible."

"Don't. I could have waited," she admitted. "I didn't have to go ahead on my own. I guess we're each of us set on having his own way."

"It's also to thank you for trying to help me with Marie," he told her. "I really appreciate that."

"I didn't get anywhere."

"That's not your fault. Marie just doesn't understand what

144

police work involves. God knows I've tried to explain. I've tried everything. I'd hoped that your marriage, the happiness and understanding you and Joe share, would be an example to her." He sounded bitter, as though he resented the very happiness he was citing.

"Well, I'm a cop myself and that's bound to make a difference."

"Hell, there are plenty of wives who aren't on the force and they understand and accept the situation. You don't know what I've done for that woman. You don't know how I've tried to make her happy. I've given her everything."

"Maybe she needs time to be by herself and think. Give her time, David. It'll work out."

He shook his head, his eyes fixed on Norah. "You know, when I first met you I thought you were all wound up with yourself. I thought you were all ambition, without any feeling for anybody else. Hard."

Norah flushed. She'd always thought that David had liked her, that they were friends. At the beginning anyway.

"I was wrong," he went on. "I wish . . . I wish I'd looked a little deeper. Now it's too late."

Suddenly, she felt sorry for him. She remembered the idealistic, hard-working, dedicated rookie detective and contrasted him with this disillusioned yet still ambitious man. Because of what she remembered, Norah glossed over the implication of what he'd just said. "It's not too late to be friends. But I can't keep the chain. I deeply appreciate your intention, but I can't keep it." She took his hand and put the chain into it.

He didn't argue anymore. He simply stuffed the chain into his pocket as though it were nothing, five-and-dime junk. At today's prices the chain must have come close to five hundred dollars. A most handsome apology, Norah thought. Impulsively, she reached out to touch him, but stopped. Something held her back.

Chapter XIII

Public outrage spread and like a rash became angrier and more inflamed. Since Norah and Joe's home address was unlisted, the sacks of hate mail went to headquarters. So did the calls. They flooded the regular police switchboard and clogged 911. They protested the "whitewash" of the "sow"; that epithet had caught on. There were threats against Norah personally and the department in general. These calls were recorded as a matter of routine, as all 911 calls were, and Norah, Joe, and Inspector Felix spent an unpleasant period each day listening to them.

"So what do you want to do?" Felix asked Norah.

"Nothing," she replied, jaw set in determination.

"The less we react, the sooner it will blow over." Joe was equally firm but he couldn't hide his concern.

"I hope so." Though he had committed himself to Norah's side, Felix was under constant pressure to remove her from the case. He didn't know how much longer he could hold out.

Meanwhile, Peter Tomasiello was discharged from the hospital. There was a picture on the front page of the *Post* of the boy on his return to his neighborhood surrounded by a cheering throng of his supporters. Norah caught the scene on the eleven o'clock news in full action, color, and sound. It took only one close-up to see that the boy was relishing the attention and gloating in his triumph. It riled Norah. Indignation coursed like a fever in her body. She jumped up and snapped off the set. Joe said nothing.

The next day Norah visited the mid-Manhattan branch of the public library at Fifth Avenue and Forty-second Street. She went looking for some bit of knowledge that might somehow trigger her subconscious. She wanted to put her jumbled thoughts and feelings into perspective.

The present juvenile system as we know it today has its roots in the 1820s and the reforming efforts of the "child savers," Norah read. These well-intentioned adults wished to correct the *abuses* that children suffered under the code of the period. Our street gangs are nothing new, she learned. In the seventeenth century violent crime by children was commonplace. They roamed the streets in groups robbing and killing. When caught, however, there was no coddling. A child of six could be tried, convicted, and sentenced if he had done something wrong. The trouble was that the code also applied to the runaways and the disobedient, to the merely mischievous, to children who had been disrespectful to their parents. Children had no rights. They were chattel. They could be, and many times were, sent out to the colonies as indentured servants for punishment. The revision of the code during the early nineteenth century was a reaction and our own present system an extension of it.

So they had come full circle, Norah thought, resting her eyes from the book. From the marauding child packs of the seventeenth century to the gangs of the twentieth, raping, warring among themselves, assaulting the elderly. As the criminal-justice system's attempt to protect the rights of the accused had resulted in depriving the victim and society of their rights, so the juvenile-justice system in attempting to protect the child had given him license.

When a juvenile offender goes into family court he does so with an unblemished record, for his prior offenses are not revealed. The purpose is to avoid influencing the judge in his decision. Once the finding is made and it goes against the juvenile, then for the purpose of disposition his past record becomes known. The point is that a record does exist in the form of Youth Cards filed at the Juvenile Bureau.

147

From Peter Tomasiello's attitude and that of his parents it was clear that the expensive stereo equipment in his room was not recently purchased: it was not, therefore, the fruit of the robberies at the Belmonde. That suggested prior forays, Norah thought. So maybe there was a card on Peter. If there was, there'd be no mention of it at his trial, if he ever came to trial. Norah closed the book and pushed back from the library table. The Tomasiellos' reaction to her visit had been normal enough, the reaction of parents to a police officer inquiring about their child—anxious, of course; guarded, naturally. And when she'd mentioned the slaughter at the zoo—shocked, appalled. That too was to be expected. They'd been protective, but they were his parents, after all.

She returned the book to the librarian.

Norah knew that getting access to youth cards wasn't easy. As David had said, the people at the bureau and those connected with family court were defensive; their initial, gut reaction to queries was to resist. A police officer carried no more clout than a civilian wandering in off the street. Norah knew they would not search the records for her. Though the evidence in those files might bear directly on an ongoing investigation, they would refuse. Unless she actually made the arrest and brought Peter Tomasiello in with her . . . Considering that she was under IA investigation on charges brought by Tomasiello, that was hardly feasible.

So Norah drove downtown. Every lot, municipal and private, was jammed. As far as street parking was concerned—forget it. She continued down to the river to a lot she knew about under the Brooklyn Bridge. The attendant shook his head at her from across the intersection. Turning left, she drove along South Street and spotted a place at last and parked, illegally, under the FDR Drive and right at the water's edge. It was a long walk back up Catherine Street to Lafayette, but finally Norah entered the new, massive, and somehow ominous building that housed the Juvenile Bureau and Family Court.

She showed her ID, murmured the name of a probation officer with whom she'd worked years back, and had no trouble being passed through.

"What's his office number again?" she asked the lobby guard.

"Four D one-five."

The building was clean and well ordered, Norah thought. People seemed to know where they were going and were treated with courtesy, in sharp contrast to the squalor and confusion of criminal court. She knew her way well enough to bypass the reception room on the fourth floor and go directly to the corridor where the probation officers had their individual quarters. Bart Kriendler's name was on his door. She knocked and walked in.

The man at the desk was in his mid-thirties, with thick, curly black hair and a thick, curly black beard. He was robust in build, and as Norah recalled, he had a cheery, informal manner. Noting that his jacket was draped over the back of his chair and that he wasn't wearing the standard white shirt and tie but a navy turtleneck, she assumed he hadn't changed. She hoped he hadn't.

The office was a small, windowless box but efforts had been made to prevent claustrophobia. One wall was painted a bright orange, the others a pale yellow. The chairs were upholstered in a clear blue. Standard but cheerful. And Kriendler had added his own touches surely to ease the tension of his young clients—signs taped to the walls:

Quiet, Man at Work
If you break it, you've bought it.
If you fool me once, shame on you; if you fool me twice, shame on me.

Suspended from the ceiling almost directly over his desk, a delicate mobile of airplanes of various World War I vintage were constructed out of silver foil and floated silently in response to the draft as Norah opened and shut the door.

Kriendler looked up. "Hi." He waited a beat. "What can I do for you?" he asked, giving her a friendly, open smile.

Apparently, the guard had not called from downstairs. "You don't remember me?" Norah asked.

"It's ungallant to admit it, but . . . I'm sorry." He continued smiling.

"Norah Mulcahaney. We worked the Vismitin and Cotter case."

"Oh. Sure. How could I not remember?" The smile remained but it was guarded. "The pictures in the papers don't do you justice."

149

"So you've read the stories and you know I'm in trouble."

"Yeah." The smile was all gone.

"I need help."

He shook his head.

"Bart . . . I need a search of your central files."

"No way. You know the situation here . . ."

"This is crucial to me personally, Bart. I did help clear the Vismitin boys and Rick Cotter," she reminded him.

Kriendler's good-natured face was troubled. "You didn't help: you did it all on your own. I know that. I was and am grateful, but I can't do what you ask. The fact that you are personally involved would make it completely unethical." He threw up his hands; he shook his head several times. "I can't."

"I understand." She did. "Couldn't you just, off the record, tell me what you know? After all, you were Tomasiello's probation officer . . ."

"No. Not me!" He broke in with relief. "Sandra had him. Sandra Palmiero. Who told you that it was me? Who . . .?" He stopped, aware that he'd made a mistake.

She looked straight at him. "I can't say."

"Yeah." He worked his lips back and forth a couple of times. "So when you go in and talk to Sandra, I'd appreciate it if you didn't tell her I gave you her name. In fact, I'd just as soon you didn't mention me."

"I never saw you," Norah promised and walked out.

Miss Palmiero's office was two doors down. As before, Norah knocked and didn't wait to enter. The office was a duplicate of Kriendler's except that it was done in shades of green and brown and that it lacked the personal, light-hearted touches. The young woman at the desk was in her early twenties, slight, almost fragile. It was hard to be sure because she was seated, but Norah put her at five feet two inches and a hundred and five pounds. The fluorescent lighting emphasized her pallor and cast a bluish aura around her dark frizzed hair. Her large, fashionable dark glasses hid her eyes and most of her face except for the tip of a delicate nose and small, pointed chin.

Norah introduced herself.

Sandra Palmiero barely glanced at the shield and ID. "Oh, yes, I know who you are." Her lips, well defined with maroon lipstick, were pressed into a tight line.

Damn, Norah thought. Well, what could she expect? Having handled Peter's case in the past, the woman would be bound to take an interest in his present situation.

"How did you get in here?"

Norah shrugged. "Just walked in."

Sandra Palmiero scowled. "What do you want?" The resistance was there and no effort was made to hide it.

"I'd like to talk to you about Peter Tomasiello."

"You shouldn't even be here. If you want information, you have to get an order from the administrative judge. Here, I'll give you the number . . ."

"I know the number, Miss Palmiero. I want to talk to you."

"The case is closed. The probation period has expired. I have nothing more to do with Peter Tomasiello."

"I see. What was the charge against him?"

"Petition." Palmiero corrected automatically. Then repeated, "The case is closed."

"The young man has important information in a homicide case that he refuses to divulge."

"I'm sorry."

"There's a strong possibility that he's involved himself."

Sandra Palmiero shook her head.

Norah considered. At least she knew that Tomasiello did have a record. Maybe she could get a court order. Or maybe IA would do it. "Thank you, anyway," she said. "I understand your position."

"Sergeant?" In a voice that was low, husky, almost a whisper, the probation officer called her back from the door. "Did he really threaten you with a knife?"

From what she could see, the young woman's face was drawn; her mouth worked spasmodically as she waited for Norah's answer.

"Yes. First he held the knife to my throat, then he lunged at me with it."

Sandra Palmiero sighed. "I can't show you the file, but I will tell you what's in it." She got up and stepped to a row of folding, louvered doors along the near wall. Opening them, she revealed a set of filing cabinets. She pulled out a drawer and with practiced fingers riffled the contents till she found what she wanted. She did not even take it out, merely glancing through. "He was picked up two years ago on October nineteenth for assault. He, along with approximately

151

twenty-two boys between the ages of thirteen and fifteen, using sticks and clubs and stones, attacked and beat up a group of vagrants down on the Bowery."

Norah recalled the incident. It had got plenty of publicity. The spectacle of schoolboys beating up on helpless bums, drunks, and addicts had shocked the city. Norah remembered that the young perpetrators were children of the middle and upper classes. "Did you process any of the other boys involved?"

"I'm sorry."

"Can you give me the names of other probation officers who might have . . ."

"I'm sorry."

Norah would push her no further. "Thank you. I appreciate what you've done."

"I have a reason." The pretty, delicate young woman turned her head and tilted her face up toward the light, then she removed the dark glasses. Both eyes were blackened. A large cut on her cheek had ragged edges which so far refused to heal.

"What happened?" Norah asked.

"One of my cases, a boy twelve, large for his age, is an alcoholic. He's been drunk in class regularly, but somehow he manages to more or less sober up by the time his mother gets home from work. He didn't appreciate my discussing his problem with her. He called it squealing."

Norah's spirits had lifted as she stepped out of the Juvenile Bureau into the gathering dusk. She could now show that Peter Tomasiello was not the exemplary young man everyone took him to be. She cautioned herself that his past record could not be introduced in evidence; nevertheless, the strain of the past few days was considerably eased.

It was the Tuesday before Thanksgiving and there was the feel of snow in the air. Actually, a few flakes floated lazily and silently around her. She turned up the fur collar of her new opossum-lined stormcoat, a birthday gift from Joe. It was bulky, but she was tall enough to carry it, and the full collar balanced her rectangular face and softened the square jut of her jaw. It was becoming; Norah knew it and took pleasure in it. The last shift of office workers, on staggered hours down here in the financial and government districts,

152

clogged the sidewalks and the traffic heading home. In another half hour, the narrow canyons and the new open plazas would all be empty and silent. She had intended going back to the office, but . . .

As she waited with the crowd to cross, the street lights came on, a magical moment for Norah always, but particularly at this season. Why not go home, too? she thought. Why not go home, have a nice hot bath with plenty of pine essence in it, then get dressed up and let Joe take her out to dinner? To Vittorio's maybe. Vittorio's was their place; they'd courted there. They hadn't been to Vittorio's in ages. They hadn't been anywhere in ages, she thought. They were in a rut and the fault was hers. She got too wrapped up in the job. She was neglecting Joe. He didn't complain, but that didn't mean he liked it. Was he happy? Norah asked herself. She thought of how David envied their marriage. Maybe she'd better put a little work into it or it might not remain enviable. She turned right past the customs court, through the Muni' arch and into Police Plaza, then down the steps to the street and along the base towers of the Brooklyn Bridge.

It looked indestructible, but like everything else in the city, the bridge was decaying dangerously. Frayed diagonal cables in the tower stacking was only part of the diagnosis. For the entire month of November the bridge was closed at night for dead-load testing. No traffic clogged its approach ramps nor hummed on the high span overhead. The cars which earlier had glutted the lots were gone so that Norah passed from crowds and lights into an eerie solitude. The traffic on the approach ramps for the FDR Drive seemed remote. She heard no sound but the slap of water against the embankment and the tapping of her own heels on the cracked and pitted pavement. The yellow sign fixed to a metal support post for the elevated highway was covered with grime but legible: PARK AT YOUR OWN RISK. Yet Norah wasn't the only one who ignored it. So when she heard the footsteps behind her she assumed it was another driver coming for his car.

She passed the first section of parked cars, then turned to walk parallel to the river. The Governor Smith houses were across and at her back, but most of the shades were drawn; neither their lights nor the street lights reached her. The Manhattan Bridge scintillated with the headlights of a dou-

153

ble traffic load. The opposite shore which had seemed so close in the daytime now appeared far away, showing here and there a twinkle from the Brooklyn Navy Yard to her left and the commercial Brooklyn docks to her right. On the Manhattan side the lights of the South Street Seaport Museum did little more than outline the masts of the schooners riding placidly at anchor. The reflections in the water enabled her just to make out her silver gray Honda about twenty yards ahead. Subconsciously, she continued to listen to that other set of footsteps that were like an echo of her own. They remained behind her, neither closer nor farther back. Deliberately maintaining the distance? To test, she stopped. He stopped. She started, so did he. She didn't quicken her pace till she was near one of the highway support posts, then slipping behind it she drew her gun.

"Police officer," she called out. "I've got a gun. Stop where you are."

She waited, straining to hear what she could not see. A rattle of loose gravel made her instinctively turn in that direction, but all she could make out was a shadow among shadows—moving fast, running in a low crouch to disappear beyond that first rank of parked cars. She blinked a couple of times but her eyes had already reached maximum night vision. Anyway, by now there was nothing to see. Whoever had been following her was gone. A mugger and she'd frightened him off. Relieved, Norah put the gun back into her handbag and came out from behind the pillar. Her car was the last in the row at the river's edge. She took out her car keys but before reaching the door, a few feet away, she stopped.

The Honda was covered with filth. A stomach-turning mess. Eggs had been splattered on the windows. A cardboard held in place by the windshield wiper had the word SOW lettered in what was probably animal blood. Feces were smeared over and piled on the hood. She felt like throwing up. She swallowed instead, tasting the bile and put the key in the lock.

Sensing movement behind her, Norah spun around in time to see a hulking figure silhouetted against the luminosity of the water. He must have doubled around and come from the opposite direction to stand now between her and the waterfront. Raising his weapon, some kind of stick or pipe, he moved in—a big man, bearded, wearing a thick wool cap pulled down to his eyebrows. As he lunged, Norah swerved sideways and once again drew her revolver. She drew fast, unfortunately not fast enough and too fast, for the blow aimed at her head hissed close and caught her hand instead and knocked the gun out of it. For several seconds she lived only in the pain that passed up her arm and into her shoulder in an excruciating wave. Clenching her teeth, Norah could only hold her right wrist with her left hand and hunker over it. She was dimly aware that her gun was skittering away from her across the slick pavement. Then she realized that he had raised the pipe and was about to strike again.

He dove at her. She stuck a foot out and sent him sprawling on his face. Now was the time to get her gun back. Oh, God, in the dark she couldn't see it. Where was it? There was no telling how far it had slid nor in what direction. The pavement slanted downward toward the water. For all she knew, her gun might have fallen in. And she had no backup gun. Though she was wearing slacks under the new coat, she hadn't worn the leg holster; she hadn't expected to be on the street. Meantime, the mugger was getting up.

"Bitch," he snarled. With the pipe clutched in both hands, he was weaving from side to side in a half crouch like a wrestler looking for a hold, determined not to miss again, determined to smash her skull to a pulp.

She'd left the key in the lock when she went for the gun, so now all she had to do was turn it and yank the door open and get in. The move took him by surprise, but he recovered in a fraction and reached the car just as Norah slammed the door shut and pushed down the locking button. For several seconds they stared at each other through the glass. Then, as he raised his weapon, Norah pushed the key into the ignition and turned. The motor caught instantly, thank God. As she released the hand brake, the pipe came crashing down against the window, shattering the glass. Instinctively, Norah squeezed her eyes shut, and also instinctively, stepped on the accelerator and the car lurched forward.

She turned the wheel hard and opened her eyes. Careening wildly, she'd managed somehow to steer clear of the other cars and the pillars and the construction equipment. She was on Catherine Street. Still, she didn't slow down, not till she was well away, not till the bridge and the highway were just an elaborate tracery against the evening sky did she even remember to turn on her headlights. Then she kept going through the now-empty streets looking for a place where there would be lights and people. She found herself on the fringe of Chinatown, and there she pulled over to the curb.

She didn't get out. She sat where she was—numb. After a while she felt over her face to make sure she hadn't been cut by any of the flying glass. Apparently, she hadn't. She double-checked using the rear-view mirror. Her heart was still pounding; otherwise, she was okay. As the heartbeat slowed, she became aware of the throbbing in her hand. Gritting her teeth, she tried to ignore it, but the pain was too severe. It was making her nauseous. Occasionally, a spasm went from her hand like an electric shock and her whole body jerked. If she had to have the hand treated then she'd have to report the incident. Until then she hadn't been aware that she was even considering not reporting it. She did so now with full intent: to report the attack would increase the pressure to have her taken off the case. Those who wanted to get rid of her would say it was for her own protection. Joe would now join them out of real concern for her safety. If she didn't report it, how would she explain the hand to Joe? How was she going to explain the condition of the car—the filth, the shattered window? She could have the car washed and the window replaced, of course. It would mean going to a garage where she wasn't known. It would be the same as lying to Joe.

Then she remembered the gun.

The worst blunder a police officer could commit was to lose his gun or to allow it be taken from him. The loss of her gun could not be covered up or glossed over. She had to report it. Unless she could find it.

She had no choice but to go back and look.

Should she go home first and get her backup gun? Joe would be home by now. One look at her and he wouldn't let her out again without the full story. Then he would come with her. The thought brought a great deal of comfort. Problem was that time would be lost, and the more time that elapsed the less chance she had of recovering her weapon. It was possible the mugger himself had it already. There was only one way to find out. Using her left hand, Norah turned on the ignition and put her right on the wheel, but with the first bit of pressure the spasm was so severe that she nearly blacked out. The hand couldn't be broken, she told herself; it couldn't be because she did have some use of it, but there was no strength in it. Fighting off the threatening darkness, she felt like a drowning swimmer in a black ocean gasping for life. She welcomed the red, yellow, and green flashes of pain like beacons on a nearby shore. Finally, she recognized them for the reality of traffic signals and knew that she could dare to move the hand from the wheel into her lap. She let it lie there limply and steered with her left.

This time when she penetrated the dark recesses under the bridge and passed from them under the highway to where she'd been parked, she had the help of her headlights and the flashlight she kept in the glove compartment with which to search. She took her time. She fanned out from the spot where she'd dropped it much farther than the gun was likely to have skidded. She followed the beam of her flashlight to the embankment where it formed a wall perhaps two feet above the pavement. So the gun could not have slid or bounced into the river. But it was gone.

She had to accept the consequences. Bowing her head wearily, Norah became aware for the first time of the filth smeared down the front of her beautiful new coat. That did it! That was the last straw! Tears welled up in her eyes and she let them flow freely. But she wasn't crying over the coat; the coat made her angry. The tears were the result of the pain which the exertion had aggravated.

Somehow, Norah got back into the car. Somehow, she drove uptown. It was late enough so that there were plenty of parking spaces on her own block. She managed to get into one and turned off the motor. That accomplished, she slumped forward against the wheel.

Wavering at the edge of consciousness, Norah experienced a montage of perceptions: she saw Joe's grave face gray with anxiety peering down into hers; she heard sirens; she was aware of being carried; and always there was the pain. The pain meant that it was all real, all happening. Then, blessedly, the pain eased. She accepted the darkness gratefully.

Norah awoke to look straight into Joe's eyes. He smiled, bent a little farther down, and kissed her.

"Good morning."

She was in a hospital. The sun was streaming in through the window. From Joe she looked down and saw that her hand was in a cast extending to the elbow and the whole thing was supported by a sling around her neck.

"What happened?"

"You tell me," he retorted. Then he grinned. "Okay, I'll go first. I was home waiting for you and starting to get a little anxious because you hadn't left any message. Then this horn started down the street. It was obviously stuck. When it had been going long enough to get on my nerves, I went down, located the car, and found you leaning against the wheel and unconscious." He indicated the sling. "Want to tell me how you did that?"

"I got mugged under the Brooklyn Bridge."

He groaned. "How many times have I told you not to park under there?"

"I know, I know. You're right." She paused. "I lost my gun. He had an iron pipe and he knocked it out of my hand. I went back, but I couldn't find it."

"You went back?"

"I had to."

Joe inflated his cheeks, blew the air out as though he were filling a balloon. It didn't release the tension. "How about the filth on the car?"

"It could have been random vandalism."

"Were any of the other cars befouled?"

"Not that I could see."

"Then it seems likely that your assailant was responsible and that suggests something more than an ordinary mugging."

What could she say? How could she argue?

"Obviously, the guy's a creep influenced by all the publicity you've been getting."

Neither of them spoke for several moments.

"And he's still out there, and now he has your gun," Joe pointed out.

"I'll be careful," she promised. "No more parking in dark, lonely, and illegal places." She tried for light humor.

"Damn right." He wasn't disposed to it. "Anyway, you're going to be in here for a couple of days and then home for at least two weeks."

"What?"

"That's right."

"Nothing's broken," she protested. "It can't be. I know . . ."

"The sheathes around the nerves in your forefinger and middle finger were smashed. The surgeon had to rebuild them. It's going to take at least three weeks for you to have any use of your hand, at least six weeks before you can handle a gun."

"Oh, no."

"So relax and enjoy, *cara*. Meantime, give me the description of your assailant so I can put out an APB."

Setting aside her disappointment, Norah drew her thick eyebrows together and set her chin as she concentrated in recreating the image of her attacker. She could have reminded Joe that it had been dark, that she'd had hardly more than a glimpse of the man, and that she'd been under considerable stress, but she didn't. He knew all that, and she was too professional to offer excuses. She did her best. "I'd say he was six feet two, one hundred and eighty pounds. He had a heavy, dark beard, and he was wearing one of those woolen fisherman's caps pulled way down to his eyebrows. With all that facial hair, it was hard to tell his age; could be either side of thirty. He was wearing baggy pants and a zippered, imitation-leather jacket." She paused. "I can still work on the case, can't I?"

Joe took another deep breath. "I didn't want to tell you till later, but . . . you would have been off the case even if this hadn't happened."

She didn't say anything, simply watched him and waited for him to explain.

"We've been hoping that the public feeling against you would die down. It hasn't. In fact, it's grown. Yesterday, Jim Felix was handed a petition with four hundred and twelve signatures, mostly people in the Tomasiellos' neighborhood, demanding your removal not only from the case but from the force."

Dismay and a sense of defeat overcame Norah and kept her uncharacteristically silent.

She looked so woebegone that Joe wanted to take her into his arms and comfort her. He knew that she wanted his active support and help, but that he couldn't give. It seemed to Joe Capretto that lately, on the rare occasions when his Norah looked to him, he failed her. Like the business with Toni: he could have been more staunchly on her side; he could have used his influence on his sister, at least he should have tried. Now, well, this was a little different. Though he was a captain, closer than most to the man he worked for and through him to the Chief, there was nothing he could do for his wife. Would he if he could? Deep down, wasn't he glad at the way things had turned out?

"It's not going to come to that, sweetheart," he assured Norah. Reaching for her hand he turned it palm up and kissed it. "Both the Inspector and Chief Deland are on your side. The thing is that now you have the perfect opportunity to get them both off the hook. Just take your normal convalescence. By the time you're fit for duty again the case will undoubtedly have been solved."

And if it hadn't? Would she be reassigned? Joe knew. She didn't want to embarrass him by asking.

As Joe had suggested, she might as well enjoy her convalescence, Norah thought as she lay in bed in her hospital room. The pain was now minimal, and she had plenty of visitors. The family came, of course; her father, Joe's mother, the sisters, their husbands and children. They alone would have constituted a steady stream and turned her room into a flower shop, but there were also her colleagues. Men and women from her old precinct, from Fifth Homicide and even from Fourth Narco, where she'd done a mere three weeks and wasn't exactly popular, came. They came ostensibly to offer sympathy for her injury, but the injury was so slight that Norah knew their real purpose was to show support. They didn't say so; they didn't need to. Never mind that she'd had to land in the hospital to get them to declare themselves.

The visit that most touched her was David Link's. He showed up wearing a dark blue suit and a white shirt—ultra straight even for David who was not given to the casual, sometimes eccentric dress of most detectives. He brought an enormous orchid plant, exotic and expensive, wrapped in clear plastic. The flowers were a deep green-yellow speckled with brown and hanging in clusters supported on a rustic scaffolding. The soil in which they grew was camouflaged with thick, deep green moss. It was gorgeous.

"David! You shouldn't have done it."

"You're not going to refuse to accept it?" he cried in alarm.

"No, no, I have no intention of refusing it. It's magnificent. I'm not leaving it behind me either; this one I'm taking home. Thank you, David."

For a short space the brooding look which had lately become the detective's habitual expression eased. "I hear you're going to be out of action for a while."

She nodded. No point going into it; David probably knew just how much her coming inactivity would be due to injury and how much to departmental policy.

"So what I was thinking was that I could kind of fill in for you. I mean, if you had any ideas, you could pass them on to me and I'd carry through. If you had any leads or . . . like, if you were working on something when this happened . . . I'll run your errands."

"That's really nice of you, David."

"What are friends for? And I'll keep you informed, naturally. We'll work together like we used to. It'll be like old times."

"That's wonderful, David."

"Then it's settled."

"As a matter of fact, I was working on something."

"Yeah?" He pulled up a chair and sat beside the bed.

She told him about her visit to the Juvehile Bureau and her discovery that Tomasiello had been in trouble before.

"So?"

"What do you mean, so? It shows he's not the perfect, underprivileged boy genius everybody makes out. That's one. Two, it reveals and establishes a cruel streak in him. We know what he did to those defenseless animals and now we know he was part of a group that beat up on a bunch of helpless winos. I thought if we could find out who else was involved in each incident we might have some other names show up twice. One of them could be the accomplice that took away the knife from Peter when I left him alone on the back stairs."

"Felix wants us to lay off Tomasiello for a while."

"How am I going to clear myself if I lay off?"

David scowled. "Why don't I just pass the info on to IA and let them handle it?" he temporized. "It's their job. That way we'll both stay clean. I'll pass it on, okay?"

She sighed. It wasn't like old times. Back then, the rookie detective David Link would have jumped on the lead without a second thought for the official policy. Experience apparently had taught him caution. She couldn't expect him to jeopardize his job for her.

"Sure, David. You pass it on."

Chapter XIV

Norah went home for Thanksgiving. As Joe was off duty on the holiday they could enjoy it together and that didn't happen often. They slept late and then had breakfast in front of the television set watching the Macy's Thanksgiving Day parade like a couple of kids. In her early days on the force, Norah had worked security for the parade in the cold and the rain; it was better this way. The shots of the happy, excited, normal children lining the route reminded her of the morally crippled and stunted children with whom she was presently dealing. Had been dealing, she corrected herself. Forget it. Think about tonight's big family dinner at Lucia's house. One of the dividends of having married into a large family, Norah reflected, was that her turn to be hostess for any specific celebration only came up once every eight years.

That night in the midst of the happy confusion, Norah could feel Lena DeVecchi watching her, trying to get her attention. With her arm in a sling, Norah was excused from helping in the kitchen after the meal, and Lena somehow managed to get out of her share of the work too. She led Norah into one of the bedrooms and closed the door. The pronounced drag of her left leg indicated she was both tired and distressed.

"The hearing was yesterday," she informed Norah without preamble.

"Yes?" From the feverish gleam in her sister-in-law's eyes and the hot spots in her cheeks. Norah prepared for the worst.

"The court found for the complainant. That's us. That's Toni."

Norah hardly needed to have the euphemisms of family court translated. She didn't mention it because Lena obviously had rehearsed what she was going to say. It did strike her as odd that she should be upset when the verdict was in their favor.

"That means the judge found the girls Toni named guilty. As I understand it, there's a lot of red tape they have to go through before placement. Oh, hell, sentencing! Why don't they say what they mean? Why don't they use plain English? The Probation Department has to make an investigation; there's got to be a psychological report. It could take months. So while we're waiting, the judge has released the girls in their parents' custody! That means they're back home, Norah. They're home living their lives just like they did before. As though nothing had happened. What's worse, they're back in school, in the same school with Toni!"

Lena's eyes were brimming; she was trembling.

"They won't lay a hand on her. They wouldn't dare," Norah strove to reassure her. "Is Toni afraid?"

"I don't think so. That's not the point I want to make. My point is that it's not fair."

"Oh, I agree with you."

"At this stage, I don't care whether those girls are ever punished or not. No, no let me finish. What I care about is Toni's reaction. How she feels seeing those girls walk around free just like before. I mean, we've brought her up, Jake and I, to understand right and wrong. To expect punishment for doing wrong. We've brought her up to respect others—their persons, their property, their feelings. Okay. What is this going to do to her moral sense? How is it going to influence the rest of her life?"

The answer Norah gave Lena DeVecchi in that quiet bedroom satisfied neither one. Joe couldn't do any better, but on Friday he was able to go back to work while Norah was left in her enforced idleness with little to distract her. She considered shopping, but there was nothing she needed or wanted. A movie? She was too restless to sit in the dark in the middle of the afternoon. She she fell back on her usual therapy and gave her apartment a down-to-the-bone cleaning. With her right hand in its sling, it wasn't easy, but she managed. Inevitably, by late Saturday that too was done.

Joe was wonderful. He called during the day and he took her out to dinner each night. They got to Vittorio's finally and it was as much fun as it had ever been. Vittorio fussed over them and they had plenty of the good red Ruffino that was their favorite. However, after Joe had left for work on Monday, Norah faced a blank day. Surely she had enough inner resources to get through it? Of course. The trouble was that she wasn't inclined to use them. It occurred to Norah as she sat at the kitchen table drinking yet another cup of coffee that she didn't really want that the Tomasiellos themselves had not joined in the march of their neighbors on the Twentieth Precinct, nor signed any of the petitions against her. They had kept and were keeping a low profile. It also occurred to her that they surely knew about the earlier orgy of violence in which Peter had taken part and that though by now it was well buried under layers of palliation and prayer, at one time a dread of repetition must have been a constant factor in their lives. When she told them about the animals in the zoo . . . Norah half closed her eyes visualizing their faces. They had not denied her allegation. They had not lashed out indignantly. They had not even asked Peter to deny it. They'd behaved as though an illness which had been in remission had suddenly erupted with new virulence. They had reacted with resignation. The Tomasiellos surely knew who the other boys were who had been with their son in the Bowery raid. Norah opened her eyes. What she wanted was to jump out of that chair, to go over there, to talk to them. But she couldn't. She had, at all costs, to stay clear of the Tomasiellos, father, mother, son. She could go back to the library though. Nobody could fault her for that.

Knowing the date of the incident made it easy to locate the edition of the newspaper that carried the story. Norah placed the cassette into the viewer, turned the adjusting wheel for focus, and read. Though it was written with the characteristic attention to detail for which *The New York Times* was known and respected, and though an even dozen of the participants had been apprehended by the police, not one name appeared in print. Not once in the original piece or in any of the follow-ups was the name of the private school which they had all attended mentioned. Each reporter did think it worthwhile to mention that the reason for the omission was that the suspects were juveniles and as such their identities were protected by law. To reveal the school which they attended would have been tantamount to destroying that protection.

Willard Dowd rose and came around to greet Norah and to help her to a chair as though it were her foot that was in the cast, not her hand.

"I was very sorry to hear of your injury."

"It isn't serious."

"I'm very glad."

Pause. They assessed each other. Sensing that the headmaster was disturbed, Norah decided to wait him out.

'I didn't expect to see you again, Sergeant," Dowd offered.

"Oh?"

"No."

A flat statement, without explanation. "This is not an official visit," Norah explained. It didn't appear to reassure him. To the contrary.

"What can I do for you, Sergeant?"

The phrasing was common enough, she thought. It was the way he said it . . . "All I want to know is whether Peter Tomasiello was a student here last year."

"Why?"

"It's an innocuous question."

"You promised to leave us alone!"

Norah raised her eyebrows at the unwarranted outburst. "I don't remember any such promise," she replied mildly. "Anyway, I can ask Peter or his parents, or any of the students. I can even get a court order to examine your files." Bluff, of course, that last; most of it, she acknowledged.

"I see. Yes, of course. I understand." He smiled, apparently completely relieved. He looked at Norah as though they shared a secret. "Peter has been enrolled for the past four semesters. If you need the exact date of his admission, you can check with Miss Harper." He indicated the outer office where his secretary sat.

Mystified by the change, Norah nevertheless took advantage of his cooperation. "I also need the names of the boys who went on the October nineteenth trip to the Bowery last year."

The smug smile disappeared. In its place was a look of surprise then outrage. He cleared his throat a couple of times; he tried out his vocal cords. The sound he finally produced was as guttural as that of a cancer victim who had lost his larynx and used his diaphragm to vibrate air into speech.

"Didn't your partner tell you?"

"Tell me what? What partner?"

"Detective Link. Isn't Detective Link your partner?"

Dowd had been nervously toying with his spent pipe; now he clenched it hard, the knuckles showing white. His face was set; beneath the grave surface turbulence lurked. "Of course, he did. Last week. Just before Thanksgiving. We had a talk."

Good for David! A smile touched the corners of Norah's mouth. He'd risked official displeasure and followed the lead she'd given him. Terrific!

"I told him what he wanted to know, of course. I had no choice."

But why hadn't David told her? "Just exactly what was the information you gave Detective Link?"

"I told him everything. That is," Dowd hurried to correct himself, "as much as I know. What you've got to understand, Sergeant Mulcahaney, is that the school was in no way responsible for what happened. It didn't happen on the outing. The outing was conducted with a view toward broadening the social horizons of the boys. As with other private schools, our students come from the privileged classes and they are insulated within their own economic environment. Other schools limit their field trips to museums, concerts, and so forth. We try to acquaint them with the way others, less fortunate, live."

"Commendable."

"Thank you. Unfortunately, it backfired. In the parents' view, the fact that the boys went down there on their own later did not absolve us from responsibility. Their attitude

167

was that we had exposed the boys to the very environment from which they paid to protect them."

For once, Norah sympathized with the headmaster. The boys had returned to the Bowery on the Saturday after the official school outing. Using sticks and bats, bricks and stones, they had attacked the derelicts without apparent provocation. Where had they got hold of the weapons? Norah wondered. No one had asked that question. They had hardly picked them up at the scene; therefore, possession was an indication of prior intent. They had beaten and stoned the helpless, befuddled, dazed men. The boys had chased the winos out of their doorways, from their street corners, out into the road and into the midst of traffic. Chaos had been the result—drivers screeching to a halt when they were able to, leaning on their horns, swerving, terrifying the pedestrians on the sidewalks. One of the vagrants was run down, his body catching in the undercarriage of the car; he was dragged for eight blocks before the driver was stopped by a group of infuriated citizens and held for the arrival of the police. Meanwhile, of course, the boys had dispersed and most of them disappeared. Only a handful had been apprehended.

"Tomasiello was at the heart of that unsavory business," Dowd exclaimed. "Just as he was at the heart of this other, recent, ugly and sickening . . ."

"Why didn't you expel him? Why didn't you expel him way back then?"

Dowd groaned. "If I expelled him, I'd have had to expel the others too, wouldn't I? Otherwise, it would have looked like discrimination, wouldn't it? The irony of it is that he's only here so that the school won't be accused of discriminating against minorities and the underprivileged."

So much for his earlier tribute to Peter's intelligence and character, Norah thought. Tomasiello was a scholarship student. For scholarship, read charity. Despite his high IQ, Tomasiello's race and economic deprivation would always keep him an outsider in the exclusive and expensive school.

Dowd reached for his pipe and tobacco pouch and occupied himself with the soothing routine of filling and tamping the bowl. "As I explained to Detective Link, that unfortunate affair cost me nearly a dozen pupils. Naturally, I'm not eager to have the whole ugly scandal revived."

"The school was never mentioned," Norah pointed out.

"Not by the newspapers, no, thank God. But once the police made the arrests, of course the boys' classmates knew and they talked and the talk reached the parents. Inevitably. It spread all over the academic community."

That explained his earlier reticence. "I can understand your feelings."

"Good." Having prepared the pipe, Dowd now leaned back and held a match over the bowl, drawing till it caught. "Then we understand each other."

"No."

"I've explained my position to you just as I did to your partner, though I shouldn't have thought it would be necessary. He assured me . . . that is, he inferred . . . Oh, my God . . ." He put the pipe down in the ashtray, his eyes searching hers and not finding what he wanted. Still, he hoped. "Detective Link promised to drop the matter."

"He couldn't do that." She hoped she misunderstood.

"He promised me the school would not be involved."

She shook her head.

"I paid him. I paid him one thousand dollars to drop the investigation insofar as it concerned the school." Then he added the clincher. "I assumed he would share the money with you."

Oh, David, David! Norah groaned inwardly. All the optimism that had buoyed her when she'd learned he had interrogated the headmaster as a result of the lead she'd given him turned to bitter disappointment. She had thought they were on the verge of recapturing their friendship. Instead, he'd used the information she'd freely shared to extract a payoff. And, by inference, he'd implicated her. No wonder David hadn't made a progress report.

The rumors of corruption within the task force that had made her wary about joining were now confirmed. For all her doubts and suspicions, not once had it occurred to Norah that the source could be anyone close, not anyone she knew so well. Or thought she did. She had questioned David's tactics, but never his motives, never. He maintained two separate establishments: the house in Queens for Marie and the boys and his own bachelor pad in Manhattan. He'd recently bought a new Cordoba—landau top, metallic black walnut interior with leather seats, wire wheel covers, the whole bit. She made more money than he did, yet she drove a modest Honda

Civic. She also thought of the lavish gifts he'd bought for her—the gold chain, the orchid plant. Marie had mentioned a mink hat he'd recently given her and two-hundred-dollar-a-pair skates for each of the children. She had not let herself speculate on where the money came from. Nor had she more than superficially questioned his style of interrogation of suspects and witnesses. She recalled now the way he'd handled Alfonse Lamont in connection with the Guthrie homicides. Had he been setting Lamont up for extortion? Extortion. The word was ugly, and in the context—sad.

Yet she had only Dowd's word for it that David had solicited a payoff. Sitting very straight, chin thrust pugnaciously forward, Norah tackled the headmaster. "That's a very serious accusation. Are you sure that you want to make it? If it should turn out to be false . . ."

"It's true."

"In that case, you're as guilty as Detective Link."

"Just a minute . . ."

"Oh, yes. Offering an officer a bribe is a serious offense."

"I didn't offer, he was the one . . . I mean . . ." Dowd stopped. He worked his mouth as though it were rubber. "Actually, what happened was that Detective Link was very understanding with regard to the reputation of the school, and he offered, of his own will and volition, to keep publicity away from us, insofar as he was legally able. Of course, I appreciated his attitude and I voluntarily made a contribution to the police fund. Naturally, I assumed that you knew about it." He ended with a look that was part beseeching and part challenging.

He's just about covered it, Norah thought, and if David should turn the money over to the PBA, well . . . she was too heartsick to pursue it—for now.

"I assume that you have the names of the boys involved in the Bowery incident?"

"Just the ones who were picked up by the police. The others . . . we never found out."

Didn't try, didn't want to, she thought. "Please write down their names."

"I gave them to Detective Link."

More leads for blackmail? Norah couldn't help asking herself. "Now give them to me."

Defeated, Dowd removed the top sheet from a memo pad on

his desk. The names were fresh enough in his mind so that he didn't need to consult a file before writing. When he was finished, he handed the paper over without one more word.

"Are these boys still students here?"

"Three of them are." Dowd took back the list and ticked off the names.

They were: Peter Tomasiello, Jr., Bud Stucke, and Rex Voight.

Chapter XV

Rex Voight was not into drugs or booze. He had no use for either and thought the whole scene was dumb. If you did drugs or booze you lost control, and Rex Voight was determined to control every aspect of his life, and that covered home and school and everything in between. There were all kinds of ways for getting what you wanted: guile—first always—then threat of force, then force itself if necessary. The main thing was you had to be smart and have the guts to do what had to be done. Rex Voight was fourteen years old.

He was blessed with a lack of imagination. He never had nightmares; in fact, he never dreamed at all. Scientists tell us that we all do dream, so undoubtedly Rex did too; what mattered was that he never remembered in the morning. He was a quiet, unprepossessing boy, slight in build, with straight brown hair and brown eyes and skin that was still clear. In fact, he was an ordinary boy with good manners and an exceptional politeness toward adults. Adults reacted almost gratefully. He was popular with his schoolmates because he worked at getting them to like him. The fact that he had lost both parents made adults feel protective and set him apart in the eyes of his peers.

Franklin and Patricia Voight had been killed in an automobile accident, incinerated along with their car. Though the tragedy was less than a year ago, Rex hardly thought about them anymore. He never spoke of them, and no one spoke to him about them. That was by tacit consent, as though by not mentioning his mother and father the boy would forget the horror of their deaths. Not that he'd had actual contact with the event. He'd been asleep in his dormitory bed when the accident happened. The minimal facts had been recounted to him and care taken so that the child's mind would not be agitated into visualizing the gruesome details. At the funeral, both caskets were closed, so he didn't see the bodies. In fact, there were insufficient remains to warrant caskets, but a cremation would have been too apposite. The traditional interment was intended to simulate normalcy for the sake of the boy and for the sake of Matthew and Katherine Voight, his paternal grandparents.

The old people clung to Rex. He'd hated the Academy in Virginia, but he didn't have to even ask to be taken out: they wouldn't let him go back. Not even to clear out his belongings. These were sent up after him. He moved in with his grandparents and was reenrolled in the Dowd School where he had been before his parents had decided that he needed closer supervision and more discipline. Franklin Voight had been an ophthalmologist, Patricia Voight an artist working in ceramics with a studio in the Village. They loved their son, but had their own lives and interests with little time left over. Time presented no problem to the elder Voights. Rex wanted to go back to the Dowd School, so that was where he went.

"Breakfast's ready, darling," Katherine Voight called out to her grandson on the Saturday of the Thanksgiving Day weekend.

"Coming, Gran," Rex replied with his usual promptness and appeared in the dark-paneled dining room on the lower floor of the duplex.

"Morning, love." The white-haired, pink-cheeked, dumpling woman kissed the boy who brought so much joy into her life. Each day Katherine Voight saw more of his father in Rex: she relived the happy memories of her son's growing up through her grandson. Sometimes she felt a pang of guilt. Sometimes she was afraid that she was too happy and that

173

she had no right to be, for if her son and his wife had not been killed, Rex wouldn't be with her. She'd be seeing him only on holidays, the odd weekend, maybe a month at their summer place at the lake. Rejoicing that he was with her every day, every week, every month, was like rejoicing in Franklin and Patricia's deaths. That feeling came over Kate Voight at that very moment and in reaction she hugged the boy tighter and held on to him a moment longer.

"What's the matter, Gran?"

"I just love you, sweetheart."

"I love you too, Gran." He returned her kiss.

He was such an affectionate child. Most boys at his age shrank from showing sentiment. Not that Rex was perfect. There had been problems, problems Frank and Patricia, God rest them, had taken too seriously. Every child steals at one time or another—change from his mother's purse, a play-mate's toys. It was part of growing up to learn respect for another's property, part of the assimilation into society. Cheating on an exam, well, that was another form of steal-ing. It wasn't that Rex had to cheat because he wasn't smart enough to pass, or that he was lazy about studying—simply that the subject hadn't interested him. Honesty too had to be taught, but with gentleness and love. Sending the boy away to that military school had been too harsh; more than a punishment, it had been a rejection. The discipline there must have been very strict—not that Rex had ever com-plained, but after the funeral when he was told that he wasn't going back, that henceforth he'd be living with her and Matthew, his relief had been pitiable. He'd thrown his arms around her and sobbed. Since then, Rex's behavior had been exemplary. Katherine Voight gave her grandson another hug and then pushed him toward his seat at the polished Sheraton dining table.

"So what are your plans for today?"

"Pete's home from the hospital, but he's not allowed out, so I thought I'd go visit him."

"That's nice, darling." Her own plans were unformed. Matt, founder of an electronics company, was going over to take a look at some new equipment recently installed in the Long Island City plant. The company had recently gone public. He was now chairman of the board, but he couldn't get over the habit of supervising every detail. She knew that what was supposed to be a quick look would turn into a full day's work. "Would you like me to come with you?"

"Sure, Gran, if you want," he answered without hesitation.

"Well . . ." She did want, but she knew better. "You boys will have a much better time without an old lady hanging around."

"What old lady? I don't see any old lady." Rex grinned. Then he turned serious. "I hate to ask you, Gran, but could I have an advance on my allowance? I think I ought to bring Pete something, don't you? Candy maybe or a record. He's big on records. I'll pay it back first thing, I promise. Okay, Gran?"

"You know you're not supposed to borrow," she chided gently. "But this is a rather special expenditure." She went into the pantry and returned with the small purse in which she kept petty cash for deliveries and change for tips. She took out a twenty and gave it to him. "Will that be enough?"

"Could you add five? I want to get old Pete something really nice." When she did, he gave her a big hug. "You're a doll, Grandma."

"And since this is a special expenditure, you don't have to pay it back. Only don't tell your grandfather," she warned, beaming.

"I love you, Gran."

Big deal, he thought. Twenty-five bucks! He had thousands coming to him. His mom and dad had left everything to him. It was over a quarter of a million: he'd asked the lawyer: he had no idea why the lawyer had been amused. The will had been read to him and explained to him. What he understood clearly enough was that he couldn't have any of the money, not a cent, till he was twenty-one. That was practically into the next century, for cripes' sake! Any extraordinary need would be considered and granted at "the discretion of the executor." That was his grandfather, so that took care of that. Except for his college education, of course. His grandfather had already indicated he'd dip into the estate for that. You could bet he wasn't going to shell out for it himself. Too tight-fisted. His grandfather wanted Rex to learn the value of money. He knew the value, better than the old man had any idea. His grandfather kept harping on Rex's learning to live within his income, that is, his allowance, to budget. He wanted Rex to keep books!

Lately, the old man had been asking a lot of questions. He wanted to know where Rex was going after school and with whom. He was very curious about Bud and Pete. Of course, that could be due to all the publicity. Rex had caught his grandfather watching him with this funny look on his face, the same kind of look his mom and dad used to have. He wondered just how much the old man knew.

He talked to Pete about it that afternoon. Pete told him to get the gun. He did, but he wasn't sure about using it. It would be better if he could figure out some kind of accident.

"Rex!" Matthew Voight called from the bathroom. "I forgot the heater. Will you bring it in, please?"

The Voights owned an elegant, Georgian style townhouse on the East Side. It had been converted so that the lower floors were rental apartments while most of the two top floors formed a duplex for the family. Living room, dining room, kitchen, and pantry were on the lower floor; bedrooms and baths, and Voight's study above. The master bathroom was large with a circular tub sunk in the center and a skylight offering a panorama of sky seen through the overhanging branches of the trees on the roof garden. Unfortunately, the expanse of glass chilled the general temperature by at least five degrees, and when the wind blew from the north or east by considerably more. The radiator just wasn't adequate, and Matthew Voight had got into the habit of augmenting it with a portable electric heater.

Voight was already in the tub soaking in one of his Foaming Mineral Bath solutions. A vigorous sixty-six, woodsman and hunter, strong Nordic skier, he was in excellent health except for an occasional bout of arthritis.

"Rex, I'm waiting!"

The boy tapped at the door as he'd been taught, then entered.

"Set it over there." Voight pointed to a glass shelf within arm's reach of the tub. "Just push those bottles to one side." He watched as Rex made room for the machine, then plugged it into the wall socket. "That's right. Now, just turn it a little more toward me . . . My God! Look out!"

The boy caught the heater just in time, just as it toppled over the edge but before it fell into the steaming water.

Matthew Voight had scrambled up and jumped out of the tub. His tanned skin had turned the color of putty, puckered with goose bumps. He was dripping wet and shaking. "My God, boy! I could have been electrocuted."

On Monday morning when he walked into his mid-Manhattan office on the twenty-second floor at 30 Rockefeller Plaza, Matthew Voight was informed by his secretary that a police officer was waiting in the reception room. With an uneasy feeling at the pit of his stomach, Voight told her to send the officer in.

David Link did not rely on the outward trappings—prestigious address and well-appointed offices; these could be and often were, a front. He had taken the trouble to look up the company in Standard and Poor's and Moody's Industrials in advance. He had checked not only the net worth and current earnings, but gone back to see how they compared over a ten-year period. Voight Electronics showed a consistent, steady rise. S and P's Directors and Officers listing gave a short background sketch of the founder, president, and now chairman of the board.

"I'm sorry to disturb you at your office," David began smoothly after having introduced himself. "I thought you would prefer my coming here rather than to your home."

Voight was not a man to avoid an issue. "Why is that, Detective Link?"

"It concerns your grandson."

David had not chosen corruption; he had slipped into it. The opportunity had come looking for him, but he had been ripe for it. Marie had been unhappy for a long time, even then talking about separation, at least on a trial basis; professionally, he'd been in a rut. In yet another re-organization of the Detective Bureau, Link had been flopped from the Fifth Homicide to precinct dick at the One-nine handling routine complaints. Meanwhile, his contemporaries were moving up. Trouble was, he wasn't black, a member of a minority, or a woman, David had reflected bitterly—they were the ones who were getting the breaks. In the midst of the gloom and frustration, a suspect in a robbery case offered him a bribe to suppress evidence against him. The evidence was circumstantial; David had already uncovered other evidence that cleared the suspect and pointed to someone else, a man who turned out to be the actual perpetrator. He was on the verge of telling the suspect so—and then came the fatal hesitation. The rationalizing.

The money gave him a feeling of well-being. When it was spent, he looked for more. Unfortunately, he began to put pressure on witnesses who might become suspects but who were probably innocent. He got no reaction. No more offers were made. So then David found himself pushing a little, suggesting, insinuating. He found that he was good at it. He got results.

Unexpectedly he was transferred to the homicide task force. He was gratified that he had not, after all, been forgotten, that he had been saved from obscurity. It was a boost to his ego; it renewed all his good intentions and ambition. He was grateful to Inspector Felix and for a while he was straight. But it didn't take long for the reaction. The work to which David was now assigned wasn't in essence much different from before—leg work, demanding no initiative, strictly, stupefyingly ordinary. The situation at home had deteriorated. He missed the extra money. At least, vice was a challenge.

"I hardly know where to begin," David Link said to Matthew Voight.

"Just say what you have to say, please."

"All right." He took a breath. It was a tricky case to make, for while the chain of logic was clear in his own mind and he had rehearsed the presentation, he found himself oddly reluctant to go ahead. "Your grandson is a student at the Dowd School, so I assume you're aware of recent incidents involving two of the students there—Peter Tomasiello and Bud Stucke."

Voight nodded.

"Bud has admitted he took part in an initiation ceremony that involved killing ahd torturing animals at the zoo on Halloween. During the spree, the night watchman was shot and killed."

Voight didn't flinch.

"Bud has implicated Tomasiello. Everything points to there having been a third boy present. I have reason to believe it was your grandson, Rex."

178

"What reason?"

The old boy was tough, David acknowledged. Well, he hadn't expected surrender at the first volley. "Rex is a close friend of the other two. The three of them were in the habit of going over to Bud's house after school every day, ostensibly to do their homework together. They horsed around in the halls—that's normal for boys of their age—but they got into an argument with one of the tenants. That tenant has identified Bud and given descriptions of the boys with him. He will make a positive identification if necessary." David was taking a calculated risk; he didn't know whether Carson could or would make such an identification.

Voight didn't challenge it, and that encouraged David.

"As you say, such highjinks are normal for boys of that age," Voight murmured. "Why should the two incidents be connected?" He shrugged. "You haven't convinced me that Rex was involved in either. I have every reason to believe," he mimicked the detective, "that on Halloween my grandson was in bed and asleep at his regular school-night hour."

"He could have slipped out."

"I will not tolerate innuendoes, Detective Link. If you have a specific charge against my grandson, make it. If not, get out."

The sweat broke out on David's brow. He didn't like being forced into a direct accusation; on the other hand, who the hell was going to know he'd made it? "I think Rex and the other boys are responsible for the robberies and murders at the Belmonde Towers."

The old man's blood seemed to drain out of him, yet he remained ramrod straight in his big, padded executive's chair.

"I'm here because I'm not sure how deeply involved Rex is." As Voight failed to rally in defense of his grandson, David's confidence was restored. "Did he actually take part? Did he actually wield a knife or a club? I'm talking now about the murder of human beings, not animals. Or was he an accomplice? Perhaps even an unwilling accomplice?" Link dangled the possibility, the hope, in front of the hard-bitten but shocked old man.

Matthew Voight was no fool. He'd been subjected to the bluffs and threats of experts in the business world. He handled this as he would any crisis situation—admitting nothing, he played for time. "You have not shown me any proof that my grandson is involved at all. Not in any of these events. You haven't offered one shred of factual evidence. Everything you've told me is conjecture."

Now, David thought, now. He dropped his bombshell. "It's based on Rex's previous record."

Voight jerked in his chair, his body pulled upward and rigid as though an electric current had passed through it. Then he went limp, slumped; sweat pouring out all over his body was plainly evident on his lean and now haggard face. "I thought . . . that is, I understood . . ."

"A year ago your grandson was charged with and found guilty of assault on a group of vagrants. The law does not permit his record to be introduced as evidence against him in the prosecution of any new charge, but the record is there. Always will be. It's interesting that the other two boys also took part in that assault and we can't forget that a death resulted." Link took his time, sure now that he was in control. "I'll be straight with you, Mr. Voight. Rex is in a lot of trouble. We know that after his arrest and conviction on the Bowery charges he was put on probation in his parents' custody and that they sent him away to military school. After their deaths, you and your wife brought him back and returned him to the Dowd School."

Voight sighed heavily. It had been the last thing he'd wanted to do. He had been set against returning the boy to the same environment, to the same companions, but he hadn't been able to resist Kate's pleading. She had wanted to keep the boy with them. She'd argued; she'd wept. Of course, she hadn't known the real reason that Rex had been sent away. She suffered from hypertension, and so the three of them, Frank, Patricia, and Voight, had decided she shouldn't be told what Rex had done. It would hurt her too much; it might even trigger a stroke. Afterward, he could hardly have added to the shock and sorrow of the tragic car accident by telling her. So, reluctantly, Voight had given in. He'd tried to get Rex into another school at least, but had been turned down everywhere he'd applied. No other private school in the city was willing to accept Rex.

"His grandmother wanted him with us," Voight told the

detective and almost immediately regretted that he'd offered even that much of what sounded like an apology.

David couldn't have cared less. "We're back to just how big a part Rex played in the murders. According to the new state law, a juvenile accused of a violent crime shall be tried by the regular adult court. As an equal partner in the crime, that's what would happen to Rex. On the other hand, if he was present but did not participate either in the robberies or the violence, his case might very well come under the jurisdiction of the family court. I don't need to tell you that there is a considerable difference in the way the case would be handled and in the sentence ultimately meted out."

"Then why are you telling me?" All of Voight's suspicions were rearoused.

David smiled ingratiatingly. "I want to make a deal."

Voight's pulse quickened. They were playing in his ballpark now. He could handle this. "What kind of deal?"

"I'll see to it that Rex is treated as an involuntary accomplice."

"And in return?"

"Rex must make a full statement telling everything he knows about Stucke and Tomasiello and the commission of the crimes."

Voight's lean, dark face had returned to its normal quiet watchfulness. Not a muscle twitched. "What else?"

David's composure was equal to the executive's. "That's up to you, sir."

Voight hesitated. He didn't want to make a mistake in reading this man. Just how much evidence did this Detective Link actually have against Rex that he wasn't putting on the table? This deal he offered—was it because he needed Rex's evidence to get a conviction on the other two as he said? Or was it a trap to implicate Rex? Or was it blackmail?

"You've given me a lot to think about, Detective Link. Now you've got to give me the time to do the thinking."

David was pleased with himself. He had mounted a double-barreled attack. He would get new information that would surely break the case and he'd get a payoff. He got up. "I wish I could say take all the time you want, sir, but I can't. I have a partner who has a tendency to get impatient."

*   *   *

181

Matthew Voight was not without connections. He investigated the investigator. He found out how much David Link was making, how long he'd been in his present assignment, when he'd been married and the current state of his marriage. He went himself to the public library and, as Norah had done and anyone could do, searched the back issues of newspapers and magazines for the stories about the crimes at the Belmonde. He read and reread. Then, waiting for a time when his grandson was at school and Kate at one of her bridge luncheons, he went through Rex's things.

When he had finished, Voight sat on the edge of the bed, head bent, face covered with his hands. This room had been his son's, Franklin's. Franklin had grown up here into adulthood, lived here right up to the day he and Patricia were married. No man could want for a better son than Franklin, and so now, whatever decision Matthew Voight took, he must consider what Franklin would have done.

Had he misjudged Voight's reaction? David Link asked himself the question a dozen times during the next two days. He grew nervous waiting for the executive's call. When it hadn't come by the third day after his visit, David decided to give him a nudge. He called Voight's office and was taken aback at being told that Mr. Voight wasn't in and that he couldn't be reached for the rest of the day. He asked to speak to Mr. Voight's private secretary, but she remained unresponsive to blandishment or threat. He called back several times; the answer was the same. He tried Voight's home. There was no answer at all.

By late afternoon David decided to go over to the house.

He heard the sirens while he was still three blocks away and had a sickening prescience of where the fire engines were headed. When he arrived, he found the quietly elegant, tree-lined block of private townhouses between Park and Lexington avenues clogged with fire engines and fire equipment, ambulances, patrol cars, and the unmarked cars that were undoubtedly official or they wouldn't be inside the barricades. Black smoke billowed from the windows of a white, colonnaded building and a black rain of ash and soil—the soil of a rooftop garden—had already formed a layer on the street and cars and people. The roof garden had been stripped, trees mangled, shrubs upended, the root balls hanging precariously over the parapet.

David pulled up to the wooden saw horse barring entrance to the block. He showed his gold shield to the guard.

"What happened?"

"Bomb. Somebody went up to the roof and dropped a bomb down through a skylight. The skylight was over a bathroom. Somebody was taking a bath at the time."

Chapter XVI

A current of cold air was sucked down through the hole where the skylight had been and poked its chilling finger into every nook and crevice of the duplex. It had long since cleared the miasma of the dirty, throat-singeing smoke, but the acrid stink of the explosives and the chemicals used to put out the fire remained. The combined residue had soaked into the very fabric of upholstery, carpets, drapes. It tainted everything. The force of the blast had ripped the bathroom door off its hinges and hurled it from the top floor through the railing of the central stair down into the foyer below. It had burst the water pipes; fortunately, the main valve in the street had been shut off before the gushing torrent did more than soak the wall-to-wall carpeting of the upper hallway.

What had been inside the bathroom had been gathered up and taken away, but blood still splattered the walls.

A multitude of men had descended on the scene—from the bomb squad in addition to the usual homicides, precinct, and technical people—all going about their business with little attention to the old lady and the boy who sat side by side on the chintz-covered sofa amid the shambles of what had been an elegant yet cozy living room. It wasn't for lack of sensitivity or compassion. Fernando Arenas who had caught the squeal for the Fourth had suggested to Katherine Voight that she and her grandson wait with a neighbor, or at least in another room, but she had refused. At the beginning, out of concern for the widow and the boy, voices had been muted and activity originating in the bathroom shielded as much as possible, but once the mortal remains of Matthew Voight had been removed, the restraint was lifted and they returned to the routine black humor that was the customary self-defense against daily horror.

It didn't matter to Katherine Voight; she was oblivious to everything. Though her arm was around Rex, it would have been hard for anyone looking at them to tell who was doing the comforting and who was the comforted, who supported and who leaned. The rosy glow was gone forever from Katherine Voight's cheeks; in the seconds it had taken her to realize what had happened to her beloved husband, the glow had turned to ashes and the plump cheeks hung like the used, raddled rubber of a deflated balloon. She had not screamed when she entered the front door of her home, nor even when they told her that Matthew had been in at the time of the explosion and that he had been taking a bath. She had uttered only a low moan, but in that suspiration her health, energy, her reason for living had gushed from her lips. She still wore the fur coat she'd been wearing when she came home to disaster, yet Katherine Voight shivered, and the brown-haired, brown-eyed, very pale and frightened youngster beside her shivered too. That was how Norah Mulcahaney found them.

Norah paused on the threshold of the open door of the duplex and looked around. Joe was attending a dinner for the police captains, so she'd been alone when she heard about the explosion on the ten o'clock news. The name Matthew Voight caught her attention. She didn't need to consult her notes to know that Rex Voight's grandfather was named Matthew. She told herself that what had happened to Matthew Voight had nothing to do with Rex. She went to the scene because she couldn't make herself believe it.

She meant to play it low key and was pleased to find Ferdi Arenas in charge. She went over to him and waited at his shoulder till he turned and discovered her.

"Sergeant!" There was no doubt he was pleased to see her too.

"I'm not official," she hastened to inform him. "I'd just like to stick around and observe, if you don't mind."

"Oh, Sergeant, sure, anything you want." He knew she wasn't there because she had nothing better to do. He knew also that Norah Mulcahaney wasn't going to try to get the jump on him. Still he couldn't resist a diffident probe. "We'd be glad of any help you can give."

On her part, Norah certainly trusted Arenas. She would have been glad to discuss what she knew, but she wanted to protect him from a possible reprimand due to her presence. There was one thing she could tell him and that he had a right to know. "The boy, Rex, goes to the Dowd school along with Tomasiello and Stucke. The three are very close."

Arenas nodded and got out his notebook. "It was a Molotov-cocktail type bomb, crude but powerful," he read. "According to the neighbors, it exploded at about a quarter of six. Everybody in the building and up and down the street heard the blast. Aside from the victim there was nobody else home but the kid. Evidently, they have daily help, a maid who leaves at five."

Norah glanced over to Rex Voight. "Did he tell you?"

"No. A neighbor. Mrs. Alice Stanley. She lives in the only other apartment on the floor. She was just starting to cook dinner when the blast occurred. She thought maybe it was a gas explosion and she turned off all her jets and ran right out into the hall. The kid was standing there outside his door."

"Did she actually see him coming out?"

Ferdi looked hard at his former boss. "She wasn't specific, and I didn't press her on it."

"Okay."

"Mrs. Stanley asked Rex what had happened, and he told her that he was in his room studying when he heard a big bang. He ran out into the hall—that would be the hall upstairs inside the apartment. He saw that the door of the bathroom had been blown off its hinges. He told her he thought his grandfather was in there, but he was afraid to look. She escorted him to her place and then went back to look for herself. She was pretty upset by what she saw."

"I don't doubt it. Where was Mrs. Voight all this time?"

186

"She got home about a quarter after six. I haven't talked to her yet. We could do it together?"

"Thanks, Ferdi."

They approached the woman and the boy together, but Norah held slightly back to give Arenas the initiative.

"I'm Detective Arenas and this is Sergeant Mulcahaney. We're very sorry for your loss, Mrs. Voight, and we regret intruding, but there are questions that have to be asked."

Katherine Voight took her arm away from Rex, pulled her mink coat a little closer around her, sat up a little straighter, clasping her hands in her lap. "I don't understand what happened. I don't understand why anyone would do this terrible thing. It must have been a mistake. A terrible, horrible mistake."

"Did your husband have any enemies?" Ferdi asked.

"Matthew? No. No. He was respected and admired by everybody who knew him."

Having knowledge of Voight's background which Ferdi at this point could not have, Norah thought it proper to step in. "I understand he was a self-made man, very successful. He built up a big business from a one-man operation in a rented garage to a complex employing thousands."

"Yes."

"Sometimes on the way up one makes enemies without realizing it. People who are bypassed resent it."

"It wasn't a matter of bypassing another employee or anything like that. Matthew was his own boss, always."

"A competitor then? Fighting for the same contract and being bested?" Norah suggested, but Katherine Voight remained adamant. "A disgruntled employee?"

"Matthew paid good wages. His was one of the first of the privately owned companies to institute a pension fund and a medical plan."

Norah let it go. Ferdi took over again. "Was Mr. Voight in the habit of taking a bath at more or less the same time every evening?"

"Yes. Right after he got home from the office. He suffered from arthritis. He used therapeutic bath salts and soaked for about twenty minutes every night. Afterward, we had two Manhattans together, and after that, dinner."

"I see."

"Matthew led a very structured life."

There was a pause.

"He was a good man. A good, decent man. Strict, demanding. He set high standards, but he was fair. And he loved us. He loved us!" Her eyes filled as Katherine Voight turned to her grandson. "What are we going to do without him? How are we going to get through the days and through the nights? How are we going to live?"

The boy, still covered with a light film of plaster over head and shoulders, sat stoic in the face of his grandmother's appeal. Shock, Norah thought. Shock, of course. He seemed an ordinary boy. No, she corrected herself, not ordinary—average. An average teenager confronted with the violent death of a member of his family. A boy who, according to her research, had very recently suffered the loss of both parents by violent death, she reminded herself. Maybe he'd learned not to allow himself to feel sorrow or to feel anything at all.

"You were in your room when it happened?" she asked Rex.

"Yes, ma'am."

"You must have felt the power of the blast."

"Yes, ma'am. It knocked me to the floor." He said it with a tinge of awe, the first emotional reaction.

"Would you take me up there to see your room?"

His grandmother held out a hand to hold him back.

"It's okay, Gran." He got up quickly almost as though he were glad finally to get away.

He led Norah and Arenas out into the foyer and then up the graceful, curving staircase to the second floor of the duplex. At the head of the stairs he made an abrupt and determined turn left, avoiding the bombed-out bathroom which was to the right.

His room was at the end of the hall: medium sized, perhaps twelve by fifteen, with two windows on the north wall and a bathroom opening off the west wall. Beyond that, it was a matter of visualizing what it had been before the explosion. A layer of white silt from the plaster of the gouged-out ceiling lay over everything. Shelves had been ripped off walls, dumping the contents on the floor in sad piles of boyish treasures. However, testifying to the capriciousness of the blast, the television set remained intact and the furniture, good, sturdy oak, was in place—even the chair at the desk.

"Did you pick up the chair and put it back?" Norah asked.

Rex scowled. "I must have."

"Or did you fall out of it?"

"What difference does it make?"

Norah wanted him to indicate a sequence of action. She also wanted to stimulate his memory of events. "Which was it?"

"I guess I fell, chair and all. Then I lay on the floor for a while till I was sure it was all over. Then I got up and set the chair back. I don't know why."

He looked around at the haphazard destruction. He showed no regret, no sense of loss for things an average boy would have prized. It was a point in his favor, she thought, that the loss of his grandfather overshadowed everything else.

"I don't know why—" Rex repeated and suddenly broke off. He walked over to a pile of rubble and reaching down fished out a Mickey Mouse wristwatch. He looked at the smashed face. He held it up to his ear. He shook it disconsolately. "My mom gave it to me a long time ago," he said and his voice quivered. Carefully, he put the watch into his pocket.

"I don't know why I put the chair back." He picked up as though he hadn't interrupted himself. "Habit. They're always after me to put my chair back when I get up from the table."

"I see." Norah nodded. "After you picked yourself up and put the chair back, what did you do?"

"I went out into the hall to find out what had happened." She indicated that he should show them.

He had told Mrs. Stanley that he had not looked into the hall bathroom, but it was now apparent to both detectives that whereas he had been able to turn his back on it on the way up the stairs, it was difficult for him to avoid looking into it on the way down. With the door blown off, he must have had at least a glimpse of what was inside. Norah, arriving after the cleanup, had been shaken by what she'd seen. The boy evidently had dealt with it by rejecting the sight. His conscious mind denied having seen it. Eyes averted, Rex Voight walked by the open bathroom and started down to the foyer and the front door.

"Where are you going?" Norah asked.

"To get help," he murmured without turning around, continuing on his way.

"Why didn't you use the phone in your own room, or downstairs?"

He didn't answer, just kept on going.

Norah and Ferdi exchanged glances. Shock, the need to get as far away as possible from the grisly scene, and the need to turn everything over to an adult could explain it, then and now.

"Was your neighbor, Mrs. Stanley, already in the hall when you came out?"

"No. I rang her bell."

"Did you?" Possibly Mrs. Stanley hadn't heard it. "Thank you, Rex," Norah said. "Why don't you go back and sit with your grandmother now."

When he was gone, by common accord Norah and Arenas headed for the roof. They used as access the stairs in the common corridor.

The viscous cloud caused by the explosion had dissipated and the full moon now shone on the blasted garden. The cold, platinum light illumined charred stumps, gnarled branches, the various constructions—air shafts, chimneys, air-conditioning units which had been artfully concealed by the plantings. Casting long shadows that shifted and distorted as reflections of the passing clouds, it was a Nevelson moonscape, eerie, futuristic, and at the same time a nightmare of our common atavism. It was easy to locate the skylight over Matthew Voight's bathroom. The glass portion had been protected by a heavy grille. This had been cut, a neat square lifted out, so that the bomb could be dropped. That made it easy for them, but how had the perpetrator distinguished the particular skylight from the others: the skylight over Rex's bathroom, the one over the guest bathroom? The glass was frosted in each instance so that even with the light on below, it would have been difficult to tell which was which and if it was occupied. It came down to foreknowledge. The perpetrator had to be aware of his victim's custom of soaking in a hot tub every night, an intimate bit of information but one which, faddist that he was, Voight might well have expounded on. However, the perpetrator also had to be able to pick the particular skylight.

"What do you think?" Norah asked Ferdi.

He was troubled. "I don't know. He says he rang Mrs. Stanley's doorbell. Even if it's true . . ."

"Did Mrs. Stanley say his apartment door was open?"

"That's right. He could have left it open on his way up to

the roof. Or he could have opened it afterward but before ringing her bell."

Norah sighed.

"I heard about a case the other day," Ferdi went on. "A girl, granted she was eighteen, still . . . She wanted a Jaguar for her graduation present. Her mother, a divorced woman, decided she couldn't afford it so she gave the girl a Chevy Chevette instead. The girl threw a glass vase at her mother. It shattered in her face causing serious lacerations. Then the girl went out, forged her mother's signature to a check, and bought the car she wanted."

Licking her lips, Norah put both their fears into words. "It's a big step to murder."

Behind them, the heavy metal roof door opened and thudded shut.

"Hi," David Link called out to Arenas. Then to Norah, "I didn't expect to see you here."

In the steely brightness of the moonlight they examined each other.

"I never know what to expect from you," Norah replied.

They were sparring, of course, but Arenas had no idea why or what about.

"I talked to Matthew Voight earlier this week," David offered by way of explanation to both of them.

He paused for comment. There was none. "I found out that Rex has a record. He participated in a gang assault along with both Stucke and Tomasiello. He was also one of the kids included in Carson's complaint to the Belmonde management. The three of them are real thick. Based on all that, I figured it was a good probability that he took part in the zoo raid and that he was an accessory in the Belmonde break-ins. I told Mr. Voight I would try to get Rex a deal from the DA. If he could get the kid to give evidence against Stucke and Tomasiello, he'd be treated as an unwilling accomplice."

Norah didn't ask whether the offer had the DA's approval, or if the DA even knew about it. "What was Voight's reaction?"

"He said he had to think about it."

Norah clenched her jaw.

"I didn't see any other way of breaking the case! One of those kids has to turn state's evidence. One of them has to give evidence against the other two. I figured Rex was the least involved and that his grandfather had a better chance of getting him to talk than you or me or anybody else."

"So you let Matthew Voight tell his grandson just exactly what the evidence against him is."

"All right, it was a mistake." Link groaned. "I know. I realize it now."

"Matthew Voight was an upright man," Norah went on. "According to Mrs. Voight, her husband hewed to the old-fashioned values and the old-fashioned morality—an eye for an eye, a tooth for a tooth."

The three stood around the gaping skylight and gazed down the shaft into the brightly lit bathroom or what was left of it. They looked not at the water line in the tub, not at the broken pipes or chunks of plaster, but at the brown streaks on the walls.

"God," Link murmured. It was the first look he'd had.

"Whoever did that had to be a hell of a lot more than an accessory," Arenas observed.

Norah continued her hypothesis. "Voight's sense of justice demanded he give the boy a hearing. After he talked to Rex, he realized there was no deal possible for the boy. Matthew Voight told his grandson he couldn't protect him. He told him he had no choice but to let justice take its course."

Not one of them raised an objection over the fact of the unnatural crime; they only grieved over it. For all the accumulation of horrors, though they were almost stunned, they could still grieve, even David. With one accord they turned away from the skylight and left the roof. Partway down the stairs, Rex's voice reached them through the open door of the apartment.

"I don't want to go, Gran. Please. I don't want to go with him. Please, Gran, please don't make me go."

They walked in on a tableau: Katherine Voight, short legs firmly planted, weariness and sorrow shucked off for the moment at least, stood embattled in her devastated home between her cringing grandson and a stranger.

"You're not going anywhere," she asserted firmly. "I told you that. Now be quiet." Her sharpness with the boy she so loved was an indication of her distress.

"What's all this?" Norah wanted to know.

Katherine Voight eagerly turned to her. "He wants to take Rex away."

"Away where?"

"Westover Military Academy," the newcomer replied.

"I won't go. I won't go!"

"Rex, be quiet!"

"Mr. Voight called the school and asked for somebody to come up and get him," the young man explained.

He was probably in his early twenties and very handsome, Norah thought. Yet what set him apart from other young, good-looking men, was not the clear, unlined face and neatly chiseled features, not his direct, unwavering gaze, but an aura of . . . innocence, an innocence rarely discernible these days except in very, very young children.

"My name is Paul Chuloy." He introduced himself first to Norah and then to the other two detectives. "I'm a teacher at Westover. Mr. Voight called early this afternoon. Rex had been a student with us and he wanted us to take him back. We agreed. He insisted that somebody should come and get the boy right away. He wanted Rex to leave for the school immediately. Tonight. He insisted."

"What time did Mr. Voight make his call?" Norah asked.

"I'm not sure," Chuloy replied. "I was told that I would be making the trip just after the lunch break, say close to two o'clock. I was told not to bother packing a bag since I'd be going right back with the student."

David looked at the boy. "When did you find out you were going?"

Instead of replying, he turned pleadingly toward his grandmother.

"Answer the question, child."

"Grandfather came and picked me up at school. He told me then." His answer was for his grandmother; he looked and spoke only to her.

It would have been useless for Rex to try denying that he knew he was going to be sent away, Norah thought. Matthew Voight had surely informed the headmaster at the Dowd School and Rex's schoolmates had surely seen him going off with his grandfather. It explained why Rex hadn't prepared a better alibi: he couldn't. It was one point clarified, one more brush stroke in the psychological portrait. She said nothing, content to let David go on carrying the ball. There was a lot she still needed to know about David.

193

"Did your grandfather tell you why he was sending you away?" David asked.

Rex Voight shook his head.

"He must have," Katherine Voight urged him gently.

"No, Gran, no. I swear." His face, which had been a blank, was now puckered like that of a child half his age.

It was in character for Matthew Voight not to have offered an explanation, David thought, at least in character as he understood him, or thought he understood, for he'd already misjudged Voight once. He had made a fatal error in judgment and he wanted now to make up for it in the only way he could—by apprehending Matthew Voight's killer.

"Where's your room?" he asked.

"Just a minute." Paul Chuloy cleared his throat apologetically. "Mrs. Voight, I don't think that you should allow Rex to answer any questions, not without a lawyer present. I don't think these officers, I assume they are police officers, have the right to go through your home at will, either."

"We do have the right, Mr. Chuloy, and here it is." From his breast pocket David Link pulled out the official paper. "This is a search warrant." He swept past the schoolteacher and past his startled colleagues. After a moment, they trooped after him.

He didn't need to be shown which was the boy's room. After a cursory look around it, Link checked the closet. "Where are the bags you packed for the trip?" he asked the boy, who had followed along with his grandmother and teacher. "I don't see them. Didn't you pack?"

Rex didn't answer; he wouldn't even look at the detective.

"Why not? Why didn't you pack?"

The answer exploded in the mind of every person crowded into that room, but the only sound was the whisper of a sigh from the boy's grandmother.

Norah touched David's arm. "I think you should read him his rights," she murmured.

"Not yet. First, I'm giving this place a toss. You can help if you want." He included Arenas in the invitation.

"What are we looking for?"

"You'll know when we find it."

They set to work. Quickly, methodically, they went through the boy's room searching all the obvious places. They examined the bathroom including the toilet tank. Nothing. Then they started on the rest of the apartment. It consisted of the two bedrooms, baths, and a paneled den upstairs; the living and dining rooms, kitchen and pantry downstairs. Even with the three of them and skilled as they were, it took time.

Katherine Voight returned to her place on the sofa along with her grandson and Chuloy to wait.

"Are you finished?" she asked when the detectives rejoined her. She was close to the limit of what she could endure and it showed. "If you are, please go away. Please go away and leave us alone."

Reluctantly, certainly filled with sadness, Norah told her, "We weren't able to get into the safe."

Link shot her a glance. What he wanted was hardly likely to be in the old man's safe. Still, she was right, nothing should be overlooked. "If you'd be kind enough to open it for us, Mrs. Voight?"

The bereaved woman got up with difficulty. Her steps were halting and she leaned on the stair rail for support with Rex helping her on the other side, but though she was slow, she didn't falter as she led the way back to the second floor and her husband's very special retreat. Here, where his aura was strongest, she swayed slightly. Link jumped forward, but she would accept no help from anyone but the boy and that only for a moment. Recovered, she walked without hesitation around the desk and to the picture on the wall. Swinging it aside, she revealed the safe. With a practiced hand, she twirled the dial; the lock clicked, the safe opened. Now she stepped back inviting any one of the three detectives to come forward.

David, standing at her shoulder, had no intention it should be anyone but himself. He looked inside and a slight, tight smile touched his lips. Bull's-eye! A quiver of elation passed through him, but he suppressed the smile; it was unseemly. He'd lucked out, he thought. Really lucked out. This was going to make everything okay. Well, not the death of the old man, naturally . . . though he couldn't be held responsible. No way he could be held responsible, he assured himself, the justification process beginning, the specious reasoning. He could not have anticipated what happened. If there was any minimal blame to be attached to his interviewing Matthew Voight it would now be wiped out. He had broken the case. Relief made him sweat. Relief made his triumph doubly sweet. Using his handkerchief, David reached into the safe for the first of the two pieces of hard evidence which would be the components of his victory. Turning around, he held the first up for all to see.

"Is this your gun, Rex?"

"No!"

Link placed the small black .22-caliber weapon on the desk. Again using the handkerchief, he reached into the safe.

"Is this your knife?" he asked, letting the light catch the long, well-polished blade before setting it down beside the gun.

The boy cringed back against his grandmother. "No."

"Then how did they get into this safe?"

"I don't know. I don't know. Gran, I swear. Please, Gran. I don't know."

"Then I'll tell you." David Link's face was grim. He spoke to the boy but for the benefit of the others. "Your grandfather put these things in there. I talked to him just three days ago. I told him that you were implicated in a series of felony murders. I also said that I believed you were only an accomplice, perhaps even an unwilling one. I think that after that he came home and searched your room and found these. He knew then that you were far more than we had feared. You were the one who shot the night watchman at the zoo. You tortured a crippled man in his wheelchair and stabbed a helpless woman in her bath. You were the instigator. You were the leader of those raids."

Katherine Voight let a soft moan escape, only that, but she stepped away from Rex; she broke their physical contact.

"Your grandfather then confronted you with the evidence and you killed him," Link concluded.

"No. I didn't, Gran." He reached for her, but she pulled away. "Gran . . ." She would not let him touch her again.

"Your grandfather loved you," Norah told the boy. "He concealed the evidence against you and called the academy down in Virginia for someone to come and take you away. For all his strong moral sense, for all his rectitude, your grandfather determined to save you. He wasn't sending you away to punish you. He was trying to put you where we couldn't get you."

"And for thanks, you killed him," Link concluded.

"Why?" Katherine Voight cried out. "Why did you do all

those terrible things? Why did you steal? What did you need that we didn't give you?" It seemed as though by focusing on the lesser aspects of his guilt she could forget, at least for a while, the greater horrors he had committed. "You have everything. We gave you everything. I always gave you everything you wanted. All you had to do was ask."

The boy stared at her. Color, an ugly, dark, mottled red crept into his sallow face. The whites of his eyes yellowed. "I've got money, lots of money. My mom and dad were rich and they left everything to me. You made me beg for what belongs to me. You made me beg for what's already mine."

Katherine Voight flinched as though he'd struck her. She stopped crying. Abruptly. Though her cheeks were still wet and her eyes still glistening, her grief had gone dry. "Take him away," she said. "Get him out of here." Rigid, looking straight ahead, she got up and walked slowly out.

They waited till she was out of sight. Then they waited till they heard the bedroom door close.

David Link hesitated. Strictly, the collar belonged to Arenas. On the other hand, he was the one who'd got the search warrant that had made it possible to turn up the evidence and break the case. Extracting the plastic-covered card from his wallet, Link began the reading of the "rights." After that he put the handcuffs on Rex Voight. As he was leading him out, he felt Norah's eyes on him. He couldn't ignore her contribution.

"Thanks," he murmured passing.

"Don't thank me," she retorted.

Chapter XVII

The weapons found in Matthew Voight's safe were examined at the lab. Bullets fired from the .22 matched the bullets removed from the body of the night watchman, Raul Pelletier. The hunting knife, in length and width of its blade, was exactly right for the wounds inflicted on Jonathan Burrell and Françoise Guthrie. Detective David Link was the principal witness called by the DA to testify before the grand jury and it was due in large part to his persuasiveness that they returned an indictment against Rex Voight for murder one. His position on the task force was assured.

He was also responsible for getting Norah off the hook with the IA.

In their examination of the murder knife, the technicians brought up two sets of fingerprints—one, Voight's, the second Peter Tomasiello's. That opened the way for an official search in which the Burrell album was legally seized and dusted and revealed the artist's own prints. So Tomasiello had at the least taken part in that robbery. It supported Norah's claim that Tomasiello had ambushed her on the back stairs, threatened her with a knife. The two together confirmed her theory of how he had got rid of the knife—namely, that a confederate, Rex Voight, had been waiting, and when she went out of the building to call an ambulance, Voight had gone in and taken the knife away.

So quietly, the charges against Sergeant Norah Mulcahaney were dropped and she returned to work. Her return was neither acclaimed nor deplored by the press or public, simply ignored. Which suited Norah just fine. There were no more threatening phone calls, no more hate mail. She was forgotten. She would have liked to recover her gun, but the chances of that were just about zilch.

Not that Rex Voight admitted taking the knife from Tomasiello on the back stairs. He neither admitted nor denied any of the charges. He answered no questions. He refused to talk at all. His grandmother engaged a lawyer and then would have nothing more to do with him. She was not interested in the suggestion that in view of his youth, the court might be disposed to grant light bail. She didn't want him home. If he were released he would have no place to go. So he stayed in jail. His arrest and indictment got comparatively light coverage by the media. The public's attitude toward adult justice for a juvenile killer was yet unformed, so the case was reported without comment and allowed to slip to the back pages.

But Norah could not so easily dismiss it—not the boy, not David's part in his arrest, not David himself.

There was still the matter of David's venality. Any lingering doubts Norah had had been dispelled when he showed up at the bombed-out Voight apartment with the search warrant in his pocket. His version that he'd offered Voight a deal on the boy's behalf to get the boy to turn state's evidence against the other two sounded okay, but gut instinct told Norah that he'd gone to see Voight to get a payoff.

She agonized, yet she did nothing about it. She kept telling herself that she had no proof. She said nothing either to Inspector Felix or even to Joe, clinging to the forlorn hope that she might still be wrong, that Willard Dowd had lied about the extortion and that the interrogation of Voight had been what he claimed and admitted—bad judgment.

Then she decided to talk once more to Alfonse Lamont.

What he told her made it impossible to keep quiet any longer.

Yet she still had to consider what the discrediting of Detective Link would do to the case against Rex Voight.

In the end, it was the boy who tipped the balance. Christmas and New Year's had come and gone, might well come and go again before Rex Voight was brought to trial. She couldn't wait that long. So on a damp, raw day in January, Norah made the trip to Rikers Island. She learned nothing she hadn't known before, but she formed an impression and reached a decision.

The weak, lemon-yellow rays of the late-afternoon sun were slanting into the squad room when Norah got back. She lingered for a moment beside the door unobserved as the shifts changed, her eyes on David Link as he tidied his desk before leaving. His movements were brisk, assured, his manner bordering on smugness. No use waiting any longer.

"David . . ."

"Oh, Norah. Hi." He could see the intensity in her eyes, in the thrust of her jaw, but he had no idea what was on her mind.

"We've made a mistake," she blurted out.

"About what?" He frowned; they hadn't been working together in recent weeks.

"Rex Voight didn't kill his grandfather."

It was a shock. He stood quite still for several moments just staring at her. He sighed. "Ah, Norah, for God's sake . . ."

"We've made a mistake," she repeated doggedly.

"The DA's satisfied that he's got a good case. The Chief is satisfied, so's the Inspector. Even Joe . . . Have you told Joe?"

She hadn't told anybody, yet.

"Rex did not drop that bomb. Matthew Voight had only told him that afternoon that he was being sent away. There wasn't time for him to go out and assemble the components and construct the device."

"We've been all over this, for God's sake. He could have had the makings from way back. He might have been planning to drop it on the grandfather. The kid was full of resentment. The news that he was being sent to the military school was the final push he needed to make him actually do it. Don't forget that he hadn't packed his bags. He knew he wasn't going."

"Maybe he hadn't packed his bags because he was relying on his grandmother not to let him go."

"You can come up with answers either way, sure," David concluded. "The whole thing is ugly. Personally, I'd like to forget it."

"I went over to talk to him."

"You mean Rex?" David groaned. "You went over to see him? Why in hell did you do that? God, you ought to know better."

"Relax. I got permission from his lawyer and from the DA." David turned pale.

"Don't you see? He ought to be denying everything. Whether he's guilty or not, he ought to be saying that he isn't. He ought to be appealing to his grandmother. He ought to be throwing himself on her pity."

"Leave it alone, Norah. Butt out."

She didn't remind him that she'd been on the case before he had. Instead she asked the question she'd been wanting to ask since the night of the bombing. "Why are you so eager to see him convicted?"

He looked around quickly to see if anyone had heard, but there was too much activity for anyone to be paying attention. "That's a hell of a thing to say." He kept his voice down.

So did she. "It's like you're trying to salve your conscience for setting Voight up."

"I don't have to take this from you, Norah."

The protest was weak, futile, and she knew she'd hit it. "You had no business offering Voight a deal."

"What's got into you? Why are you doing this to me?"

"Willard Dowd says he gave you one thousand dollars to keep the name of the school out of the papers."

"He's a liar."

"*You* lied when you told Jim Felix you were late getting to our meeting with the Tomasiellos because you had a flat. *You* lied when you told me that you were actually meeting with an informant. The truth is that were with Alfonse Lamont. You had an early date with him and he was delayed. That delayed you. You couldn't tell me because you got a payoff from him. He gave you twenty-five hundred dollars to play down his relationship with Mrs. Guthrie. You were supposed to take care of me too. Please don't bother to deny it, David," she said sadly. "Don't bother."

He sat down, bowed his head.

In Dowd and Lamont, David had chosen his marks well, Norah thought. Both had paid off without resistance. However, he'd misjudged Matthew Voight. Voight had decided not merely that he wouldn't pay, but had determined to save his grandson. David felt responsible for Voight's murder. He wanted the boy to be guilty to salve his own conscience.

"Just exactly what did you tell Matthew Voight?"

"I outlined the case against his grandson. I had every right to do that."

"Did you mention the names of the other boys involved?"

He scowled. "I may have. I don't remember. Probably, I did. What the hell difference . . ."

"So suppose Mr. Voight did some investigating on his own. Suppose he went to see Peter Tomasiello? Suppose it was Peter who decided the old man knew too much?"

"Suppose, suppose . . ."

"Both Peter and Rex left prints on the knife," she reminded him. "Peter had the only known spoils from the robbers, the Burrell album, in his possession."

"Rex had both the gun and the knife in his."

"That doesn't prove he used them." ·

David's face was black with anger and with frustration. His eyes glittered; his jowls hung slack. He was a changed man, no longer handsome, but corrupted. It showed. Involuntarily, Norah flinched as he got up and towered over her. Maybe because of where they were, or because of what he had once been, he held himself back.

"It's good enough for me," he said and stolidly walked out.

David Link's last look at Norah had been a challenge; it had asked no quarter. Though it was her quitting time too, she didn't go home. She went to her own desk and got out all her notes and sketches and all the material she'd accumulated going back to the very beginning. She consulted her own rough drawings rather than the more precise official diagrams and photographs because in the heaviness or lightness of her own pencil, in the underscorings and circlings, she could revive her emotional memory.

Certainly, she had firsthand evidence that Peter Tomasiello knew how to handle a knife. It was therefore logical to assume that he was the one who had used it throughout the series of crimes. Had he also carried the gun as backup, to use at long range, or against an opponent too strong or too resourceful to be overcome by the knife? Most perpetrators relied on the one weapon; used the same MO over and over. In this case from zoo holocaust to robberies, the pattern was the same but the weapons varied. The bombing, of course, was out of pattern, but that could be explained by the urgency of the situation or by the young perpetrator's not having the nerve to face Matthew Voight. That certainly suggested Rex but didn't rule the other boy out.

Norah studied the drawings of the Burrell living room, noting where and in what direction the invalid victim's wheelchair had been toppled and the attitude in which the body had fallen. It didn't tell her anything new. She went on to the Guthrie file. There were two sketches: one of the foyer where the girl, Sylive, had been choked; the other of the bathroom where Mrs. Guthrie had been stabbed as she rose up out of her tub. Though the direct cause of death had been drowning, the intent, Norah believed, had been to kill with the knife and pushing her and holding her under had been part of the struggle. She had no reason now to change her mind, still she continued to stare at the drawing of the bathroom.

The water had still been in the tub when the police arrived. On her sketch, Norah had marked the level at just below half. She had indicated that the bathwater had been tinged pink. She had also scrawled a note to the effect that there were stains on the tile floor, some spots darker and more viscous indicating blood had been spilled but not diluted. It had suggested that when the victim rose to fight for her life some of her blood had splattered outside the tub. Had she managed to inflict any damage on her assailant? Could she have turned his own knife on him, thus forcing him to push her down and under the water?

Was some of that blood that Norah had seen on the floor and marked on her diagram—his?

Had anybody tested it?

Heart beating fast, cheeks flushed, Norah reached for her telephone and dialed Asa Osterman.

The Medical Examiner answered it himself. He listened and then replied glumly. "No, nobody was smart enough to think of it."

"Including me at the time," Norah reminded him. Now it was too late, the floor had been mopped, God only knew how often. Still, looking at the diagram which lay beside the telephone, it occurred to her that when the perpetrator pushed Mrs. Guthrie down into the tub, he would have been leaning over and some of his blood might have mixed with hers. "I don't suppose anybody analyzed the bathwater."

"You suppose correctly."

Norah noted that she'd marked the torn shower curtain which the dying woman must have clung to as she was shoved under. She'd also marked another item. "I wonder . . ."

"What?"

"Roland Guthrie closed the apartment and moved to a hotel almost immediately after the murders. I wonder just how much of a cleaning job was done in there before he left."

"Why?"

"There was a sponge floating in that bathwater."

The lush, luxuriant potted plants that had transformed Françoise Guthrie's bathroom into a tropic bower were still there in their niches, but without the moist warmth and without any watering, they had withered and died. They gave off a rancid odor in the enclosed space. Norah wrinkled her nose but surveyed this sign of neglect with a surge of optimism. The cleaning woman had let the water out of the tub and she'd scrubbed the ring. The torn shower curtain had simply been bunched to one side; the sponge fished out and set to dry in a corner. If the rest of her work was an indication, she hadn't rinsed it, probably not even squeezed it. God bless her laziness, Norah thought.

She reached over for the sponge. It was natural, not plastic, with irregular-sized, relative pores. Such sponges were usually a light yellow-beige in color. This one was a dark, mottled, reddish brown. Norah dropped it into the plastic bag she'd brought along for the purpose.

Within the past decade lab techniques had become breathtakingly sophisticated. There was neutron activation analysis, which made it possible to identify the most minute quantity of a substance, and electrophoresis, a new procedure specifically for blood. Amounts which at one time were simply not sufficient for testing now yielded a plethora of infoɪ mation. Norah knew that Asa would use every available technique to identify the blood type in that sponge.

It took time. The tests took time; even getting on the machine took time: it was booked in advance like a computer. Asa called her back five days later.

"And? What happened, Asa? What did they find?"

"Two blood types."

She sucked in.

"Type A in volume . . . Well, you're not interested in the technicalities. Type A was in the larger quantity and is, in fact, the victim's blood type. In a lesser quantity was type B negative."

"The killer's type!"

"I think we can safely assume that."

"That's great! Fantastic, Asa! Now all we have to do is check the blood types of the two suspects. I could have done it in advance, but I didn't. I was superstitious about queering our chances," she admitted ruefully. "I'll get right on it now. Tomasiello was recently hospitalized, and we can check the school medical . . ."

"I can save you some trouble," Osterman cut in. "I went ahead and checked."

"Oh?" Norah sensed disaster. She heard it in the Medical Examiner's flat intonation and in his dry cough; she felt it in the pit of her own stomach. "And?" she prompted.

"Neither Tomasiello nor Voight is type B negative."

That left one possibility, and checking his blood type was as simple as checking the others' had been. He too had recently been hospitalized.

"The little squirt with the broken jaw?" Joe exclaimed.

"That's the one," Norah replied. She sat for a long time after the hospital called back with the information before going into Joe's office to tell him. It was little satisfaction that she'd been right about Rex Voight's innocence.

"The runt? The one with the Prince Valiant haircut?" he marveled.

"Right."

Joe sighed. "God."

Crisply, Norah detailed the reasoning that had led to the blood analysis. While doing so, she was at the same time trying to gain insight into the character of these three boys. She couldn't. She couldn't understand them or today's children. Or what the violence of these children portended for society. It seemed to Norah, who believed in the rule of law, that an atavistic strain had been spawned in this generation. Side by side with scientific advance, there was a return to barbarity. It was ominous and frightening.

"That gives us what I think is conclusive proof that Bud Stucke stabbed Françoise Guthrie," she concluded the report.

Joe nodded. "It doesn't let Rex or the other boy off. It doesn't solve the bombing or the other crimes."

No matter how hard she tried, Norah could find nothing to excuse the boys, no mitigating circumstance. Peter Tomasiello had above-average intelligence and came from good, hard-working parents. Rex, perhaps neglected by his parents and overdisciplined by his grandfather, had certainly not lacked for love; his grandmother had showered it on him. His railing at her at the time of his arrest had shocked Norah. As for Bud, of the three, he had seemed to her the most normal.

"I know," she agreed. "It does shift the assumption of guilt."

He reached for her hand. "Let's go in and see what Felix has to say."

"I just got through talking to the DA who just got through talking to Osterman," Jim Felix informed them. "He's not enthusiastic about making the arrest on purely technical evidence. He's even less enthusiastic about releasing the Voight boy. He figures Voight is implicated. The question is the degree."

"I don't understand why the boy won't talk," Joe remarked.

Norah had asked herself that question over and over. Even the visit to Rikers Island had not suggested an answer.

"If he's guilty, you'd expect him to be denying it up and down. Why doesn't he yell it out? Scream it? To us, to his lawyer, to the media, to everybody. If he's innocent, then all he has to do is tell who's guilty."

"That's it!" Norah cried out. "He's afraid to tell who's guilty. He's afraid that the same thing that happened to his grandfather will happen to his grandmother. He's protecting her. That's why he won't talk. He loves her enough to sit in

206

jail and take the blame to protect her." It didn't make everything all right, but it helped. She felt a lot better.

The two men looked at each other, then at Norah. "Maybe." Joe was cautious. "Suppose we offered protection for her and for him?"

"We could do that," Felix agreed. "Okay. Suppose Voight decides to give evidence. Isn't the jury going to be skeptical? They could, with reason, regard the testimony as one teenager accusing the other, one kid trying to get himself off the hook by accusing the other."

Norah nodded. "The jury is going to be very sensitive to the fact that they're dealing with a juvenile. They're going to be understandably nervous about being criticized later. So they'll want incontrovertible evidence, plain and easy for all to understand."

"Exactly," Felix said. "What they'd really like is for whoever did it to be caught redhanded."

"Sure. That would make it nice for them," Joe commented. "And for us."

"I was thinking the same thing," Norah said.

Jim Felix knew Detective Mulcahaney long enough to recognize the signs; she had a scheme and she was getting ready to make a pitch for it.

Being married to her, Joe could guess what she had in mind. "You want the DA to release Rex."

"Yes. In his grandmother's custody."

"I thought she didn't want him," Felix observed. "I thought she refused to take him."

"His grandfather was willing to give him a second chance," Norah reminded them both. "I think she will be too."

Chapter XVIII

Felix set it up in consultation with Joe, first defining the parameter of the stakeout, then getting down to specifics, including assignments. It was not an area into which Norah would normally presume to intrude, but she was in the position of knowing of a possible leak. If she didn't speak, the whole thing might go down the drain. She had to speak. Hearing her own assignment, she took that as her opportunity.

"I was thinking—someone from the Fourth should be with me inside. It is their case."

"Right," Felix agreed. "I figured on Arenas, since he's carrying."

He'd intended that, of course, without her suggestion. It had been her way of opening up the subject; now came the touchy part. "Would that mean leaving David on the outside? He did make the case against Rex. I'm not saying that would influence him, but he would be less than sympathetic. Two inside is enough . . ." She just couldn't get it out in plain language.

Joe was puzzled by her hesitancy. Felix's thick, scraggy eyebrows were drawn together as he watched her and let her flounder. When it was apparent that she had finished, he spoke.

"I hadn't intended using David inside or out. He's resigning."

"From the task force?" Joe was surprised; he had been very much aware of Link's struggle to make a secure place for himself.

"From the department. He wants out—for good."

"Did he say why?" Norah asked.

"His wife has agreed to go back to him and to make another try at the marriage if he quits. You did know that they were separated?"

"Oh, yes," Norah said.

Joe nodded.

"He thinks that he can get work as security officer in some big company or department store. He wanted to know if I'd recommend him." Felix looked straight at Norah.

She sat very still. Did he know? Did James Felix guess? Since her last meeting with David in which so much had been said and so much more left unsaid, she had been struggling with her conscience. She'd justified her continued silence by the fact that David hadn't blackmailed anyone who was actually guilty of a crime. He had not diverted justice. Not yet. Maybe he was afraid that he might one day. Maybe he knew it was inevitable and he'd decided to quit before it happened. Norah was mortally certain that David Link had worked alone. Which was not to say there weren't others. If there were, Felix was now alerted, and he would rout them out.

"I think David would be well suited to that kind of work," she said.

Felix's face was grave. "I agree."

Joe sensed that something passed between them. He could discern the almost imperceptible easing of tension in the set of Norah's shoulders, the relaxation of her jaw. Her blue eyes were soft. It involved David, he thought. A few days back Felix had mentioned that David Link had turned over a sizable contribution to the PBA welfare fund—apparently, he'd been collecting for it a long time. Was there a connection between that and his resignation? Norah knew, had borne the burden of knowing alone. He should be more receptive; he should make it easier for her to share her burdens with him. He would in the future. His dark eyes told her so.

"So." Felix got back to the business at hand. "Norah and

Ferdi will work together. The two of them will go in with Mrs. Voight and Rex."

The building was covered front and rear; most importantly, men were stationed up on the roof. Under Captain Capretto's direction, detectives from the task force carrying walkie-talkies were stationed at each end of the block with outposts on both Lexington and Park. The bomb squad had thoroughly checked the apartment to make sure it was clean before Mrs. Voight and her grandson were allowed to enter. It had been decided that Norah and Ferdi Arenas should not be seen with them, so they had gone ahead and were already up there waiting.

There was no way of knowing how long it would take.

The DA's office had made the same deal with Peter Tomasiello that David Link had ostensibly been trying to make with Rex through his grandfather. In other words, Tomasiello had been offered a reduction of the charges against him in exchange for cooperation. He'd accepted and, coached by Sergeant Mulcahaney and Captain Capretto, and in their presence, had made the call to Bud Stucke.

Now they had to wait.

The apartment had been restored. What could not be repaired had been replaced. New wallpaper and reupholstering could not erase the miasma of what had occurred. Matthew Voight's aura lingered, the manner of his death and his grandson's part in it. As dusk fell Katherine Voight made a tour of both floors, turning on the lights everywhere. It was done mechanically as a set routine. It would be a long time, Norah thought, before Katherine Voight could sit comfortably with her shadows.

At seven she brought in sandwiches and coffee. No one was particularly hungry, but everyone ate. It passed the time. No one talked; there was nothing more to be said. No one suggested turning on the radio or television, for despite the tight surveillance above and below, each person in that apartment was depending on his own perception to catch the first warning footfall, the first creak of a floorboard. Ferdi and Norah were veterans of stakeouts, but they were as tense as the targets they were there to protect.

After the meal was finished, and Mrs. Voight had cleared

and washed up with Rex's help, there was no other activity with which to fill the hours.

At eleven, Norah advised Mrs. Voight that she and Rex should go up and try to get some rest.

"I couldn't," Mrs. Voight protested. She had agreed to the scheme reluctantly, out of a sense of duty. Though from the moment of his release Rex had stuck close to his grandmother, she held herself aloof from him. She had not touched him. If possible, she avoided looking at him. "I'm sorry, Sergeant, I couldn't."

"Try," Norah urged. "It should look as though you're following your normal routine."

"I'm afraid," the widow admitted.

"Don't be. There are men around the house and up on the roof," Norah reminded her. "The instant he makes his move they'll grab him."

"I know that. I understand. I just can't help myself." She shuddered.

"Oh, Gran, Gran . . . I'm sorry. I'm so sorry!" Rex cried out in desperate appeal.

It cost her an effort, but she made herself turn and look at him.

In response to that searching gaze, his face quivered and the tears welled in his eyes and coursed freely down his cheeks. His voice was choked as he repeated, "I'm sorry, Gran."

Her ravaged face remained impassive. Her voice was flat and cold. "Being sorry doesn't help."

He reeled. Being sorry had always been enough before. How many times, how many scrapes had he got out of with those magic words, *I'm sorry!* Norah could see that he was trying to adjust, rallying to find another formula.

"I didn't mean for anything to happen to Grandfather. Honestly, Gran. I didn't mean for anything bad to happen."

"But it did."

"I'm sorry . . ." By rote he started again, but cut himself off. "Gran, forgive me. Please . . . forgive me."

For the first time in her life Katherine Voight looked at her grandson and saw not the reflections of her desires for him, but the reality of what he was. She saw a selfish child, spoiled, a child with an evil streak which his parents had recognized and tried to correct. She had loved Rex too much.

211

She had indulged him. Her heart was a cold, hard lump in her chest—a painful weight. Desolation which had fallen on her since Matthew's terrible death grew heavier and darker. She had not thought that was possible. It was close to insupportable. She felt that the only way she could retain her sanity at this moment was to shriek out her sorrow, to fling herself on the boy, to shake him, to drag her nails down that deceitful face, to rake it and make the blood run in the channels left by his facile tears.

"Forgive me, Gran."

"I can't."

It was the second blow Rex had sustained and his dismay showed. His eyes widened and the tears stopped.

Katherine Voight felt a clutch of uncertainty. In indulging Rex hadn't she actually been indulging herself? Didn't that give her a share in the responsibility for Matthew's death? As she had indulged her love, was she now indulging her grief? "I can't," she repeated, but this time her voice quavered. "Not yet." She turned away quickly lest she show her weakness.

Norah saw it. "I have a suggestion. You and Rex can stay here, but we'll put out the lights. He'll think you've gone up to bed, but you'll be here with us."

Katherine Voight shrugged; she was too spent to even be afraid.

So room by room, the downstairs lights were put out and the vigil continued in the dark. Of course, the darkness wasn't complete—street lights, lights from other buildings, illumined the room in which they sat. Nevertheless it caused a lowering of the life flow. What little conversation there had been now ceased entirely. The woman and the boy fell into a kind of semiconsciousness. On Norah and Arenas, the partial darkness had the opposite effect. Their vision gradually adjusted, their pulses quickened, their perceptions were sharpened.

It was after midnight when Norah's walkie-talkie emitted a low crackle.

"A kid, right height and weight, has been spotted coming up Third," Joe said. "He's at the corner. He's just passing under a street light. It's him. He's carrying a small flight bag." There was an interval of silence, then Joe's voice. "He's walking up the front steps to the door. He's got a key."

No one in the dark room spoke, but Norah sensed that the

212

woman and the boy had heard and were now as alert as she and Ferdi.

There was another pause and then again Joe's voice. "He's inside. No more transmissions till we've got him."

Now they strained to hear the whine of the elevator, but the building was old, well constructed, more soundproof than most ultramodern edifices whose thin walls could make the lack of privacy embarrassing. Since she couldn't hear his approach, Norah tried to estimate the time it would take him to get up to the top floor and listened for the opening and closing of the elevator door at the end of the hall, but she couldn't hear that either. Footsteps would be muffled by the heavy hall carpeting. Well, he ought to be on the stairs to the roof by now, she decided. The men on the roof had been alerted by Joe just as she and Ferdi had. They would be ready. As he approached the skylight, as he got his home-made bomb out of the flight bag, they would close in.

At any moment it would happen. At any moment they'd hear the scuffling overhead, the shouts. Instinctively, Norah tilted her head up. So did the others.

Why was it taking so long? She felt Ferdi edge close.

"What do you think?" he whispered.

He should have been up there by now. They both knew it. He should have made his move and been apprehended. It should have been all over. Norah didn't dare break radio silence to ask what was going on.

"I don't like this," she whispered back.

"What can he be up to?" Ferdi wondered.

The answer came to both of them at the same time. They smelled it.

"Dios mio!" Ferdi exclaimed, still remembering to keep his voice down so the other two wouldn't hear.

"Put on the lights," Norah whispered. "Put them on," she repeated in a normal tone; Mrs. Voight and the boy had to know. They'd be smelling the smoke themselves soon enough. While Ferdi groped for the switch, Norah used her walkie-talkie. "Joe? He didn't go up to the roof. He set a fire—out in the hall, I think. I can smell the smoke." She knew, before Ferdi even hit the light switch, that the smoke was curling in under the front door, for her eyes were beginning to smart. Just the same, when the lights did come on, she was shocked at how much smoke had already infiltrated.

213

"We've got to get out. We'll go through the back."

She led them through the kitchen and opened the back door to the service area which had no elevator, only stairs.

"Take them down one flight, then ring the bell of the apartment below," she told Arenas. "They're going to have to evacuate, too, so you can go through their place to the front and take the elevator down the rest of the way."

"What are you going to do?"

"Take a look around."

"Sergeant . . ." Arenas hesitated. Norah was his superior and even now he couldn't overstep the boundary. "Don't wait too long, Sergeant."

"I won't."

When they were gone, she used her walkie-talkie. "Joe? Have you spotted him? He ought to be coming out."

"Not yet. I think he made us."

"Maybe he'll wait for the fire engines and try to slip away in the confusion."

"Maybe. Meantime, you come on out."

"As soon as I can."

She switched off. Drawing her newly issued gun from her handbag, Norah started up the back stairs. Here, the air was still clear; there was no indication yet that a fire raged on the other side of the building. At the top of the flight she found that the bolt on the roof door was still in place. She wasn't surprised or deterred. If he'd gone up, he had used the front way. Norah drew the bolt and pushed the door open and stepped out into the cold, dark January night.

The moon, which had been full and relentlessly bright the last time she'd been up here, was on the wane and clouds in ominous masses partially obscured it as they converged from the north and east. However, there was enough light to see that all traces of the blasted garden, the trees and the shrubs, the shattered planters and mounds of soil, had been cleared and there was no indication left that a garden had existed. What Norah looked at now was an ordinary, flat black tar roof enclosed by a low retaining wall with iron pickets embedded along the top. There was nobody around. The men of the task force were gone; they would have been ordered down at the first warning of fire.

Undoubtedly Bud Stucke had counted on exactly that. He'd probably waited somewhere and watched them go down

214

before coming up here himself. And then what? Scanning the empty expanse, Norah decided that he must have climbed the wall to the adjoining roof and gone down through that building to the street. He shouldn't be that far ahead of her. She went to the wall and looked over. The adjoining roof was lower by a drop of about eight to ten feet. Stuffing the gun back into her purse, hanging the walkie-talkie by a clip to her belt so that both hands were free, Norah swung one leg over the iron palings, then the other, and clutching the bars, let herself down till it was just a matter of dropping free the last few feet. Her knees flexed on landing and she came up bouncing. Nothing to it.

The roof was smaller and narrower than the Voights'. Through a break in the clouds, the moon poured down an icy-blue shaft of light that showed every structure in stark relief—air-conditioning unit, chimney stacks, ventilators. The door housing loomed largest. Norah went to it and grasped the handle and pulled. It wouldn't budge.

She had no choice but to contact Joe again. She unclipped the communicator from her belt.

"He appears to have crossed over next door to Thirty-four. He'll probably be coming out the back there."

"It's covered. You come on down. Now, Norah. Now, Sergeant."

"I'd like to, Captain, but I can't. He's bolted the door on me. This roof is lower. I can't climb back up."

"Terrific!" Joe groaned. "Okay, I'll send someone up to get you. Stay put."

"There's no place for me to go," she observed ruefully and switched off and pushed the aerial back into its socket.

"You're so right, Sergeant."

Whirling, Norah saw a figure detach itself from the rear of the door structure. The figure's right arm was raised high above the head. "Don't go for the gun, Sergeant. I've got plastic explosive here. Actually, I prefer it to the other stuff; it's easier to carry but it makes just as big a bang."

She had no choice but to believe that what he held was what he claimed it was.

"I'll take that—" He indicated the two-way radio and reached his other hand out for it. With an expert fling and never taking his eyes off Norah, he tossed the radio over the fence and up to the higher roof. "Now the pocketbook. Just

215

slip the strap off your shoulder, nice and easy. That's right."
After he'd got rid of that, he grinned. "You thought you were
outsmarting me, didn't you? I was on to you all along. I knew
there was no way old Pete would make that phone call on his
own. I knew you had the pressure on him."

She could see now that the grin consisted of a mere separation of the lips; it was the twin scars of the surgery on his
broken jaw that provided the upward tilt at the corners.

He was, in all, an antic figure. The spindly legs encased in
pipestem jeans contrasted with the balloon bulk of a down-
filled jacket and splayed-toed earth shoes. He was bareheaded
and the moon's light turned his stringy blond hair white,
faded his sparse lashes and eyebrows to platinum, tinted his
skin and lips a ghostly blue. He looked like an albino even to
the red-rimmed, gray-to-colorless eyes. For a moment, Norah
had the illusion that she was confronting a ghoulish old man,
the old man he would become—if he lived long enough. She
shook her head and the vision cleared. She faced a thin,
undersized fourteen-year-old with a maniacal grin stitched
into his face.

"If you knew it was a trap, why did you come?" she asked
Bud Stucke.

"I figured I could get Rex and the old lady right from under
your noses. And I came close."

"Why did you hang around? You could have been long
gone."

"There's plenty of time. I wanted to talk to you."

"Why me?" she almost asked, but didn't. She knew the
answer. It was because he'd had to do the dumb, slow, humble
bit with her. It had been rankling. He wanted *her* to know
what he really was. How smart, how superior to her and
everybody else. To brag. To gloat. To rub it in. Then afterward, maybe, probably, he'd use the plastique. Okay. She'd
give him all the opportunity he wanted to brag.

"You sure fooled me. When you fingered Peter Tomasiello,
I assumed he was the one who beat you up. You let me think
so and you let me think he did it to keep you from telling
what you knew. You encouraged me to believe he was the
brains behind the raids. I know now it was you. You were the
one who planned and directed everything. And he didn't beat
you up. You fought each other. Why?"

216

Let him tell it, Norah thought. It would feed his ego—not that it needed feeding.

"We were setting up the Guthrie hit. Pete was supposed to be making a play for Sylive so that we could get the layout and pick the best time to go in." The street jargon was awkward spoken in his private-school diction and rigorously inculcated grammar and he was obviously uncomfortable using it. "Well, he fell for her. Her people were very social— East Hampton and Palm Beach. Old Pete had visions of being accepted into that crowd." Bud sneered. "There was no way a guinea was going to get into that league. But he thought he had a shot and he wanted us to lay off. Naturally, that was out of the question. Anyhow, I couldn't let him tell me what to do. If I let that happen once, I'd lose control."

That was the key, Norah thought. Bud Stucke was the youngest of the trio, the smallest and weakest physically, but he controlled Tomasiello who was older, tall and handsome, and had the highest IQ in the school.

"Once we got inside, he turned chicken. Left Rex and me to do it alone."

"Rex was with you?" Rex Voight, despite his meager allowance, was the richest boy in the school.

"Just in case I needed an extra pair of hands," Bud deprecated. "I didn't."

Norah had to clench her teeth together; she didn't trust herself to speak.

Of course, Bud couldn't overlook Tomasiello's running out. He had taken on the older, stronger boy in physical contest knowing that he would sustain serious injuries and then he'd used those very injuries to turn himself from loser to winner. Norah sighed. She felt a terrible depression of spirit. "Why did you have to kill Sylive and her mother? And the others, why did you have to kill them?"

"So there wouldn't be any witnesses."

He said it so calmly as though the logic should be obvious even to her.

"We made a point of not taking anything that could be traced," he explained condescendingly. "What was the use of being so careful if we were going to leave witnesses behind to identify us?"

Was that his idea of how the pros did it? And where did he get it from? Books, movies, TV? Who was responsible for him

217

and other youthful criminals? What dreadful contaminant in our society was producing these morally deformed children? "Peter took a record album from Jonathan Burrell," she told him.

"I know." He scowled. "I shouldn't have let him keep it."

So far it was his only regret and very likely part of the reason why there'd been no mercy for Pete's girl. Norah sighed. "Let's talk about the weapons. I understand how Rex got the knife—he took it from Pete on the back stairs. Pete used the knife earlier and Rex the gun."

"No. They were both mine." At Norah's raised eyebrows, he told her the rest. "Pete took the knife from me in the fight." He shrugged. "Well, he's bigger than me." He wasn't justifying, simply stating a fact.

"How come their prints are on the knife and not yours?"

"I wore gloves."

Of course. "Shouldn't Rex after he got the knife from Peter have got rid of it?"

"Why? He wasn't under suspicion."

"How did Rex come to have the gun in his possession? Did you plant it on him?"

Bud Stucke laughed. He threw his head back and laughed stridently. After a while, he stopped. "I lent it to him," he said and Norah's obvious dismay delighted him. "Rex came to me all shook up about his grandfather. Seems Mr. Voight was asking a lot of questions, and Rex was afraid he was on to us. So I gave Rex the gun and showed him how to use it. He didn't have the guts."

"That left it up to you to get rid of Matthew Voight."

"Yes," he said. Then he added, "It really wasn't my responsibility."

The petulance made Norah shudder. She glanced sideways at the roof door. Whoever Joe was sending to open it for her should be there at any moment. He would come unsuspectingly bursting through and the advantage would stay with Bud and the plastique. If she could keep the teenager's attention fixed, the officer might grasp the situation . . . She had to keep Bud talking. There was only one more question she could think of to ask.

"Why?"

"Why what?" He had explained the murders; he had explained the need to dominate.

218

"Why the robberies? You didn't need the money. Why break into somebody's home and steal?"

He was silent. Stumped. Apparently, he hadn't thought about it before. He did so now and came up with an answer. "To see if I could pull it off."

Norah stared. "That's it?"

He shrugged. "That's it."

The cloud which had remained stationary overhead having massed its thunderhead into an ugly, blue-black rumbling phalanx now resumed its advance across the sky. Gathering speed it swiftly blocked out the moon, plunging Norah and the boy on the roof from glaring brightness into dark. For the second time that night Norah had to strain to keep her bearings, to know where she stood in relation to the boy. The concentration which had encapsulated them both was broken by this need. First, she became aware of a gust of wind, warm when it should have been bitter cold, acrid and singeing her throat when it should have been clean and invigorating; of lights in apartments across the way that had been dark before. There were people leaning out of those windows, she saw. Across on the corner of Lexington, a small knot of spectators had gathered. The howl of approaching fire engines wiped out all other impressions. Their headlights strafed the night-empty streets. They screeched to a halt directly below. Men shouted instructions to each other and issued orders to the public through loudspeakers. They were calling for evacuation of the burning building and the buildings adjacent. Superfluous, Norah thought; by now everybody was out—that could get out.

The fire had eaten up and through the Voight roof. Norah could see flickering tongues of flames, playful, skipping and hopping to form small, sporadic circles like bonfires on a beach of a summer's night. Even as she watched, they grew and threw off sparks which spawned new fires that would work their way back down toward the source. By their blazing, roaring light, Norah saw Bud again. He was looking around at his handiwork.

"May I ask you a question, Sergeant?"

Still that private-school politeness. "Go ahead."

"I suppose that Rex and Mrs. Voight got out?"

"They did."

219

"How? I made sure the door to the service stairs was locked."

And still the arrogance, too. "I made sure I had a key."

Respect, a mere hint of it, flickered in the pale eyes. "There was no way I could start two fires, front and back. So . . ." He dismissed it. "Time to go."

As he turned, Norah reached down and pulled the gun from her ankle holster. Before she could issue the official warning, he had stopped of his own accord.

"You did tell them that I'd be going down through this house, through Thirty-four, didn't you?" He gave no indication that he was aware of the gun, if, in fact, he was.

Suddenly, she realized that he couldn't have gone down that way, and couldn't now, because the door was bolted from the other side. He hadn't planned that far ahead. She'd given him too much credit.

"You heard me say so."

"Thank you."

He stuffed the alleged plastique into the side pocket of his jacket as carelessly as though it were . . . *Silly Putty*. Then he headed back the way they both had come—the higher roof. He was young enough and agile enough to scale the wall where she couldn't, Norah thought, watching as Stucke jumped and grasped the iron bars of the railing. Hanging from them, he probed for and found toeholds in the brickwork and somehow scrambled to the top. He had meant all along to go that way.

Holding the gun in both hands, Norah got ready to call out the formal order to *freeze*. It wasn't necessary. Bud Stucke wasn't going anywhere. The fire barred his way. The isolated flames had joined into a line of snarling, howling, slavering beasts that he could not pass. His only option was to come back down to Norah.

But Bud Stucke didn't take it. He stayed where he was—on the wall between the two buildings. He had finally and fatally miscalculated.

Below, the firemen had rigged spotlights and now began a slow sweep of the buildings and the roofs. One of them found the boy and stayed on him.

Bud blinked in the glare. He raised one arm to shield his eyes, then walked forward along the wall till he was out on

220

the overhang and looking down into the street. He seemed a lonely and frightened figure.

The crowd caught sight of him through the swirling smoke. First one bystander then another saw him and passed the word along till everybody was looking up, pointing and shrieking. They begged him to get back. They yelled to the firefighters to get him. A cherry picker was cranked up carrying a man in heavy slicker and hat in its basket. The crowd exhorted the operator of the big crane to hurry. Norah ran to the base of the dividing wall as far toward the street edge as she could get. She leaned out.

"Don't jump!" she yelled as loudly as she could over the noise. "Don't jump, Buddy," she pleaded. "Please, don't jump." She reached a hand out to him.

He ignored the hand and looked at her, face dead white, pale eyes red-rimmed and scornful. "I'm not going to jump. You think I'm crazy?" His lips stretched beyond the surgeon's stitching into a clown's painted grin. "They're not going to do anything to me. I'm just a kid."

She watched as the cherry picker swung over and the boy climbed aboard into the arms of his rescuer. Down below, the crowd broke into wild cheers.

Buddy was right.

His friends Pete and Rex were tried in family court and received suspended sentences. They were remanded to the custody of their parents—in Rex's case, that of his grandmother.

Bud would be tried in adult court, but customary plea bargaining could get the charge reduced to manslaughter: "commission of a homicide while influenced by extreme emotional disturbances." A good lawyer, and surely he would have the best, might even get it reduced to manslaughter in the second degree. Depending on the deal, Bud Stucke might very well "walk" on a conditional discharge.

Freed on bail after booking, he could go home without ever having spent a night in jail.

Buddy was right.

The odds were in his favor, and Norah knew it.

221

FOR MOST VIOLENT
TEENS, CRIME PAYS

NEW YORK, March 24 (AP)—Only 442 juveniles out of 3000 prosecuted as adults in New York City under the tough new state law were eventually convicted, a report released today discloses.

The report by the state Division of Criminal Justice Services shows that 897 of the juvenile cases were dismissed outright and another 1069 were found ineligible for prosecution under the law, which was passed 28 months ago and permits 13-, 14- and 15-year-olds to be tried as adults if they commit certain violent crimes.

The borough with the best conviction record—80 per cent—was The Bronx.